Aubrey De Vere

Essays, Chiefly on Poetry

Aubrey De Vere

Essays, Chiefly on Poetry

ISBN/EAN: 9783337427573

Printed in Europe, USA, Canada, Australia, Japan

Cover: Foto ©Andreas Hilbeck / pixelio.de

More available books at **www.hansebooks.com**

ESSAYS

CHIEFLY ON POETRY

BY

AUBREY DE VERE, LL.D.

IN TWO VOLS.

VOL. II
ESSAYS, LITERARY AND ETHICAL

London
MACMILLAN AND CO.
AND NEW YORK
1887

TO THE MEMORY OF

SCOTT AND SOUTHEY,

IN WHOSE POETRY

IMAGINATION EVER WALKED SIDE BY SIDE WITH

VIRTUE AND HONOUR,

THIS VOLUME

IS DEDICATED

CONTENTS OF VOL. II

SIR HENRY TAYLOR'S POETRY

PAGE

VII. EDWIN THE FAIR 1

VIII. LATER PLAYS . . . 28

IX. MINOR POEMS 69

X. THE TWO CHIEF SCHOOLS OF ENGLISH POETRY.
POETIC VERSATILITY. SHELLEY AND KEATS . 100

XI. LANDOR'S POETRY . . . 143

XII. THE SUBJECTIVE DIFFICULTIES IN RELIGION:
Does Unbelief come from something in Religion
or in the Unbeliever? 189

XIII. A SAINT 229

XIV. THE HUMAN AFFECTIONS IN THE EARLY CHRIS-
TIAN TIME; Or The Eremite Ambrosius his
Epistle unto Marcella, A.D. 410 . . . 265

XV. RECOLLECTIONS OF WORDSWORTH . 275

VII

EDWIN THE FAIR

IT is neither from its devotion to industrialism nor to inductive science that the spirit of the age has largely become wanting in dramatic aptitudes. Its moral qualifications also appear not exactly of the right sort. It is deficient in simplicity, in earnestness, in robustness—in that intrepid and impassioned adventurousness which desires to watch and join the great battle of the passions on the broad platform of common life ; and in that elasticity of soul which makes renewed vigour the natural recoil from suffering, and a deeper self-knowledge with a firmer self-government the chief permanent results of calamity. These are the heroic virtues of our nature ; and the Drama is the heroic walk of Poetry. Without these qualities it is as impossible heartily and practically to value a great dramatic literature as it is to produce it. We may be drawn to the theatre by the fame of a successful actor, or the splendour of scenic decoration, but all that is deepest and best in the drama will be thrown away upon us. Everything else we may have, things better

or things worse, but not this.   We may write excellent
descriptive poetry, or the noblest lyrics, or the most
profound philosophical pieces.   We may descend into
the depths of meditative pathos, or ascend into the
regions of the mystic and the spiritual; but dramatic
poetry we shall aim at in vain, unless we appreciate
those manly qualities which are the firm foundation
of real life, and therefore of imitative art.   This is the
reason that the time at which the drama rises up is the
heroic period of a nation—the heroic period not yet
extinct, though passing into the intellectual, and therefore at once present in power and beginning to be
associated with the records of a legendary past.   We
put off our coat-of-mail to assume the buskin and the
tragic robe; and the first sound from the stage is the
note of self-gratulating strength—

Now are our brows bound with victorious wreaths.

It is while we still thirst for great enterprises that we
desire to see them represented, and before our youth
has relinquished its reckless humours or its ideal and
half-fantastic elevation.   It is before the social principle has become merged in the selfish instinct that
the popular feeling so necessary for all true art, and
so useful both by exhibiting the average and spontaneous judgment of men under very various circumstances of life, and by enkindling through sympathy
the deepest powers of the artist, retains its unity and
its collective force.   This social and sympathetic
principle has been materially impaired by the exclusive

character of modern intercourse, and by those arbitrary distinctions which break up society into cliques and sets. It is before the principle of division and mechanical arrangement has supplanted the essential ties by the conventional modes of life, and weakened the tone of the individual mind even while increasing its stores and multiplying its implements, that the poet possesses that many-handed versatility of resource combined with that fiery and yet majestic intensity of mind, which is necessary to awaken his dramatic faculty and endow its creations with life and reality. Life, however, is life in every age, and there can never be a time in which dramatic art will not find its resources if the impulse of the poet be strong enough to bear him up against circumstances. Of this we have proof in such a work as *Edwin the Fair*.

The subject of this Saxon drama abounds in variety of interests, political, ecclesiastical, personal, and romantic; and not less various are the modes of treatment. It is the privilege of the mixed drama to reconcile many different styles. In the following extract the songs of the two fortune-tellers foreshow the fortunes of the Earls Athulf and Leolf—

> *A Thane.*   Hark ye! are we blind?
> The Princess was led in by brave Earl Athulf;
> And didst thou mark the manner of it, ha?
> *Scholar.* Methought she leaned upon him and toward him
> With a most graceful timid earnestness;
> A leaning more of instinct than of purpose,
> And yet not undesigned. But think you then . . .   [*They pass.*

Heida (sings to a harp).

> She was fresh and she was fair,
> Glossy was her golden hair ;
> Like a blue spot in the sky
> Was her clear and loving eye.
>
> He was true and he was bold,
> Full of mirth as he could hold ;
> Through the world he broke his way
> With jest, and laugh, and lightsome lay.
>
> Love ye wisely, love ye well ;
> Challenge then the gates of Hell.
> Love and truth can ride it out,
> Come bridal song or battle shout.

First Priest. Our gallant Heretoch, the good Earl Leolf,
Should have been there methought.
 Second Priest.   He should have been ;
But there are reasons, look ye,—reasons—mum—
Most excellent reasons—softly—in your ear— [*They pass.*

Thiorbiorga (sings).

> He stood on the rock,
> And he looked on the sea,
> And he said of his false Love,
> " My Love, where is she ?
>
> " Have they bought her with bracelets,
> And lured her with gold ?
> Is her love for her lover
> A tale that is told ?"
>
> From the crest of the wave,
> In the deep of the gulf,
> Came a voice that cried, " Save !
> For behold the sea-wolf !"
>
> He stood on the rock,
> And he looked at the wave,
> And he said, " Oh, St. Ulfrid !
> Who's this that cries Save !"
>
> Then arose from the billow
> A head with a crown,

And two hands that divided
The hair falling down.

As the foam in the moonlight
The two hands were fair,
And they put by the tangles
Of seaweed and hair.

He knew the pale forehead—
A spell to his ear
Was the voice that repeated,
" The sea-wolf is here !"

" I come, Love," he answered.
At sunrise next day
A fisherman wakened
The Priest in the Bay :

" For the soul of a sinner
Let masses be said—
The sin shall be nameless,
And nameless the dead." [1]

These are good songs, and there are few things
which it is so difficult to write. The moment we
endeavour to give completeness or wholeness to a
song the true lyrical spirit is lost. It is a vain labour
to balance part against part ; to elaborate some central thought, and illustrate it with metaphors. A
song is essentially fragmentary. It is a mass of closely
charged feeling suddenly finding vent, catching in its
passage a stream of imaginative thought—melting into
it, and scattering itself abroad in harmonious words.
One characteristic of a good song, and a reason why
in modern poetry we have so few, is its objectivity.
The passion expressed is unconscious of itself : it is
borne by a happy instinct at once to its object : it

[1] Pp. 87-91.

sinks into that object and loses itself. There exists a remarkable analogy between the lyrical and the dramatic faculties. The mind of a dramatic poet must, like the island of Prospero, be

full of noises,
Sounds, and sweet airs, that give delights and hurt not.

The ground should be firm and strong, but the air which hangs above it must swell and undulate with music ever ready to shoot a sweet note through the discords of the world below, to sustain courage in the midst of mischance, and to promise better things for the future. The characters of a drama are not mere individual men : they belong at least to a generic, if not to a moral ideal. Nor is nature in poetry mere nature : it borders more closely than common life on an archetypal region of justice and of glory. Throughout the whole drama there must thus be infused a certain lyrical spirit—that is, a spirit of elevation, buoyancy, and vitality. Songs are this spirit condensed and made visible : they are the sudden and electric flashes of this poetical element concentrated, mating itself to new forms, and restoring the equilibrium of imagination and passion.

The Greek Tragedy, as is well known, originated in the choral ode, and retained to the end of its nobler period a predominance of the lyrical character. This circumstance is alone sufficient to account for the ideal structure of that drama, as well as its elevated spirit, and in part for the impassioned rapidity of its action, in which event followed event with a turbulent precipitance like the successive notes of a triumphal song. In England the species of poetry which, before the period of the drama, had most found its way to the hearts of the people was the narrative ballad; and if we suppose the ballad to have had something of the same influence in suggesting our Historical Drama as was exerted by the ode on the Greek Tragedy, the conception will facilitate our understanding the great difference between those two species of composition. We shall thus observe the necessary superiority of the classic Tragedy in poetic loftiness, and its inferiority in variety, in detail, in familiar pathos, in local associations, and in picturesque effect. In some of these latter qualities the Historic Drama has an advantage over our own Tragedy also. One remarkable difference between our romantic Tragedy and Historic Drama is forcibly recalled to our recollection by the work before us. In pure Tragedy there is, or there ought to be, more of intensity, of concentrated energy, and consequently of elevation, than in the Historic; but in the latter species of composition the deficiency may be atoned for by a greater breadth of effect and more of philosophical thought. Hence too the historic drama presents us with a calmer and more widely instructive picture of human life. In Tragedy the problem of life is pressed upon our attention: in the Historic Play it is solved. The former, from its very superiority in compactness, does not leave, as it were, room for light: the different characters stand so close together

as to overshadow each other; the struggle of the
action is, to a large extent, a battle in the dark;
and the reader's interest partakes, therefore, of a
certain breathless and supernatural awe.   It is not,
however, when the nerves of feeling are strung to a
degree of extraordinary tenseness that we can appreciate the average motives of men—or trace out the
threads of the web woven by human beings, as they
move by a natural instinct through the concentric
circles of domestic, social, and political life.   To learn
this lesson we must observe the course of action and
of passion developing themselves, by a process more
leisurely and relaxed.   It is thus that we shall recognise in man a being who, as an individual indeed,
is invested with a freedom which renders his desires
and designs inscrutable, but who at the same time,
as a social being, is subject to a Law that moves in
him without his consciousness, and by virtue of which
Society becomes capable of possessing a natural
history of its own.   In Tragedy the general law is
often lost in that disproportionate development of
individual Will which is necessary for the resistance
of overwhelming circumstance : in the wider and less
tempestuous expanse of the Historic Drama, we have
opportunity and patience to follow out the working of
the general law as it influences the actions even of
men whose motives appear most different.   The
great idea of all high Tragedy includes to a large
degree what it was pre-eminently in the Greek—viz.
that of Fate : what, then, is the idea of the Historic

Drama? It is a very different idea—that, namely, of Providence: we trace the circle all round, and, observing the converging lines to point to one spot, we find the solution of the complex system of actions and reactions in the words Διὸς δ ἐτελείετο βουλή. We acknowledge a Power from above, not a hand from the shades—a Providence, not oppressing and subduing man, but working with his strivings while it works beyond them; and thus, while it unconsciously vindicates the ways of God, the Historic Drama instructs us likewise in the philosophic lore of nature and of man.

Dunstan, Wulfstan, Leolf, and Athulf, are characters of primary importance in this drama; and Odo, Archbishop of Canterbury, though age has deprived him of the keener part of his intellect, and Dunstan's predominant power of that weight which would otherwise belong to his vehement and uncompromising temper, remains, on the whole, a considerable person from his past energies and present station. Clarenbald, the chancellor, may be described in a few words: —orderly, upright, versed in affairs, and efficient. The young king, though, from youthful precipitance not equal to the needs of the time, is worthy of his throne, brave as well as gentle, single-hearted and royal-minded, and exciting a deeper interest as we become acquainted with his strength through his trials. The queen-mother is the darkest of all the figures introduced, and has least to redeem her: malignant, wrong-headed, and narrow-hearted; blundering on with a paralytic obliquity of mind; her religion a fear;

her maternal love an animal instinct. Of a very different order is Wulfstan the Wise :—a recluse and a philosopher; subtle of intellect, yet simple as a child; a mind rather than a man; searching all things for their inner laws, and scarcely noticing their outward effects; seeing *through* all objects, and therefore seeing them not; drawing his manifold wisdom from the springs of intuitive and discursive reason, and yet, with amusing and not unnatural perverseness, fancying his especial gifts to be knowledge of the world, and skill in the conduct of business: by the very largeness of his being, exempted from the agitations of life, like a ship which lies along too great an expanse of waves to feel their shocks; yet prompt in sympathy as well as daring where need is, and at a word of kindness moistening his visionary eyes with dews that rise from no Olympian spring. This character could hardly have belonged to the age illustrated here; but it is deeply conceived, and beautifully set forth. Very exquisite too is the sketch of the Princess Ethilda, though it is too slightly drawn to be generally appreciated. She is one of those beings whom in real life we love without exactly knowing why, or caring to know—innocent, devout, solicitous, yet trusting, and adding the gracefulness of her illustrious descent to that of her youth and sex. She has in a singular degree that charm which consists in the absence of self-asserting or disproportionate qualities; and we grow to understand her not a little through the impression she makes on others. The scholar, the minstrel, the soldier, all love her; and even the queen-mother does not hate her. Earl Athulf is described by Wulfstan—

> As one whose courage high and humour gay
> Cover a vein of caution : his true heart,
> Intrepid though it be, not blind to danger,
> But through imagination's optic glass
> Discerning, yea, and magnifying it may be,
> What still he dares. . . .
> . . . prompt for enterprise
> By reason of his boldness, and yet apt
> For composition, owing to that vein
> Of fancy which enhances, prudence which wards
> Contingencies of peril.[1]

This character seems drawn mostly from observation,—that of Dunstan from reflection and imaginative induction. Leolf, more than all the rest, bears the impress of that poetic sympathy on the part of the author which is so essential to the vividness of the picture as well as to its accuracy. He is thus presented to us as he paces the seashore near his castle at Hastings—

> *Leolf.*   Here again I stand,
> Again and on the solitary shore
> Old ocean plays as on an instrument,
> Making that ancient music, when not known?
> That ancient music, only not so old
> As He who parted ocean from dry land,
> And saw that it was good. Upon mine ear,
> As in the season of susceptive youth,
> The mellow murmur falls—but finds the sense
> Dulled by distemper ; shall I say—by time?
> Enough in action has my life been spent
> Through the past decade, to rebate the edge
> Of early sensibility. The sun

Rides high, and on the thoroughfares of life
I find myself a man in middle age,
Busy and hard to please.   The sun shall soon
Dip westerly,—but oh! how little like
Are life's two twilights!   Would the last were first,
And the first last! that so we might be soothed
Upon the thoroughfares of busy life
Beneath the noon-day sun, with hope of joy
Fresh as the morn,—with hope of breaking lights,
Illuminated mists and spangled lawns,
And woodland orisons and unfolding flowers,
As things in expectation.—Weak of faith!
Is not the course of earthly outlook, thus
Reversed from Hope, an argument to Hope—
That she was licensed to the heart of man
For other than for earthly contemplations,
In that observatory domiciled
For survey of the stars?   The night descends,
They sparkle out.

Known rather by his misfortunes than his actions, King Edwin, though sufficient to supply the whole interest of a romantic poem, could hardly have held, except nominally, the chief and central place in the plot of a Tragedy.   But the periods of history most fit for a historical drama are not always those in which the conspicuous sufferer is also the great man.   Thus much Shakespeare's *Richard the Second* proves.   A personal interest does not suffice where a social and political problem has to be solved.   Strange escapes, sudden exaltations, unforeseen calamities,—these will never appeal in vain to the sympathies of the most careless reader; but such events, if they involve no moral lesson, yield no field for the highest art of the historical dramatist.   He requires one of those periods of social fermentation during which the national ener-

gies are evolving themselves according to some internal
law; in which principles that have grown up naturally in the human heart, and matured themselves in
the mind of the recluse, receive a mission to go forth
and wield the destinies of social man; in which several
such principles meet together in a war-struggle, and
manifesting through opposition their latent might,
attest the great truth that the progress of nations, like
that of men, is the progress of mind, and depends not
merely on the transmission of outward impulses.
Such a state of affairs is presented to us by the contest between the monastic orders and the civil power
in England's Saxon days.

The subject of *Edwin the Fair* is then, on the whole,
well chosen, though it possesses not the advantage of
concentrating the interest on an individual character as
imposing as that of Artevelde.   Without a principle of
unity, indeed, no dramatic work can possibly be good;
but that harmony of effect which is produced by some
one predominant character, is only one mode of giving
unity.   In painting and in sculpture, it is not merely
by means of a central figure that unity is imparted to a
group.   When the persons constituting that group, or
the larger number of them, fix their attention on a
common object or a common action, there we have
unity; and we feel it the more strongly if something
of a common expression be found in the different
faces.   Variety is, of course, necessary also; but where
variety exists there may be found a generic likeness.
There may exist in the various faces a resemblance, as

of kindred ; or they may express the same passions in different degrees and stages ; or the passions which they express may be allied to each other, or supplemental to each other.   Such is the unity which we so often find in pictures of the old masters : and every one who has understood them will admit that the effect of harmony thus conveyed to the mind (whether through a science now forgotton, or by the unconscious genius of the early artists) is often far more full and satisfactory than that which we receive from modern works, designed according to the strictest rules of composition.

Of this nature is the unity which pervades *Edwin the Fair*.   Throughout it we find one spirit ; the spirit, namely, of England in the time of that struggle which raged with such violence between the "men of arms and the men of thought."   Throughout the whole play we trace this spirit working its way in different characters according to their constitution, varying with their varieties, but everywhere active.   No one is too high or too low to take a part in this great contest. The queen-mother's "mean and meagre soul" attaches itself to Dunstan as the only defence, while persecuted by her "past misdeeds and ever-present fears."   The princess, too, has caught the infection, though it has not tainted "her pleasant purity of spirit."   The monks are "raving of Dunstan," and see signs and wonders in his mode of coughing and discussing the weather ; the nobles allow themselves to be marshalled at his pleasure in the field of battle.   The Archbishop of

Canterbury grows jealous ere long; but endeavours in
vain to separate his fortunes from those of the master-
spirit of the age. The characters arrayed on the other
side are not less deeply impressed with the antagonist
principle. Elgiva is hardly more earnest in her love
for Edwin than in her hatred of the monastic party:
the Earls Leolf and Athulf are full of the indignation
of nobles who have long felt themselves supplanted in
the affections of the people, and at last find themselves
assailed even with their own weapons of military force.
The king's jester has learned to value a sharp saying
against Dunstan above his other witticisms: even the
recluse philosopher, Wulfstan the Wise, though, as he
rather unnecessarily assures us, "never factious or
inflamed," forgets his secluded habits to mingle in the
tumult of the time, and gives an account of Dunstan's
character, which, however applicable to a part of that
strange complex, does not intimate that the philosopher
has in this instance exercised his great faculties with
an entire fairness—

> *Wulfstan.*   His, Sir, you shall find
> A spirit subdolous, though full of fire.
> A spider may he best be likened to,
> Which creature is an adept not alone
> In workmanship of nice geometry,
> But is beside a wary politician:
> He, when his prey is taken in the toils,
> Withholds himself until its strength be spent
> With struggles, and its spirit with despair:
> Then with a patient and profound delight
> Forth from his ambush stalks.

Mr. Taylor has acted with reference to Dunstan's

character as he tells us he has done with regard to incident, "choosing from amongst the accounts of the reign given by its early historians, where they conflict, those which best suited his purpose." The dramatist is, however, bound at least to observe ideal truth when historical veracity is impossible ; and the chief inquiry, therefore, which his readers will make is whether the character, as conceived by him, be consistent with itself. Mr. Taylor's Dunstan is not altogether evil : far from it. He has great aspirations, great thoughts, great, though not invariable, self-control. Nay, in an important sense, he is sincere. He believes in the reality of his struggles with Satan, and esteems himself the chosen instrument for promoting the glory of God in the world—

> Spirit of speculation, rest, oh rest !
> And push not from her place the spirit of prayer !
> God, thou 'st given unto me a troubled being—
> So move upon the face thereof, that light
> May be, and be divided from the darkness !
> Arm thou my soul that I may smite and chase
> The spirit of that darkness, whom not I
> But Thou through me compellest. Mighty power,
> Legions of piercing thoughts illuminate,
> Hast Thou committed to my large command,
> Weapons of light and radiant shafts of day,
> And steeds that trample on the tumbling clouds.
> But with them it hath pleased Thee to let mingle
> Evil imaginations, corporal stings,
> A host of Imps and Ethiops, dark doubts,
> Suggestions of revolt.[1]

Contemplating, however, the Supreme Being chiefly as a God of Power, and forgetting that He is no less a

[1] P. 13.

God of Truth and of Goodness, Dunstan, as here set forth, can only conceive His glory promoted by the bringing of all secular powers under submission to the Church ; and regarding himself as that Church's chief champion, the result is a species of self-inebriation, which heats and hardens his soul almost to madness. Such a mind by its ardour resolves all the solids and liquids of social life into their aërial form, and then rushes forward, scarcely conscious of an obstacle, or even a resisting medium. He is represented as one with high aims but boundless spiritual pride and no scruples, acting mainly through his genius and power of will on men, and, when those resources fail, resorting to the weapon of craft. The device, however, attributed to him in conjunction with the queen-mother against the honour of Elgiva is a blemish in the drama ; and it is also superfluous, as regards the delineation of one, whose craft is abundantly exhibited elsewhere in a manner less painful and improbable.

Such, then, is the character of Dunstan, as delineated in *Edwin the Fair :*—a fanatic working on the religious affections of others for his own exaltation, but also for that of what he deems a great cause :—in youth not exempt from offences which in later life he so easily suspects in others :—a lover of science and of art in an age when the former was accounted for witchcraft, and the latter for paganism :—while young attaching himself to the sect of those who touch the viol or harp cunningly, and work in iron and brass ; learning ere long to subordinate the artist to the leader, to play on the heart of man as an instrument, to heat society to the temperature of glowing metal, and mould it at his pleasure, trampling underfoot those ties of life which he in fact did not understand, and yet shrinking with constitutional softness from shedding blood, except in a case of necessity; mortifying his flesh, yet exalting his spirit; vehement yet patient; wary yet precipitate.

Mr. Taylor's conception of Dunstan is powerfully brought forward in the second scene of the third act.

> *Dunstan.* Kings shall bow down before thee, said my soul,
> And it is even so.   Hail, ancient Hold !
> Thy chambers are most cheerful, though the light
> Enter not freely ; for the eye of God
> Smiles in upon them.   Cherished by His smile
> My heart is glad within me, and to Him
> Shall testify in works a strenuous joy.
> —*Methinks that I could be myself that rock*
> *Whereon the Church is founded,*—wind and flood
> Beating against me, boisterous in vain.
> I thank you, Gracious Powers ! Supernal Host !
> I thank you that on me, though young in years,
> Ye put the glorious charge to try with fire,
> To winnow and to purge.   I hear your call !
> A radiance and a resonance from Heaven
> Surrounds me, and my soul is breaking forth
> In strength, as did the new-created Sun
> When Earth beheld it first on the fourth day.

The synodial scene is the centre on which the main interest of the drama turns.   Dunstan has discovered, through his emissaries, that the archbishop has secretly deserted him, and that a large proportion even of his own friends have resolved on making peace with Edwin.   He arms himself, however, for the conflict, and not in vain.   When, after a stormy

debate, the synod is about to acquiesce in the terms
proposed, he comes down into the battle, and as usual
he carries all before him—

[DUNSTAN *throws himself on his knees, and bows his head on
      the ground.*
    Sidroc. He bends before the storm.
    Wulfstan.   Will he not speak?
    Sidroc. I know not—yes—he is in act to hatch
A brood of pestilent words, if I mistake not.
He stirs, he moves—few moments are enough.
    Wulfstan. They say a louse that 's but three minutes old
May be a grandsire; with no less a speed
Do foul thoughts gender.
    Sidroc.   Ha! we'll see anon—
Faith of my body! up he goes—sit—sit.
    Dunstan (*rising slowly*). I groan in spirit.   Brethren,
          seek not in me
Support or counsel.   The whole head is sick,
The whole heart faint; and trouble and rebuke
Come round about me, thrusting at my soul.
But, brethren, if long years of penance sore,
For your sake suffered, be remembered now,
Deem me not utterly of God forsaken,
Deem not yourselves forsaken.   Lift up your hearts.
See where ye stand on earth; see how in heaven
Ye are regarded.   Ye are the sons of God,
The Order of Melchisedeck, the Law,
The visible structure of the world of spirit,
Which was, and is, and must be; all things else
Are casual, and monarchs come and go,
And warriors for a season walk the earth,
By accident; for these are accidental,
But ye eternal; ye are the soul of the world,
Ye are the course of nature consecrate,
Ye are the Church! one spirit is throughout you,
And Christendom is with you in all lands.
Who comes against you?   'Scaped from Hell's confine,
A wandering rebel, fleeting past the sun,
Darkens the visage of the Spouse of Christ.
But 'tis but for a moment; he consumed

Shall vanish like a vapour, She divulged
Break out in glory that transcends herself.
The thrones and principalities of earth,
When stood they that they stood not with the aid
Of us and them before us?   Azarias,
Azias, Amaziah, Saul himself,
Fell they not headlong when they fell from us?
And Oza, he that did but touch the ark?
Oh then what sin for me, what sin for you,
For me victorious in a thousand fights
Against this foe, for you as oft redeemed,
That now we falter!   Do we falter?   No!
Thou God that art within me when I conquer,
I feel thee fill me now!   Angelic Host,
Seraphs that wave your swords about my head,
I thank you for your succours!   Who art thou
That givest me this gracious admonition?
Alas! forgive me that I knew thee not,
O Gabriel![1]

Suddenly a voice—*Absit hoc ut fiat*—is heard from
the remoter end of the hall.

*Most of the Assembly fall prostrate.   There is a pause of some
moments.   Then* DUNSTAN, *who had remained erect, with
his hands stretched towards the Crucifix, resumes.*
Oh precious guidance!   Oh ineffable grace!
That dost from disobedience deliver
The hearts of even the faithless!   We obey,
And these espousals do we now declare
Avoided and accursed.   The woman espoused,
By name Elgiva, from the man called Edwy
We separate, and from the Church's pale
We cast her forth; and with her we cast forth
Those three that have been foremost to uphold her,
Earl Athulf, and Earl Leolf, and Earl Sidroc.
Them we proclaim, by sentence of the Pope,
From Christian rites and ministries cut off,
And from the Holy Brotherhood of the Just
Sequestered with a curse.   Be they accursed!
Accursed be they in all time and place,
Accursed be they in the camp and mart,

---

[1] Pp. 173-176.

Accursed be they in the city and field,
Accursed be their flying and abiding,
Accursed be their waking and their rest—
We curse the hand that feeds them when they hunger,
We curse the arm that props them when they faint ;
Withered and blasted be that hand and arm !
We curse the tongue that speaks to them, the ear
That hears them, though it be but unawares :
Blistered and cankered be that tongue and ear !
The earth in which their bodies shall be buried
We curse, except it cast their bodies out :
We shut the gates of Heaven against their souls,
And as this candle that I fling to the ground,
So be their light extinguished in the Pit ! ![1]

Dunstan's speech is an extraordinary instance of dramatic art. He begins apparently in a state of entire prostration, in order that the lofty courage of his subsequent harangue may appear inspired, and not his own. Gradually he rises into a tone of elevation, which in turn ere long passes into a loftier strain of genuine passion. Still, however, he keeps his faculties in hand, economises his enthusiasm, and balances his assumed and his real inspiration, until, kindling at last as with the velocity of his own motion, his suppressed ardour bursts into a flame which communicates itself at once to the assembly; and he triumphs. Equally well imagined is Dunstan's change of tone when crowned with success. No more poetical raptures or mystical visions, but words, sharp, plain, and concentrated, comprising a brief enumeration of the offenders, and definition of their punishment.

The introductory address of the archbishop is of

---

[1] P. 176.

not less artistic merit, though that merit is of a less obvious sort. That speech is a business speech, and seeks to be no more. But several of the lines are worthy of study, from the manner in which, by a subtle alternation of succinct with periodic writing, they illustrate the occasional outbreaking of the Primate's vehement temper through the official dignity which keeps it on the whole in restraint. The speech of Cumba, the conciliatory priest and meek man of the world

> Whose faith is mounted on his charity,
> And sits it easy—

is a felicitous example of that wisdom which remembers that to convince before you have persuaded is a process as painful as shaving without soap, and which understands also how dishonesty may be kept within such bounds as neither to hinder a man's fortunes, nor, in case his ambition extends to posthumous honours, to hurt his epitaph.

Dunstan, who has roused the country people into rebellion, appears next ordering about the military leaders as unceremoniously as he had before made bishops and monks his puppets. Retribution has begun. At first he had carried all before him; but England's intestine divisions have drawn the Danes down upon her.

> *Dunstan.* No more of Wittenagemóts—no more—
> Councils and Courts we want not.—Get ye back,
> Back to your posts, and pluck me forth your swords,
> And let me hear your valiant deeds resound,
> And not your empty phrases. Ecfrid, Gorf,
> Look to your charges—Nantwich stands exposed—
> Whitchurch lies open to the enemy—

> Burley and Baddeley have sold themselves—
> Wistaston is as naked as Godiva,
> And not so honest.   Eadbald, Ida, Brand,
> What seek ye here, when honour is in the field?
> Forth to your charges!
>
> .   .   .   .   .   .
>
>   *Æthelric.* You will not hear, my Lord.   We have no
>   charge—
> We have no force.   Our men are slain—ourselves
> Escaped by miracle.   The Northmen, led
> By Sweyne and Olaf, landed yesternight
> In Porlock Bay and clipped us round at Stoke,—
> And, thinned as we had been, we fell perforce
> An easy prey.   Not twenty men are left
> To tell the tale.
>   *Dunstan.*   In Porlock Bay!   At Stoke!
> —Have I not bid you to your posts, my Lords,
> And must I bid you twice?   Get ye hence all.
> If news ye came for, ye have heard it.—Stop,
> Ceolwulf.   Whither go the Northmen next?
>   *Ceolwulf.* To Glastonbury it is thought, my Lord.
>   *Dunstan.* To Glastonbury do they go?   Alas!
> My mother there lies sick.

Before we meet Dunstan again a further change
has come over him.   His mother is dead—dead in
consequence of the success which has attended her
son's pernicious intrigues.   She was to him the one
object of human affection; and even his strong being
is cleft in twain by her death.   Thirsting for revenge
on the Danes, he proffers terms to the young king:
they are rejected, for he too has suffered an irreparable
wrong, and he too seeks but revenge.

Near the end is a scene marked by a pathos which
makes it unique in this work.   Elgiva escapes from
her prison through the aid of the lover whom she has
forsaken for the young king.   A little before the
arrow pierces her heart they converse.   This scene is

the only one which suspends for a moment the precipitated movement of the fifth act; and it is the more touching for its stillness in the midst of commotion, as it hangs like one of those little woody islands which often divide the waters of a river just before they reach the rapids—

> *Elgiva.*   Oh Leolf! much
> I owe you, and if aught a kingdom's wealth
> Affords could pay the debt. . . .
> *Leolf.*   A kingdom's wealth!
> Elgiva! by the heart the heart is paid.
> You have your kingdom, my heart hath its love.
> We are provided.
> *Elgiva.*   Oh! in deeds so kind,
> And can you be so bitter in your words!
> Have I no offerings of the heart, wherewith
> Love's service to requite?
> *Leolf.*   The least of boons
> Scattered by Royal charity's careless hand
> O'erpays my service.   To requite the rest
> All you possess is but a bankrupt's bond.
> This is the last time we shall speak together;
> Forgive me, therefore, if my speech be bold,
> And need not an expositor to come.
> I loved you once; and in such sort I loved,
> That anguish hath but burnt the image in,
> And I must bear it with me to my grave.
> I loved you once; dearest Elgiva, yes,
> Even now my heart doth feed upon that love
> As in its flower and freshness, ere the grace
> And beauty of the fashion of it perished.
> It was too anxious to be fortunate,
> And it must now be buried, self-embalmed,
> Within my breast, or, living there recluse.
> Talk to itself and traffic with itself;
> And like a miser that puts nothing out,
> And asks for no return, must I tell o'er
> The treasures of the past.
> *Elgiva.*   Can no return

Be rendered?   And is gratitude then nothing?
    Leolf. To me 'tis nothing—being less than love.
But cherish it as to your own soul precious !
The heavenliest lot that earthly natures know
Is to be affluent in gratitude.
Be grateful and be happy.   For myself,
If sorrow be my portion, yet shall hope
That springs from sorrow and aspires to Heaven,
Be with me still.   When this disastrous war
Is ended, I shall quit my country's shores,
A pilgrim and a suitor to the love
Which dies not nor betrays.—What cry is that ?
I thought I heard a voice.
    Elgiva.   Oh Leolf, Leolf !
So tender, so severe !
    Leolf.   Mistake me not.
I would not be unjust : I have not been ;
Now less than ever could I be, for now
A sacred and judicial calmness holds
Its mirror to my soul ; at once disclosed
The picture of the past presents itself
Minute yet vivid, such as it is seen
In his last moments by a drowning man.
Look at this skeleton of a once green leaf :
Time and the elements conspired its fall ;
The worm hath eaten out the tenderer parts,
And left this curious anatomy
Distinct of structure—made so by decay.
So, at this moment, lies my life before me,—
In all its intricacies, all its errors—
And can I be unjust ?
    Elgiva.   Oh, more than just,
Most merciful in judgment have you been,
And even in censure kind.
    Leolf.   Our lives were linked
By one misfortune and a double fault.
It was my folly to have fixed my hopes
Upon the fruitage of a budding heart.
It was your fault,—the lighter fault by far,—
Being the bud to seem to be the berry.
The first inconstancy of unripe years
Is Nature's error on the way to truth.
But, hark ! another cry !   They call us hence.

The last scene of *Edwin the Fair* in its tragic strength contrasts signally with the milder pathos of this one. It is in the Cathedral of Malpas where the monks have been performing a service of thanksgiving for their victory. On a bier in the transept lies the body of Elgiva awaiting burial, where it is found by Edwin, who, mortally wounded, has risen from his bed in the delirium of fever and made his attendants conduct him to the church in which his wife is to be interred. The wanderings of the young king on recognising the corpse, and the breaking out of his mind into light and passion the moment before his death, can find a parallel only in the greatest among the Elizabethan dramas. In this scene the injurer and the injured are once more, and for the last time, confronted.

> *Edwin.* Thy hand is very cold,—Come, come, look up;
> Hast not a word to say to so much love?
> Well—as thou wilt—but 'twas not always thus,
> So soon to be forgotten ! Oh so soon !
> And I have loved so truly all this while!—
> I dream—I do but dream—I think—What's here?
> 'Tis not the dress that thou wert wont to wear.
> This is a corpse ! Attendance here ! What, ho !
> Who was so bold to bring a stone-cold corpse
> Into the King's apartment? Stop—be still—
> I know not that. Give me but time, my friends,
> And I will tell you. . . .
> *Dunstan.* Bridferth, mount the tower
> And look abroad.
> *Edwin.*   That was a voice I knew—
> It came from darkness, and the Pit—but hark !
> An Angel's song ! 'Tis Dunstan that I see !
> Rebellious monk ! I lay my body down
> Here at thy feet to die, but not my soul

Which goes to God.   The cry of innocent blood
Is up against thee, and the Avenger's cry
Shall answer it.   Support me, Sirs, I pray ;
Be patient with me . . . there was something still . . .
I know not what . . . under your pardon . . . yes . . .
Touching my burial . . . did I not see but now
Another corpse . . . I pray you, Sirs . . . there . . . there ?

[Dies.

Bridferth (*from the tower*). My Lord, my Lord, Harcather
      flies ; the Danes
Are pouring through the gate.   Harcather falls.
Dunstan. Give me the crucifix.   Bring out the relics.
Host of the Lord of Hosts, forth once again !

LATER PLAYS

A Sicilian Summer occupies a peculiar position, both in Mr. Taylor's poetry and in modern literature. Since the earlier part of the seventeenth century we have had but few comedies after the genuine Shakespearean model. Our modern comedies have been comedies of wit and manners: they have dealt with the humours, not the heart of man, and aimed but to combine a skilful plot with a brilliant, superficial sketch of society. Such was the comedy of Sheridan, whose works are perhaps the happiest specimens of the style to which they belong. But the Shakespearean comedy was another order of composition. In spite of the gay scenes with which they are so delightfully varied, such plays as the *Merchant of Venice*, *The Tempest*, and *As You Like It*, are as full of serious purpose as Shakespeare's tragedies themselves. Those trifles on the surface of society with which they sport so buoyantly do not hinder them from descending into the heart of the humanities. In them joy and sorrow are allowed to alternate their voices, as they do in the

long dispute of human life, although the brighter
genius has the last word.   It is from the imagination
and the reason that all genuine poetry springs, the
imagination claiming in it first place.   The higher
drama is thus competent to measure itself with the
whole of human life.   There is a music in human
laughter as well as in sighs, of which reason alone can
discern the law; and there is a depth in the humorous
which the imagination alone can fathom.   Ages before
a Shakespeare had been raised up to prove the truth
of the assertion, the great critic of antiquity had
affirmed that the intellect capable of the highest
greatness in tragedy must be competent in comedy
no less.

A Sicilian Summer is as bright and musical as the
southern clime it illustrates, and it is full of that wisdom
which is never wiser than in its sportive moods.   It
is not, however, every reader who will appreciate it.
Strength touches all : but strength refined into grace
addresses itself to a select circle.   Tragic passion, be
it remembered, challenges the personal as well as the
imaginative sensibilities; and as such it affects not
only a better class, but many likewise who, if they
sometimes respond to what is truly great, yet as
frequently burst into raptures at the clumsiest appeals.
It is far otherwise with those passages of a finer grain
—those delicate hair-strokes of felicitous thought and
finished expression, which to be apprehended at all
must be fully appreciated.   By many poetry is liked
best for the accidents with which the noblest poetry

is most willing to dispense. In its inmost essence it reveals itself but to those who prefer the distant flute-tone to the rattle of wire and wood, and enjoy most the odour that floats upon the breeze.

The scene of *A Sicilian Summer* is chiefly at Palermo, where Silisco, Marquis of Malespina, in the prodigality of youthful spirits and vast wealth, fills his old palace with a perpetual revel. His generosity and his magnificence make him the delight of the young; but the old prognosticate his speedy ruin,—a catastrophe not the less probable because the young nobleman, after the fashion of the time, is merchant too. He charters a ship to Rhodes, mortgaging the remaining portions of his estates to three Jews. Spadone, the captain of the ship, conspires to betray at once his employer and his crew. He is to sink his vessel on his return, and escaping in a boat with his fellow-conspirators, to secrete amid the catacombs near the seashore the jewels and ingots of gold which he has brought from Rhodes. In the meantime Rosalba, daughter of the king's chamberlain, Count Ubaldo, comes from Procida to Palermo, accompanied by her chosen friend Fiordeliza. The revels at Silisco's palace are soon given exclusively on Rosalba's account, Fiordeliza being wooed at the same time by Ruggiero, the friend of Silisco, though the severest censor of his waste. Count Ubaldo has, however, contracted Rosalba to Ugo, Count of Arezzo, the wealthiest of the Sicilian nobles, desiring to preserve her from spendthrifts and fortune-hunters, and seeing nothing

amiss in a bridegroom of between sixty and seventy
years. At the king's entreaty Ubaldo relents so far
as to say that he will not insist on his daughter's
engagement if Count Ugo can be induced to forego
it, and if Silisco is able, on the return of his ship, to
redeem his lands of Malespina, impledged to Ugo.
Silisco is not less successful in his suit, and Rosalba
promises to be his, if, through a change in her father's
purpose, she should find herself free. She leaves her
lover, at his own prayer, till All Saints' Day, to work
upon her father's will.

The second scene of the play illustrates the revels
of the prodigal—

Silisco. Off with these viands and this wine, Conrado ;
Feasting is not festivity : it cloys
The finer spirits. Music is the feast
That lightly fills the soul. My pretty friend,
Touch me that lute of thine, and pour thy voice
Upon the troubled waters of this world.
Aretina. What ditty would you please to hear, my Lord ?
Silisco. Choose thou, Ruggiero. See now, if that knave . . .
Conrado, ho ! A hundred times I've bid thee
To give what wine is over to the poor
About the doors.
Conrado.   Sir, this is Malvoisie
And Muscadel, a ducat by the flask.
Silisco. Give it them not the less ; they'll never know ;
And better it went to enrich a beggar's blood
Than surfeit ours ;—Choose thou, Ruggiero !
Ruggiero.   I !
I have not heard her songs.
Silisco.   Thou sang'st me once
A song that had a note of either muse,
Not sad, nor gay, but rather both than neither.
What call you it ?
Aretina. I think, my Lord, 'twas this.
Silisco. Yes, yes, 'twas so it ran ; sing that, I pray thee.

Aretina sings—

> I'm a bird that's free
> Of the land and sea,
>   I wander whither I will ;
> But oft on the wing,
> I falter and sing,
>   Oh fluttering heart, be still,
>   Be still,
>   Oh fluttering heart, be still.
>
> I'm wild as the wind,
> But soft and kind,
>   And wander whither I may,
> The eye-bright sighs,
> And says with its eyes,
>   Thou wandering wind, oh stay,
>   Oh stay,
>   Thou wandering wind, oh stay.
>
> .   .   .   .   .

The prodigal is neither a sensualist nor a mere trifler.   His nature has strength and sagacity in it, and it is only the edge of the wave that breaks into froth and loses itself.   Yet his heedlessness tends to worse than the loss of his lands, as is intimated by the reply of Fra Martino to a friend who has found it impossible to refuse him aid in his difficulties—

> Give thou to no man, if thou wish him well,
> What he may not in honour's interest take ;
> Else shalt thou but befriend his faults, allied
> Against his better with his baser self.

We are early introduced to the heroine of the play, and to Fiordeliza.   They are coming from Procida, and Silisco waits on the seashore, with Ruggiero, to receive them.   The friends converse of their expected guests—

Ruggiero. In the soft fulness of a rounded grace,
Noble of stature, with an inward life
Of secret joy sedate, Rosalba stands,
As seeing and not knowing she is seen,
Like a majestic child, without a want
She speaks not often, but her presence speaks,
And is itself an eloquence, which withdrawn,
It seems as though some strain of music ceased
That fill'd till then the palpitating air
With sweet pulsations ; when she speaks indeed,
'Tis like some one voice eminent in the choir,
Heard from the midst of many harmonies
With thrilling singleness, yet clear accord.
So heard, so seen, she moves upon the earth,
Unknowing that the joy she ministers
Is aught but Nature's sunshine.
    Silisco.   Call you this
The picture of a woman or a Saint ?
When Cimabue next shall figure forth
The hierarchies of heaven, we'll give him this
To copy from.   But said you, then, the other
Was fairer still than this ?
    Ruggiero.   I may have said it ;
I should have said, she's fairer in my eyes.
Yet must my eyes be something worse than blind,
And see the thing that is not, if the hand
Of Nature was not lavish of delights
When she was fashion'd.   But it were not well
To blazon her too much ; for mounted thus
In your esteem, she might not hold her place,
But fall the farther for the fancied rise.
For she has faults, Silisco, she has faults ;
And when you see them you may think them worse
Than I, who know, or think I know, their scope.
She gives her words the mastery, and flush'd
With quickenings of a wild and wayward wit,
Flits like a firefly in a tangled wood,
Restless, capricious, careless, hard to catch,
Though beautiful to look at.[1]

---

[1] Vol. iii. p. 13.

The young countess lands, and Silisco's fate is changed.   It is thus he ruminates—

> Hope and Joy,
> My younger sisters, you have never yet
> Been parted from my side beyond the breadth
> Of a slim sunbeam, and you never shall;
> Already it is loosen'd, it is gone,—
> The cloud, the mist; across the vale of life
> The rainbow rears its soft triumphal arch,
> And every roving path and brake and bower
> Is bathed in colour'd light.   Come what come may,
> I know this world is richer than I thought
> By something left to it from paradise;
> I know this world is brighter than I thought,
> Having a window into heaven.   Henceforth
> Life hath for me a purpose and a drift.[1]

The venture of the merchant - prince promises success.   In good time his ship reappears in the offing.   All day long it is watched from the harbour tower by one of the Jews.   Then its treacherous captain, Spadone, executes his plot.   About sunset the good ship *Maddalena* suddenly sinks.   Writs are immediately sent out by the Jews against Silisco, who flies for refuge to the catacombs on the seaside. Spadone has already lodged his booty there.   His two accomplices watch for him in a boat outside; but on the appearance of Ruggiero, who is walking on the shore, they take to their oars.   Spadone commits his booty to his mistress Aretina, and leaves her, with directions to send him word as soon as he can safely return.   In an agony of terror at the crime of which she has just heard, Aretina meets Silisco, and is on the point of telling him all she has learned when

[1] Vol. iii. p. 17.

Spadone, who has lurked near them, stabs her. He endeavours to kill Silisco also; but after a short combat, falls covered with wounds. Silisco, not knowing with whom he has been engaged, drags him out of the cave, leaves him at the door of Gerbetto, the king's physician, who lives on the beach, and again secretes himself. Ruggiero learns soon after from the lips of a half-drowned sailor, sole survivor of the *Maddalena's* crew, the villainy by which the rest have been destroyed. His eye has already been attracted by the signs of guilty terror with which the mate and boatswain fled at his approach; he leaps into a boat, and with the help of the rescued sailor gives them chase.

Rosalba finds herself thus deserted by her lover, and loses in his ruin all hope of a changed intention on the part of her father. She still resists the marriage with Count Ugo, till assured by Gerbetto, on the word of the dying Spadone, that Silisco had been faithless to her, and had induced Aretina to be false also. She then consents to wed Count Ugo. Silisco lies hid on the lands of Malespina, which have now passed into Ugo's hands. He is there joined by Ruggiero, who, after giving chase for a night and a day to the fugitives, saw them go down at sea, as he supposed, with Silisco's lost treasures, and had then himself languished in fever for months on the coast of Calabria. Ruggiero resolves to make an effort to prevent the marriage; but it has already taken place before his tired horse can bear him to Palermo. The evening, however, of the marriage-day is kept with masque and pageant. Ruggiero attends the festival, and removing his mask, arraigns the bride for her falsehood. Her reply brings out the statement made by the dying Spadone respecting Arctina, which Ruggiero at once confutes, revealing the crime of Spadone, of which Silisco's ruin had been the consequence. In the midst of the grief of the bride, and her father's anger, the aged bridegroom displays a magnanimity for which none had given him credit. He declares that he can never recognise as valid an engagement contracted under such circumstances, and that the calamity which has befallen them is the punishment of his own sin. On the death of his first wife, he had vowed to go on a pilgrimage to the Holy Sepulchre. Upon that pilgrimage he goes forth at once, and alone.

Rosalba, quitting the court, takes refuge in the castle of Malespina. There she lives in a seclusion, partaken only by her friend Fiordeliza. The maiden solitude of the friends is a charming idyll of rural life, rich in fancy, quaint in humour, and set forth chiefly in that finer and more delicate prose, the cadence of which is hardly less rhythmical than that of verse. At last, word is sent to her by her father that he who in name only has been her husband has died at Jerusalem, and that she must return to Palermo, there to do homage for the lands that have now become her own. She obeys; but before her has returned a pilgrim, Buonaiuto, from the Holy Land. The pilgrim is Silisco, who, on hearing that Count Ugo had set out upon a journey, the hardships of which could scarcely be surmounted by the young and strong, had accompanied him in disguise, and saved his life in numberless dangers. Silisco has returned in time to see Aretina, who tells him just before her death that it was from jealousy, as well as fear, that Spadone had stabbed her, and that the treasures carried off from the wreck had not, as he supposed, been lost at sea, but were buried in the catacombs. The last scene unravels all the threads of a plot very skilfully woven. It is in the royal palace of Palermo. The king sits on his throne, surrounded by his court, when Rosalba advances at her father's command to receive investiture of Count Ugo's lands. Is it certain, the chief justiciary demands, that the count has made no will? Gerbetto, who at the king's command had attended Count Ugo, and was with him at his death, presents the will of the deceased count. It prescribes that his possessions shall devolve on Rosalba if she remains single; but that if she marries they shall pass to the pilgrim Buonaiuto. Silisco advances. His suit is not long resisted by Rosalba. Ruggiero, who had been cast off by Fiordeliza, and vindictively pursued by the king, in consequence of unfounded jealousies, stands forth at the same moment, and with Gerbetto's aid refutes the charges that had been brought against him, receiving from the king pardon and restitution, and from Fiordeliza a gift that he values more.

There are many dramatic writers whose powers are rendered nugatory by the want of one great gift—a

light hand.   The gift may seem a slight one, but its
absence soon proves its importance.   Here is a
specimen of it—

> *Fiordeliza.* Let me alone, I say ; I will not dance.
> *Rosalba.*   Not if Ruggiero ask you ?
> *Fiordeliza.*   He indeed !
> If the Colossus came from Rhodes and ask'd me,
> Perhaps I might.
> *Rosalba.*   Come, Fiordeliza, come ;
> I think, if truth were spoken, 'tis not much
> You have against that knight.
> *Fiordeliza.*   Not much you think :
> Well, be it much or little, 'tis enough ;
> He has his faults.
> *Rosalba.* Recount me them ; what are they ?
> *Fiordeliza.* I'll pick you out a few ; my wallet : first,
> He's grave ; his coming puts a jest to flight
> As winter doth the swallow.
> *Rosalba.*   Something else,
> For this may be a merit ; jests are oft
> Or birds of prey or birds of kind unclean.
> *Fiordeliza.* He's rude ; he's stirring ever with his staff
> A growling great she-bear that he calls Truth.
> *Rosalba.* The rudeness is no virtue ; but for love
> Of that she-bear, a worser vice might pass.
> Again ?
> *Fiordeliza.* He's slow,—slow as a tortoise,—once
> He was run over by a funeral.
> *Rosalba.* He may have failings ; but if these be all,
> I would that others were as innocent.
> *Fiordeliza.* Oh, others ! Say, then, who ?
> *Rosalba.*   Nay, others—all ;
> I wish that all mankind were innocent.

This theme is resumed in a later part of the play,
with that deep moral seriousness which underlies the
gaiety of this play—

> *Ruggiero.* Why hither ? It can bring you little joy
> To look upon the lands that you have lost.

Silisco. To look upon the *days* that I have lost.
Ruggiero, brings me less ; and here I thought
To get behind them ; for my childhood here
Lies round me.   But it may not be.   By Heavens !
That very childhood bitterly upbraids
The manhood vain that did but travesty,
With empty and unseasonable mirth,
Its joys and lightness.   From each brake and bower
Where thoughtless sports had lawful time and place,
The manly child rebukes the childish man ;
And more reproof and bitterer do I read
In many a peasant's face, whose leaden looks
My host the farmer construes to my shame.
Injustice, rural tyranny, more dark
Than that of courts, have laid their brutal hands
On those that claim'd my tendance ; want and vice
And injury and outrage fill'd my lands,
Whilst I, who saw it not, my substance threw
To feed the fraudulent and tempt the weak.
Ruggiero, with what glittering words soe'er
We smear the selfishness of waste, and count
Our careless tossings bounties, this is sure,
Man sinks not by a more unmanly vice
Than is that vice of prodigality—
Man finds not more dishonour than in debt.[1]

In those self-reproaches we find the development
of that better life which dawned on Silisco when he
first met Rosalba.   The change thus worked in him is a
very different one from that imputed to beauty by dramatists whose moralising vein is often at least as dangerous
as their immoralities ; dramatists who reform a rake
by a virtuous woman's smile, and confirm the rickety
virtue thus produced by the grace of matrimony—

Since that eve
When, as you landed in the dimpled bay

---

[1] Vol. iii. p. 42.

From Procida, I help'd you from the boat,
And touch'd your hand, and as the shallop rock'd,
Embolden'd by your fears I . . . , pardon me,
I should not make you to remember more,—
But since that moment when the frolicsome waves
Toss'd you towards me,—blessings on their sport !
I have not felt one kindling of a thought,
One working of a wish but you were in it ;
The rising sun, that striking through the lattice
Awaken'd me, awaken'd you within me :
The darkness closing shut us up together :
I saw you in the mountains, fields, and woods ;
Flowers breathed your breath, winds chanted with your voice,
And Nature's beauty clothed itself in yours.
Then think not that my life, though idly led,
Is tainted or impure or bound to sense,
Or if incapable of itself to soar,
Unworthy to be lifted from the dust
By love of what is lofty.[1]

Silisco becomes at the end but that which potentially he was from the beginning. Rosalba had not failed to detect the inner strength that lurked beneath the outward lightness—

Three long days had past
(Long though delightful, for they teem'd with thoughts
As Maydays teem with flowers) since I had first
Beheld him, standing in the sunset lights,
Beside a wreck half-buried in the sand
Upon the western shore.   I see him now
A radiant creature with the sunset glow
Upon his face, that mingled with a glow
Yet sunnier from within.   When next we met
'Twas here, as you have said ; and then his mien
Was lighter, with an outward brightness clad,
For all the Court was present ; yet I saw
The other ardour through.[2]

The following passage embodies Mr. Taylor's

[1] Vol. iii. p. 25.   [2] Vol. iii. p. 77.

philosophy of art. This play may be considered as a practical exemplification of it.

> *Silisco.* We'll have the scene where Brutus from the bench
> Condemns his son to death. 'Twas you, Ruggiero,
> Made me to love that scene.
> *Manager.*   I think, my Lord,
> We pleased you in it.
> *Ruggiero.*   Oh, you did, you did ;
> Yet still with reservations : and might I speak
> My untaught mind to you that know your art,
> I should beseech you not to stare and gasp
> And quiver, that the infection of the sense
> May make our flesh to creep ; for as the hand
> By tickling of our skin may make us laugh
> More than the wit of Plautus, so these tricks
> May make us shudder.   But true art is this,
> To set aside your sorrowful pantomime,
> Pass by the senses, leave the flesh at rest,
> And working by the witcheries of words
> Felt in the fulness of their import, call
> Men's spirits from the deep ; that pain may thus
> Be glorified, and passion flashing out
> Like noiseless lightning in a summer's night,
> Show Nature in her bounds from peak to chasm,
> Awful, but not terrific.
> *Manager.*   True, my Lord :
> My very words ; 'tis what I always told them.
> Now, Folco, speak thy speech. . . .
> *Ruggiero.*   'Tis a speech
> That by a language of familiar lowness
> Enhances what of more heroic vein
> Is next to follow.   But one fault it hath :
> It fits too close to life's realities,
> In truth to Nature missing truth to Art ;
> For Art commends not counterparts and copies,
> But from our life a nobler life would shape,
> Bodies celestial from terrestrial raise,
> And teach us, not jejunely what we are,
> But what we may be when the Parian block
> Yields to the hand of Phidias.[1]

---

[1] Vol. iii. p. 7.

The criticism of Silisco on the histrionic art is applicable not less to the art poetic. We live in a "fast age," but if "he that runs may read," it is to be feared that he will prefer what is written in the largest and coarsest characters, to what requires a more steadfast attention. Loud words, big words, odd words, will recommend themselves more than the unobtrusive witcheries of common "words *felt in the fulness of their import.*" But what the eye takes in as quickly as the advertisements that adorn a railway station, it forgets no less rapidly. The poetry that lasts is that which embodies thoughts, but so embodies them that they sink at once upon the slumbering feeling and wake it into life.

Mr. Taylor's latest tragedy is entitled *St. Clement's Eve.*[1] This play takes up the tale of European society where it was left off in *Philip van Artevelde*, but illustrates it as it existed in France, not Flanders. Charles the Sixth, the boy-king, by whom so bright a light was thrown over the second part of Van Artevelde, is presented to us again, but this time in eclipse. He was subject to recurring fits of madness, during which the kingdom was torn to pieces by the rivalries of the Duke of Burgundy, the king's cousin, and the Duke of Orleans, his brother. It was perhaps about the worst and most anarchical period of the middle ages. The king was loved by his people, and deserved their love, for in the intervals of his malady he devoted himself to their interests with a tender and profound

---

[1] This noble play is greatly improved in the latest edition.

solicitude.   He is described in this play with a mournful pathos.

The Duke of Burgundy is a man of blood, fierce, with a shrewd intellect, the instrument of ungovernable passions, a domineering pride, and a will that knows no law.   The Duke of Orleans has not escaped the contamination of a dissolute court, more disposed to respect religion in its outward forms than to obey its commands, but he has about him much that is good, and more that is specious.   He is frank, generous, loyal, and devotedly attached to his brother, whom he resembles in his personal beauty and in love for his country.   His kindly and courteous manners make him a favourite of the people, while his learning and accomplishments recommend him to the clergy. He represents the chivalry of his age; but it was a chivalry dying out.   The spirit of self-sacrifice, the virtuous zeal, and the reverence for purity had left it, and consequently the childlike faith of the middle ages was daily becoming more enervated by those childish superstitions from which neither orthodoxy nor heterodoxy secures the unspiritual and sensual. Chivalry retained its bright accost and winning grace, but the graver heart had departed from it, and the savage fierceness of the feudality it had covered was working out again through the thin disguise.

St. Clement's Eve is, in power and ability, among the best of Mr. Taylor's dramas, but in some respects it is less satisfactory than it is remarkable.   Both in its success and its shortcomings it signally illustrates the philosophy of the drama. It is as masculine a work as *Philip van Artevelde.* It is also far more condensed, and the action is more rapid. But the subject throws a gloom over the play darker than that which tragedy requires. We leave it with a feeling of sadness, the result not merely, or chiefly, of a fatal catastrophe, but of the absence of noble characters sufficient to balance the ignoble and the wicked. We have no right to quarrel with a dramatist either for selecting a corrupt period of history for illustration, or for representing it faithfully, yet he certainly loses not a little by such a selection. Whatever the pride of art may affirm, the abiding charm of a poem will ever bear a proportion to the moral beauty it enshrines,— not merely the beauty which the poet has created, but that which he has found ready-made in his theme. A favourite book is generally one fortunate in its subject, as well as one that makes the most of that subject. The poet works against the tide unless the theme and the characters he describes work with him, and tend to a result which, even if painful, still is such as the higher imagination can muse on with satisfaction and peace. There must be a due proportion of sunshine to the shadow, and even the saddest events must be something more than sad ; they must illustrate poetical justice ; they must leave behind them the sense that the world we inhabit, though it has its sorrows, has yet its method and order, that it is a region into which angels of chastisement are indeed sent as well as angels of love and joy, but that it is not a jungle beset by wild beasts, or a labyrinth, the haunt of mocking spirits.

A perfect tragic theme is one that presents us with greatness in all forms. There must be great sorrows, but there should also be great characters; there should be a scope for great energies: the event should be the result of great, even though of erring, passions, not of petty infirmities and base machinations. Many a striking theme does not include such materials, abundant as it may be in stirring action and picturesque positions, just as many a fair landscape is deficient in that which a picture requires. Let the subject include the characteristics we have named, and very numerous defects, with which the critic may cavil, will detract but little from the reader's pleasure. He will recur to the work when the first effect of surprise, and the admiration produced by the sense of difficulties overcome, have worn off. A poet will be wise to choose a theme that does much for him. It is the one for which he can do most, as, in the long-run, it is the best land which best repays the husbandman's toil.

The subject of *St. Clement's Eve* combines the barbarism of prolonged civil war with the corruptions of a court, and exhibits a social condition in which simplicity has ceased to exist, while refinement has not yet come. It supplies but one wholly noble male character, that of the hermit, Robert de Menuot. Montargis and Burgundy are men without conscience or honour, or even that regard for reputation which often passes for honour. The two monks, or supposed monks, are equally prompt at the burning of a witch or the composition of a philtre. Such characters, in their due place, may doubtless be portrayed both justly and usefully. But the higher charm of the drama requires, and historic truth no less, that specimens of a nobler order of character should be introduced in a compensating measure. The best periods have their villains, and the worst have often their saints and heroes: nature commonly produces such intermingling, and art requires it. The chronicles of the time described, full as they are of violence and wrong, delight us also with many a trait of generosity, magnanimity, loyalty, fidelity, and self-abnegation, which need no aid from the romance of chivalry to give them interest. Virtue becomes perfected by the very trials and temptations to which it is subjected, and though at particular periods injustice and wrong may occupy an unusual prominence upon the surface of society, yet true virtue must coexist with these, both in high places and in low, or society could not long continue to exist. It has but small place in this play. Even characters so rarely presented to us that their vices contribute nothing to the carrying out of the plot, are sketched in colours of arbitrary gloom. The Archbishop of Paris is made a servile old pedant. This is gratuitous. The metropolitan sees were in those ages commonly occupied either by men of ability and force of character, or by the representatives of some great family,—by one, in short, whose faults were not likely to be those of a schoolmaster turned courtier. We find here something of that confusion between the middle ages and the *ancien régime* which M. de Montalembert alludes to as so common. Such bishops would have been less easily found in the middle ages than in the seventeenth century, when in most parts of Europe an oriental despotism had risen up upon the ruins of feudalism. In still more repulsive colours is the Abbess of the Celestines represented. Of the younger female characters, Flos, though energetic and sparkling, is not intended to interest our deeper sympathies.

Such are the faults, not of the poet, but of his theme. It is more difficult to speak, without the appearance of exaggeration, of the drama's merits. Its manliness might startle a literary age as effeminate as ours. Not a few of its readers will exclaim—

> What doth the eagle in the coop,
> The bison in the stall?

In its vigour, both of thought and of language, some readers will find a strangeness like that which we find in the organic remains of a remote age. That vigour belongs, not only to the serious scenes, but to the lighter also, which are of a very different character from those of *A Sicilian Summer*, and preserve something of fierceness even in mirth. Its songs have the buoyancy, terseness, and dramatic impulse which belong to those of Mr. Taylor's earlier plays. In none of his works, perhaps, is his style so consummate. It is at once classical and idiomatic, and it has the polish, with the strength of steel. Above all, it is invariably clear, letting the thoughts shine through it, like objects seen through transparent air. This last characteristic is becoming rare in our day, owing, in some measure, to the degree to which certain special merits of style have been carried. At present, in not a little of our popular poetry, language has been so strained in search of expressiveness, and has thus become such a richly-coloured medium, that it sometimes seems to be a beautiful substitute for thought rather than a revealer of thought, thus resembling those water-colour drawings in which the aërial effects swallow up mountain and plain, and in which the picture might be described as mist with trees in it. In this play, condensation has, perhaps, been carried too far. The introduction of a few interstitial scenes would be useful, not only as thus allowing the enrichment of poetry and philosophic thought, but yet more in suspending the course of an action so rapid as to hurry us out of breath. That action is occupied chiefly by the jealousies of the royal cousins. They had also their occasional reconciliations, one of which is thus humorously described—

> To-day they rode together on one horse,
> Each in the other's livery. To-morrow
> They are to sleep together in one bed.
> The People stare and deem the day is nigh
> When lamb and lion shall lie down together.
>   *De Chevreuse.* Rode on one horse!
>   *D'Aicelin.*   Yea, Orleans before,
> And Burgundy behind.
>   *Gris-nez.*   'Twas so they rode:

Two witches on one broomstick rode beside them ;
But riding past an image of Our Lady
The hindmost snorted and the broomstick brake.
   De Cassinel. Would I were sure my gout would be as
     brief
As their good fellowship.
   De Vierzon.   To see grim John
Do his endeavour at a gracious smile,
Was worth a ducat ; with his trenchant teeth
Clinch'd like a rat-trap.
   De Cassinel.   Ever and anon
They open'd to let forth a troop of words
Scented and gilt, a company of masques
Stiff with brocade, and each a pot in hand
Fill'd with wasp's honey.

The most characteristic illustration which can be
given of *St. Clement's Eve* is the following denuncia-
tion of both the royal dukes, pronounced by Robert
the Hermit before the Council. It is also, perhaps,
the finest piece of poetry in the play—

   Robert.   . . . The tenth night
A storm arose and darkness was around
And fear and trembling and the face of death.
Six hours I knelt in prayer, and with the seventh
A light was flash'd upon the raging sea,
And in the raging sea a space appear'd
Flat as a lake, where lay outstretch'd and white
A woman's body ; thereupon were perch'd
Two birds, a falcon and a kite, whose heads
Bare each a crown, and each had bloody beaks,
And blood was on the claws of each, which clasp'd,
This the right breast and that the left, and each
Fought with the other, nor for that they ceased
To tear the body.   Then there came a cry
Piercing the storm—" Woe, woe for France, woe, woe !
Thy mother France, how excellently fair
And in how foul a clutch ! "   Then silence ; then,
" Robert of Menuot, thou shalt surely live,
For God hath work to give thee ; be of good cheer ;
Nail thou two planks in figure of a cross,

And lash thee to that cross and leap, and lo !
Thou shalt be cast upon the coast of France ;
Then take thy way to Paris ; on the road,
See, hear, and when thou com'st to Paris, speak."
" To whom?" quoth I.   Was answer made, " The King."

    .   .   .   .

    The King. Good hermit, by God's mercy we are spared
To hear thee, and not only with our ears
But with our mind.
    Burgundy.   If there be no offence,
But take thou heed to that.
    Robert. . . . Nigh forty days I sped from town to town,
Hamlet to hamlet, and from grange to grange,
And wheresoe'er I set my foot, behold !
The foot of war had been before, and there
Did nothing grow, and in the fruitless fields
Whence ruffian hands had snatch'd the beasts of draught
Women and children to the plough were yoked ;
The very sheep had learnt the ways of war,
And soon as from the citadel rang out
The larum peal, flock'd to the city gates ;
And tilth was none by day, for none durst forth,
But wronging the night season which God gave
To minister sweet forgetfulness and rest,
Was labour and a spur.   I journey'd on,
And near a burning village in a wood
Were huddled 'neath a drift of blood-stain'd snow
The houseless villagers : I journey'd on,
And as I pass'd a convent, at the gate
Were famish'd peasants, hustling each the other,
Half-fed by famish'd nuns : I journey'd on,
And 'twixt a hamlet and a church the road
Was black with biers, for famine-fever raged :
I journey'd on—a trumpet's brazen clang
Died in the distance ; at my side I heard
A child's weak wail that on its mother's breast
Droop'd its thin face and died ; then peal'd to heaven
The mother's funeral cry, " My child is dead
For lack of food ; he hunger'd unto death ;
A soldier ate his food, and what was left
He trampled in the mire ; my child is dead !
Hear me, O God ! a soldier kill'd my child !
See to that soldier's quittance—blood for blood !

Visit him, God, with Thy divine revenge!"
The woman ceased; but voices in the air,
Yea and in me a thousand voices cried,
"Visit him, God, with Thy divine revenge!"
Then they too ceased, and sterner still the Voice
Slow and sepulchral that the word took up—
"Him, God, but not him only, nor him most;
Look Thou to them that breed the men of blood,
That breed and feed the murderers of the realm.
Look Thou to them that, hither and thither tost
Betwixt their quarrels and their pleasures, laugh
At torments that they taste not; bid them learn
That there be torments terribler than these
Whereof it is Thy will that they shall taste,
So they repent not, in the belly of Hell."
So spake the Voice, then thunder shook the wood,
And lightning smote and splinter'd two tall trees
That tower'd above the rest, the one a pine,
An ash the other.   Then I knew the doom
Of those accursèd men who sport with war
And tear the body of their mother, France.
Trembling though guiltless did I hear that doom.

   .   .   .   .   .   .

Oh cruel, cruel, cruel Princes, hear!
For ye are they that tear your mother's flesh;
Oh, flee the wrath to come!   Repent and live!
Else know your doom, which God declares through me,
Perdition and the pit hereafter; here
Short life and shameful death.[1]

The chief female characters in the play are Flos
and Iolande.   Flos is betrayed and deserted by her
lover Montargis.   Wooed by another, she tells him that,
before he wins her favour, he must avenge her wrong—

Give me thy hand again.   It is too white.
I dedicate this hand to truth and love,
And hatred and revenge.   White as mine own!
Dye it and bring it back to me to-morrow,
And I will clasp it to my heart.   Farewell!

---

[1] Vol. iii. pp. 125-128.

Father Renault moralises well—

> How swift
> The transformation whereby carnal love
> Is changed to carnal hate! I have heard it said,
> There is no haunt the viper more affects
> Than the forsaken bird's nest.

Iolande has a delightful freshness, and a purity capable of "disinfecting" the bad air in which she lives. She is tender in heart and soaring in aspirations, one of those who, if reproached as visionaries, might reply, with the author of *Guesses at Truth;* "Yes, a visionary, *because* he *sees*." But fate and fortune conspire to take from her the respect of others and her own. She has been saved by Orleans from Montargis, who attempted to carry her off, and she loves her preserver before she knows he has a wife. On the discovery she breaks the tie ; but her heart is neither restored to liberty nor left in peace with its sorrow and its humiliation. Orleans implores her—"O pious fraud of amorous charity"—if she renounces him, at least to befriend his sick brother. At his entreaty she undertakes to exorcise the king's malady by means of a relic, the healing virtue of which depends upon the spotless purity in heart and life of her who touches with it the sufferer's brow. She makes the attempt, and fails. The ordinary reader will account for her failure, not by her unworthiness, but by the circumstance that she was but a dupe, practised on by impostors. This is not her view of the subject, nor the hermit's ; and if accepted as just, though it exculpates the victim it leaves her death wholly unredeemed by poetic justice. In Shakespeare imposture is treated with the contempt so sorry a thing deserves; it is exhibited, detected, and flung aside. The catastrophe of a tragedy is never made to depend on it. In this play the noble efforts of the hermit for the restoration of France are frustrated, and the most interesting characters swept into ruin by instrumentalities too petty for such a catastrophe.

This part of the plot forces our sympathies into a painful region of poetic casuistry. The struggle between human love and heavenly love, where each so easily puts on the semblance of the other, is perplexing to the imagination. We know not how far we are to condemn, and how far we may pity. There is a pity which is "akin to love," and another pity which is "akin to contempt"; and in the misty region of insincere and equivocal action and passion, the two run into each other. The hopes and aims of Iolande are noble; her heart was liegefully given to heavenly things, and was worthy of a human love also that should have elevated, not degraded her. There is something surely beneath the generosity of art (equally great when it dares and when it forbears), in the exhibition of a contest like that to which she is subjected—one entered upon so unwittingly, waged so bravely, and yet ending so ignominiously, as well as disastrously. By the only elevated characters in the play, the healing power of the relic is accepted as certain. In that case its failure must have seemed to them the condemnation of one who, with deficient purity, had dared to profane it.

In many parts of Mr. Taylor's poetry we find a singularly keen appreciation of the kindred art of painting.　The following description will at once enable the reader to determine the school to which the picture described belongs.　We are much mistaken if it be not the Venetian.

> *Painter.*　There is a power in beauty which subdues
> All accidents of Nature to itself.
> Aurora comes in clouds, and yet the cloud
> Dims not, but decks her beauty.　Furthermore
> Whate'er shall single out a personal self
> Takes with a subtler magic.　So of shape ;
> Perfect proportion, like unclouded light,
> Is but a faultless model ; small defect
> Conjoint with excellence, more moves and wins,
> Making the heavenly human. . . .
> 　　　　　　　　　　I spared no pains.
> Look closer ; mark the hyacinthine blue
> Of mazy veins irriguous, swelling here,
> There branching and so softening out of sight.
> Nor is it ill conceited.　You may mark
> The timbrel drooping from her hand denotes
> The dance foregone ; a fire is in her eye
> Which tells of triumph, and voluptuous grace
> Of motion is exchanged for rapturous rest.[1]

This picture has very serious consequences.　Montargis, pretending zeal for a friend,

> 　　　　　　　　Whose soul
> Lies in the hollow of her Grace's hand
> Soft fluttering like a captured butterfly,

persuades the painter to lend it to him.　It is the portrait of the Duke of Burgundy's wife, from whom

[1] Vol. iii. p. 170.

he has long been estranged. Resolved to procure
the assassination of Orleans, who had rescued Iolande
from him, Montargis secretly conveys this portrait into a
chamber of the Duke of Orleans's palace, reported to
be hung round by the portraits of all those ladies who
had successively become the favourites of a prince as
dissolute as he was captivating; and having carefully
prepared the train, he introduces the Duke of Burgundy
into the apartment, among the boasts of which is this
witness to his dishonour. This is the critical scene,
upon which the plot of *St. Clement's Eve* turns; and
there are few passages in the English drama in which
a vehement outburst of passion is more intensified by
every art of skilful delay and artificial stimulus. To
appreciate the full force of this scene, one must previously be acquainted with the ferocious, though by no
means callous, character of Burgundy. He is thus
described early in the play—

> Other clay,
> Dug from some miry slough or sulphurous bog,
> With many a vein of mineral poison mix'd,
> Went to the making of Duke Jean-Sans-Peur.
> This knew the crafty Amorabaquin.
> When captives by the hundred were hewn down,
> 'Twas not rich ransom only spared the Duke.
> 'Twas that a dying Dervise prophesied
> More Christian blood should by his mean be shed
> Than ere by Bajazet with all his hosts.
> Therefore it was to France he sent him back
> With gifts, and what were they? 'twas bowstrings made
> Of human entrails.[1]

This is the man who, after years of contest with

<hr>

[1] Vol. iii. p. 111.

his cousin of Orleans, has been forced into a temporary reconciliation with him.   As daring in his wild fits of half-savage frolic as in ambition, he has entered the palace, nay, the inmost and secret chamber, of one whom he knew to have been his successful rival in power, but whom he has never suspected of rivalry in love.   The first sight of the "galaxy of glowing dames" delights him—

> Ha ! were it not a frolic that should shake
> Grim Saturn's self with laughter, could we bring
> The husbands hither, each to look round and spy
> The blazon of his dire disgrace.

Then comes a series of pictures, accompanied by corresponding descriptions of character, presented in a few masterly touches, and strangely contrasting, by the tranquillity that belongs to such delineations, with the storm that follows—

> *Burgundy.* And then the next !
> *Montargis.*   Which ?   This ?
> *Burgundy.* She with the timbrel dangling from her hand.
> *Montargis.* I know not this ; this was not here before.
> The one beyond it . . .
>   *Burgundy.*   Not so fast ; this face
> I surely must have seen, though not, it may be,
> For some time past ; it hath a princely grace
> And lavish liberty of eye and limb,
> With something of a soft seductiveness
> Which very strangely to my mind recalls
> The idle days of youth ; that face I know,
> Yet know not whose it is.
>
>   .   .   .   .   .   .
>
>   . . . Death of my soul !
> It is my wife.
>   *Montargis.*   Oh no, my Lord, no, no,
> It cannot be her Highness.
>   *Burgundy.*   Cannot—cannot—
> Why, no, it cannot.   For my wife is chaste,

And never did a breath of slander dim
Her pure and spotless fame ; no, no, it cannot ;
By all the Angels that keep watch above
It cannot be my wife . . . and yet it is.
I tell thee, Bastard of Montargis, this,
This picture is the picture of my wife.
   Montargis. And I, my Lord, make answer it is not.
I would as soon believe that Castaly
Had issued into Styx.   Besides, look here,
There is a mole upon the neck of this
Which is not on your wife's.
   Burgundy.   That mole is hers ;
That mole convicts her.
   Montargis.   What ? a mole ?   Well, yes,
Now that I think of it, some sort of smirch,
A blot, a blur, I know not what . . .
   Burgundy.   That mole—
Oh see, Montargis, look at her, she smiles,
But not on me, but never more on me !
Oh, would to God that she had died the day
That first I saw that smile and trusted her ;
Though knowing the whole world of women false,
Still trusted her, and knowing that of the false
The fairest are the falsest, trusted still,
Still trusted her—Oh my besotted soul !
Trusted her only—Oh my wife, my wife !
Believing that of all the Devil's brood
That twist and spin and spawn upon this earth,
She was the single Saint—the one unfallen
Of this accursed Creation—oh my wife !
Oh the Iscariot kiss of those false lips !
With him too—to be false with him—my bane,
My blight from boyhood.

   .   .   .   .   .

 .
                    I'll have his blood . . .
Ere the sun sets.
   Montargis.   A later hour were better ;
We want not daylight for a deed like this.
   Burgundy. I sleep not till he's dead.   Come thou with
      me
And take thy warrant.
   Montargis.   Sir, at your command.

Burgundy. Look here, Montargis; [*Drawing his sword.*
                              Should a breath be breathed
That whispers of my shame, the end is this.
                      [*Stabs the portrait in the heart.*[1]

A succession of stirring scenes follows. The populace of Paris, infuriated by the return of the king's madness, demands the death of the maiden who had undertaken his cure. The Duke of Burgundy, sitting in council, pledges his word that she shall die. To save her Orleans hastens to the council, attended only by his page. As he makes his way in the dusk, through the snow-covered streets, Montargis, who, after receiving Burgundy's warrant, has lain in wait within the gate of a house, springs upon his prey, and slays him. All Paris is in commotion, and the crowds soon swarm around the council-chamber where the Duke of Burgundy is sitting with the king's uncles, the Dukes of Bourbon and Berri, and the Titular King of Sicily. The chamberlain, entering, announces the murder. The Provost of Paris, who follows him, demands permission to search for the assassin in all places alike, the royal residences, in spite of their ordinary privilege, not being excepted. The other royal dukes consent. Burgundy alone refuses, and on being challenged by the rest, suddenly avows his guilt, leaves the council, and with his attendants escapes from Paris. In the meantime the body of Orleans has been carried to the convent of the Celestines, where Iolande watches beside it. Montargis, who enters with a warrant for her apprehension and

[1] Vol. iii. pp. 179-181.

death, is himself stabbed by De Vezelay. Immediately afterwards a tumult is heard without. The infuriated crowd, rolling on like a raging sea, have reached and beleaguered the convent. The hermit entreats Iolande to fly by the wicket. She answers—

<blockquote>
It is I
Must speak and vindicate the fame of him
Whose lips are silent ;
</blockquote>

and advances to the window, when an arrow from below strikes her. She falls and dies.

In estimating Mr. Taylor's position among the English poets, both of recent and earlier days, and in comparing the modern dramatists with those of the time of Elizabeth, we must bear in mind that the dramatists of the earlier period are themselves to be divided into two classes. Shakespeare by himself constitutes one of these, while the whole of his contemporaries and immediate successors constitute the other. The rest, with all their differences of species, are still generically one, while Shakespeare is a "hierarchy in himself." Each of Shakespeare's greater plays is, in the highest sense of the word, a poem as well as a play. It possesses an *interior* unity, a unity proceeding from the one great idea that created the whole, the predominant sentiment that inspired it, and the exquisite subordination of the details to the general effect. This unity, piercing at once and comprehensive, belongs alone to great creative genius, and Shakespeare's contemporaries seldom had it. Ben

Jonson, with all his learning and classical predilections, lacked it as much as Marlow or Webster. Shakespeare worked "from within"; the process was one of growth, and the unity latent in the parent germ manifested itself in every leaf and spray of the developed plant. This is the secret of that marvellous judgment which, as Coleridge remarks, equalled his imagination itself. Starting with a genuine idea, he shrank instinctively from whatever obscured it, whether by disproportion or by incongruity. The other dramatists worked "from without," and mechanically. They found their materials in life and books, and with great ability, but not always a true inspiration, they combined them. In multitudes of cases the result is a painful discord; in few is it a complete harmony.

The reader who turns to their Plays in a complete edition, after reading the splendid fragments detached from them in Lamb's *Specimens*, will often think the finished work more fragmentary than the fragments. Again and again, the finest scenes in our early drama lose half their value from the inappropriateness of their position. Take, for instance, Ford's best play, *The Broken Heart:* nothing can exceed in suppressed passion the concluding scene, in which the princess, receiving secretly and successively the tidings of the death of her father, of her friend, and of her lover, with a Spartan's fortitude replies indifferently, keeping up the court pageant almost to the moment of her death. Shakespeare would have cast the whole play so as to have foreshadowed the dreadful catastrophe; and

in approaching it we should have felt as men feel when
their boat is swept towards the rapids. In Ford's
work we see little of the princess, and care little for
her ; nor is there anything in her character to suggest
the marvellous conclusion which suddenly confronts us
like a precipice without a mountain-range to back it.
This want of judgment in our early dramatists is often
a moral even more than an intellectual deficiency.
It proceeds from too great a love of the startling, and
too slight a sense of the becoming, the fitting, and
the orderly. Those great men were also great sen-
sationalists.

Another difference between Shakespeare and his
contemporaries is the amount of extravagance and
rant in the latter. Strength was the great quality our
early dramatists valued. When it came to them in the
form of real passion, they knew how to exhibit it in
perfection, intermixing the most delicate with the most
vigorous touches. In the absence of real passion they
were often content with its coarse imitation. Giovanni,
in a too celebrated play, makes his appearance at the
revel with the heart of Annabella, whom he has just
slain, on the point of his dagger ! Yet this outrage
against all genuine passion, as well as against decency,
almost immediately follows a scene of the truest
pathos.

The same exaggerated love, either of strength itself
or of bombast mimicking strength, prevented Shakespeare's contemporaries from even aiming at his profound conception of character. Their own characters

were formed on a different principle, and one for their coarser purposes more effective. To a great extent they are but abstractions, vividly described as are the circumstances among which they are placed. In *The Broken Heart*, Bassanes is not a jealous man so much as jealousy itself embodied, while Shirley's Traitor is not an example of fearless perfidy, but its impersonation. In the comedies the characters are often not even representations of qualities; they are but the embodiment of some personal whim or transient folly of society. Thus, in Ben Jonson's *Epicæne*, the chief character, Morose, might be defined as "a nervous gentleman's dislike to noise in the street." How different is this from Shakespeare! Before his mighty mind there ever stood the great idea of humanity; and each of his characters is worked out of that one manifold type. In shaping it, as much is withdrawn from the universal as is necessary to present the particular, but the universal remains. This is the cause of the infinite light and shadow of Shakespeare's characters; in them the passions are influences working in conjunction with all else that belongs to their moral being, not tempests blowing on them from without. Characters thus delineated are so softened and rounded off by imperceptible gradations that they can only be effective in the hand of a genius who combines with the force of Nature her infinite variety, grace, and subtlety. Those only can appreciate the strength shown by Shakespeare who appreciate also the profundity, the completeness, the many-sidedness, and the refinement which he never sacrificed in order to gain the appearance of strength.

The most important point of diversity remains to be noticed—the moral sense. The true greatness of Shakespeare is by nothing so proved as by his superiority to his contemporaries in this respect. Shakespeare does not bring out his moral in didactic vein ; but the great moral that always belongs to Nature herself belongs to him who best knew how to delineate her. In him there are no moral confusions, no substitution of rhetorical sentiment for just feeling, no palliation of vice, no simulations of virtue. The dramatic form of composition by necessity gives a great prominence to the passions, and must also keep in the distance that region of the supernatural and the infinite in the immediate presence of which the passions are cowed. But from that remote and awful background no doubtful flashes are sped to bear witness that this life, with all its tumults, is circled by a vaster one. There are occasionally moral blemishes in Shakespeare's plots, and there is not seldom a license of language to be seriously regretted ; but this last is far less than in the other writers of his time, nor do we know how much of it is owing to the interpolations of those players whom he commands to deliver "no more than is set down for them."

It is far otherwise with almost all Shakespeare's contemporaries. When, some half-century ago, our earlier dramatic writers emerged once from obscurity, the public thought that all their offences ought to be condoned to make up for the neglect under which they had long lain. But the interests of literature itself require that in all cases justice should be done. The sins of our dramatists in the reign of Elizabeth and James the First were not exceptional, nor were they but superficial blemishes. The plays of Charles the Second's time were so far worse, that they possessed no compensating merits; but their positive offences could hardly have proved more injurious, both to the cause of poetry and of society. In multitudes of our early plays the whole plot turns upon vice in its grossest forms, or a second and foul plot is joined to a sound one, like a dead body bound to a living form. Fletcher's *Faithful Shepherdess* is rich in poetry from which Milton borrowed in his *Comus;* yet it is disgraced by whole scenes of ribaldry; and in the *Maid's Tragedy* the grief of the forsaken Aspatia is similarly dishonoured. Massinger offends less than most of the other dramatists, yet in his *Fatal Dowry* sin almost rejects the plea of temptation; and even his *Virgin Martyr* is deformed by the excrescence of scenes which were reverently omitted in a recent and separate edition of that play.

Such offences have commonly, when not condoned by the false charity of indifference, been regarded only from the moral point of view. The boundless injury inflicted by them on literature has hardly been adverted to. The Greeks were so well aware of the relations between virtue and the liberal arts, that even when the morals of Paganism were at the lowest, a high moral standard was maintained in serious literature. The indirect losses sustained by our early dramatists, in consequence of their defects in this matter, were even worse than the direct ones. They found in coarseness and license so easy a means of amusing the audience, that they were rarely forced to elicit their own deeper powers. Strength to excite and ribaldry to amuse sufficed, and they too often spared themselves the trouble of addressing the finer affections, the reason, or the moral sense of their audience. Their works consequently, in spite of some splendid exceptions, lacked those passages of quiet beauty, of pathos, of philosophy, of imaginative grace, and of moral power, which are our principal inducements to return to a book when the interest of story is exhausted. The same fault blunted the best faculties of the early dramatists, and allowed others to lie fallow. The moral sense thus obscured, man was known to them in his animal relations chiefly. To them the passions were often but appetites intellectualised and directed to exclusive objects. They knew little of the connection of the passions with the affections and the moral sense; in other words, all in them that is ennobling, and all that subjects itself to law they ignored. Hence those causeless changes from evil to good, or from passion to passion, which evince so superficial a knowledge of human nature. Hence that lack of gradation, and those movements, fierce and lawless as the movements of wild beasts. They knew man socially, but did not also know him in his personality, and therefore their knowledge was empirical. The inner scope of man's faculties had escaped them. In man, for example, the faculty of Observation does not act separately, but in subordination to that interior wisdom which alone teaches him how to observe; they, on the other hand, frequently delineate it as though the observing eye were that of a dog, not that of a man. The faculty of Reflection, similarly, as they delineate it, works apart from that *mens melior* which alone sustains it with the true food of reason, and inspires its nobler aims. Society as illustrated by them seemed often a thing gregarious rather than human. Imagination emptied her urns to bathe and irradiate the wastes of the senses: the understanding directed those actions the root of which was in the appetites; but the inmost spirit of the spectator starved amid abundance, for the same hand which pampered the body had "sent leanness into the soul."

That these early dramatists were men of great intellects and great energies cannot be denied. They possessed marvellous gifts, had they but known how to use them aright; and their genius could have failed in no attempt, had it cared to subject itself to the true and the good. But the imagination which works for the senses loses its spiritual heritage, and sells its birthright for a mess of pottage. They wrote down to those low tastes which it is the duty of the drama to raise. Their offences were those of their age, for they did not rise superior to it. Our age has

offences of a different kind, and our literature reflects
them.   Their offences would not be tolerated in our
day ; but, while acknowledging the moral improvement
evinced by modern literature, we have yet almost
always to lament an inferiority, on the part of our
recent poets, as regards intellectual keenness and
energy.   That inferiority of itself has disqualified
them for the higher drama.   Ben Jonson said of a
young competitor, " My son Cartwright writes all like
a man."   Among our modern dramatic aspirants
some have written like women, and some like philosophers, but few like men.   Mr. Taylor is an exception.   There is in our earlier dramatists nothing more
manly and vigorous than his writings ; and that
manliness is enhanced by their grace.

The speciality of his genius consists in its uniting the
masculine strength of our early drama with the richer
variety, the thoughtfulness, and the purer sentiment
of our best later poetry.   Others among our modern
poets have carried farther, some one, some another high
poetic merit.   His characteristic consists in his being
a connecting link between the two chief periods of
English poetry.   It would be curious to compare the
different modes in which the poets of different periods
have gone through their poetic education.   In our
own time it is often said that Nature is the only true
instructress, and that the mountains and forests are
the colleges in which her sons must graduate.   Our
earlier dramatists generally began with the universities,
and then precipitated themselves upon the society of

the metropolis, as exhibited at the theatres, where they often combined a great deal of undigested learning with not a little of debauchery. In such a career there was more to develop the animal intelligence than that part of our being in which the intellect and the moral sense blend ; that part of it from which the most permanent poetry proceeds. It is likely that, at least for some departments of poetry, the training of professional, public, or official life, may be as auspicious as either of the other modes. It occupies the mind seriously, and not for the purpose of diversion, with persons at once and with things, and thus disciplines, while it elicits conjointly, the faculties of observation and reflection, supplying an undesigned aid doubtless to the writer of dramatic poetry which at heart is ever a serious thing. In the university poetic the aspirant takes many degrees ; and the author of these dramas had early "proceeded" *Statesman*—a title borne by one of his ablest volumes.

MINOR POEMS

A LONG poem, if fortunate in its theme, has its advantages over short ones, especially those of comprehending a larger sphere of interest, employing a greater number of the poetic faculties, and including more various elements in a richer harmony. On the other hand, it is seldom conceived, as a whole, with the completeness which belongs to the design of a short poem; and that portion of it which did not enter into the original conception is in danger of hanging about it clumsily. Again, no amount of executive skill can wholly atone for defects in the subject matter; and the subject of a long and elaborate composition is apt to reveal, at the last moment, some defect, as provoking as the black spot which sometimes comes out in the marble, when the statue is all but finished.

A short poem has several advantages over a long one. It is rendered buoyant by a fuller infusion of that essential poetry which pervades, rather as the regulating mind than the vivifying soul, a body of larger dimensions. The particular beauty which results from symmetry is most deeply felt, when the piece lies within so small a compass that the grace of proportion is recognised by an immediate consciousness, and not merely detected by patient analysis. Poems consisting of a few lines only, for the most part, will have been suggested by something experienced or observed, and thus touching nature at many points, will draw strength from contact with their native soil; whereas a longer work, even though not abstract in its subject, joins thought on to thought and image to image, without remanding the poet to the common ground of reality; and being thus "carved out of the carver's brain," is apt, if not of firstrate excellence, to meet with a cold response from men whose associations are different from those of the poet. It may be added that short poems bring us more near to the author; and to impart and elicit sympathy is among the chief functions of poets, who may be called the brother-confessors of mankind—for however devoid of egotism he may be, he must unavoidably present more aspects of his own many-sided being, when expatiating on many themes, and in many moods, than when engrossed by a single task. Their brevity also makes them more minutely known, and more familiarly remembered.

Mr. Taylor's short poems are characterised by the same qualities which distinguish his dramas. That strength which belongs to truth, and that grace which flows from strength when combined with poetic beauty, are exhibited in them not less distinctly. Their subjects, as well as their limits, exclude Passion in its specific *tragic* form ; but, on the other hand, they are wrought out with a more discriminating touch than his dramas. There is in them a majestic tenderness ennobled by severity ; and, at the same time, a sweetness and mellowness, which are often missed in the best youthful poetry, before time has seasoned the instrument, as well as perfected the musician's skill. Retaining the same peculiar temperament, light, firm, and vigorous (for true poetry has ever a cognisable temperament, as well as its special intellectual constitution), their moral sympathies are wider, and respire a softer clime. They are uniformly based upon those ethical qualities, simplicity, distinct purpose, and faith in man's better nature, which are not less essential than any intellectual gifts to excellence in poetry. Modern poetry includes many Elegies. Here is one written in the rare and exquisite metre of *Lycidas*, and worthy of it. It is called " Lines written in remembrance of the Hon. Edward Ernest Villiers "—

> A grace though melancholy, manly too,
> Moulded his being : pensive, grave, serene,
> O'er his habitual bearing and his mien
> Unceasing pain, by patience tempered, threw
> A shade of sweet austerity. But seen
> In happier hours and by the friendly few,
> That curtain of the spirit was withdrawn,
> And fancy light and playful as a fawn,
> And reason imped with inquisition keen,
> Knowledge long sought with ardour ever new,
> And wit love-kindled, show'd in colours true
> What genial joys with sufferings can consist.
> Then did all sternness melt as melts a mist
> Touched by the brightness of the golden dawn,

Aerial heights disclosing, valleys green,
And sunlights thrown the woodland tufts between,
And flowers and spangles of the dewy lawn.

And even the stranger, though he saw not these,
Saw what would not be willingly passed by.
In his deportment, even when cold and shy,
Was seen a clear collectedness and ease,
A simple grace, and gentle dignity,
That failed not at the first accost to please ;
And as reserve relented by degrees,
So winning was his aspect and address,
His smile so rich in sad felicities,
Accordant to a voice which charmed no less,
That who but saw him once remembered long ;
And some in whom such images are strong
Have hoarded the impression in their heart,
Fancy's fond dreams and memory's joys among,
Like some loved relic of romantic song,
Or cherished masterpiece of ancient art.

.   .   .   .   .   .

But farther may we pass not ; for the ground
Is holier than the Muse herself may tread ;
Nor would I it should echo to a sound
Less solemn than the service for the dead.
Mine is inferior matter,—my own loss,—
The loss of dear delights for ever fled,
Of reason's converse by affection fed,
Of wisdom, counsel, solace, that across
Life's dreariest tracts a tender radiance shed.
Friend of my youth ! though younger yet my guide,
How much by thy unerring insight clear
I shaped my way of life for many a year,
What thoughtful friendship on thy deathbed died !
Friend of my youth, whilst thou wast by my side
Autumnal days still breathed a vernal breath ;
How like a charm thy life to me supplied
All waste and injury of time and tide,
How like a disenchantment was thy death !

"The Eve of the Conquest" is an impassioned
narrative of those events in King Harold's life which

connected themselves with the Norman invasion.   The
event described, paramount as it was in political
importance, was but proportionate to the characters
of the two men who at that great crisis stood opposed
to each other, not only as the heads of hostile armies,
but as the representatives of contrasted principles and
contending races.   The character of Harold was one
of heroic material and heroic dimensions; and, with
one exception, it was without stain.   Of that fatal error,
his engagement to William,—imposed upon him, it is
true, iniquitously, but sacrilegiously violated,—Harold,
as here described, is deeply sensible, although he is no
penitent.   A great character, with one great flaw in it,
appears to present us with the truest tragic effects ; for
without such a flaw no place is reserved for poetic
justice.   The night before the battle Harold sends for
his daughter, and makes her the depository at once of
his confession, and his vindication.

It is thus that the king concludes his narrative—

> "Here we stand opposed ;
> And here to-morrow's sun, which even now,
> If mine eyes err not, wakes the eastern sky,
> Shall see the mortal issue.   Should I fall,
> Be thou my witness that I nothing doubt
> The justness of my doom ; but add thou this,
> The justness lies betwixt my God and me.
> 'Twixt me and William. . . ."

> Then uprose the King ;
> His daughter's hands half startled from his knee
> Dropt loosely, but her eye caught fire from his.
> He snatched his truncheon and the hollow earth
> Smote strongly that it throbbed : he cried aloud—
> "'Twixt me and William, say that never doom

> Save that which sunders sheep from goats, and parts
> 'Twixt Heaven and Hell, can righteously pronounce."
> —He sate again, and with an eye still stern
> But temperate and untroubled, he pursued :
> "''Twixt me and England, should some senseless swain
> Ask of my title, say I wear the Crown,
> Because it fits my head."

This brief poem contains not fewer than five admirable portraits.   The most powerful is that of William ; the most beautiful that of Adeliza, his daughter—

> " A woman-child she was : but womanhood
> By gradual afflux on her childhood gain'd,
> And like a tide that up a river steals
> And reaches to a lilied bank, began
> To lift up life beneath her.   As a child
> She still was simple,—rather shall I say
> More simple than a child, as being lost
> In deeper admirations and desires.
> The roseate richness of her childish bloom
> Remain'd, but by inconstancies and change
> Referr'd itself to sources passion-swept.
> Such had I seen her as I pass'd the gates
> Of Rouen, in procession, on the day
> I landed, when a shower of roses fell
> Upon my head, and looking up I saw
> The fingers which had scattered them half spread
> Forgetful, and the forward-leaning face
> Intently fixed and glowing, but methought
> More serious than it ought to be, so young
> And midmost in a show."

The chief characteristic of Mr. Taylor's narrative verse, as well as of his poetry in general, is a vivid and practical reality, using the word reality, not less as contrasted with the poetry of abstract thought, than with the miscreations of morbid passion, capricious fancy, or convention. This quality of reality is one the searching nature of which has seldom been appreciated, although that small department of it which relates to the picturesque has been much insisted on. The form of reality most saliently exhibited in the poem from which we have last quoted, is that of character. Poetic reality, in this primary form, has for many years been little expected and seldom found. Modern representations of character have for the most part been feeble, vague, and superficial. The cause of this great defect is yet more to be deplored. The delineations of the poet have been copies of copies, or arbitrary creations of fancy, only because the poet has no longer had frequent opportunities of studying from living models. What was once said, a little invidiously, about "matter too soft a lasting mark to bear," applies no longer exclusively to that sex in which the fault might most easily be pardoned. If modern society has reached a higher average of decorous virtue ; yet individual robustness,—and therefore character,—like intellectual greatness, is rarer than it was in ruder times. The aids and appliances which are now multiplied round men, enfeeble them. The shield of law renders it no longer necessary that every man should be competent to his own defence : and the division of labour has forestalled the necessity of intellectual self-reliance, and of that large yet minute development of faculties which was produced when, for the work of one man, the most opposite qualities were required. In-dustrialism, likewise,—while the prosperity which is its just reward too often betrays it into selfishness,—

is a sedative to the more distinctive passions. A certain social uniformity ensues, which exercises a retarding force like the resistance of the air or the attrition of matter, and insensibly destroys men's humours, idiosyncrasies, and spontaneous emotions. It does so, by rendering their concealment an habitual necessity, and by allowing them neither food nor sphere. Besides—the innumerable influences, intellectual and moral, which, at a period of diffused knowledge like the present, coexist and co-operate in building up our mental structure, are often completely at variance with each other in origin and tendency; so that they neutralise each other's effects, and leave a man well stored with thoughts and speech, but frequently without aim or purpose. If to these considerations we add the fact, that greatness and strength are only produced where they are reverenced, and only reverenced where required, we shall have gone far to account for that want of robustness which belongs to modern character, and that tameness with which, consequently, it is portrayed.

These obstacles are indeed less formidable in narrative than in dramatic poetry, because in the former a less vivid sympathy with character is required. While in dramatic poetry character is conceived by the intuition of a passionate sympathy,—in narrative, and especially in epic, it is the offspring largely of an imaginative contemplation. The tragic poet looks on human action from all sides, and with the eyes of all men; the epic poet regards it from above and with the eyes of the Muse. Tragic poetry is for this reason the more versatile and the more intense. Narrative, when it takes its highest form, that of the epic, is the more comprehensive, impartial, and sublime.

The poem of "Ernesto" is remarkable for its deep pathos and romantic interest; and yet more for its truth to character. It opens with a striking retrospect—

> Thoughtfully by the side Ernesto sate
> Of her whom, in his earlier youth, with heart
> Then first exulting in a dangerous hope,
> Dearer for danger, he had rashly loved.
> That was a season when the untravelled spirit,
> Not way-worn nor way-wearied, nor with soil
> Nor stain upon it, lions in its path
> Saw none,—or, seeing, with triumphant trust
> In its resources and its powers, defied,—
> Perverse to find provocatives in warnings
> And in disturbance taking deep delight.
> By sea or land he then saw rise the storm
> With a gay courage, and through broken lights,
> Tempestuously exalted, for awhile
> His heart ran mountains high, or to the roar
> Of shattered forests sang superior songs
> With kindling, and what might have seemed to some,
> Auspicious energy;—by land and sea
> He was way-foundered—trampled in the dust
> His many-coloured hopes—his lading rich
> Of precious pictures, bright imaginations,
> In absolute shipwreck to the winds and waves
> Suddenly rendered.

Profoundly sad, and yet more beautiful, is the conclusion of the love-story—

> ——Once again
> He sate beside her—for the last time now,
> And scarcely was she altered : for the hours
> Had led her lightly down the vale of life,

> Dancing, and scattering roses, and her face
> Seemed a perpetual daybreak, and the woods
> Where'er she rambled, echoed through their aisles
> The music of a laugh so softly gay
> That Spring with all her songsters and her songs
> Knew nothing like it.   But how changed was he !
> Care and disease and ardours unrepressed,
> And labours unremitted, and much grief,
> Had written their death-warrant on his brow.
> Of this she saw not all—she saw but little—
> That which she could not choose but see she saw—
> And o'er her sunlit dimples and her smiles
> A shadow fell—a transitory shade—
> And when the phantom of a hand she clasped
> At parting, scarce responded to her touch,
> She sighed—but hoped the best.
>   When winter came
> She sighed again ; for with it came the word
> That trouble and love had found their place of rest,
> And slept beneath Madeira's orange groves.

The vivid reality predominant in Mr. Taylor's poetry is its attribute, because Truth belongs to it more than to that of any other modern poet except Wordsworth.   Truth in Wordsworth's poetry is more often ideal truth than in Mr. Taylor's, where it may more properly be termed truth to fact, consisting as it does mainly in its affinities with life, action, and circumstance.   It is not the trifling mind alone which fails to appreciate the need of veracity in poetry.   The ultra-admirers of the abstract and recondite are apt to underrate its importance also.   Without denying that a deep philosophy must underlie the highest poetry, it should be remembered also that the foundations of a building may well remain underground.   A certain degree of plainness is absolutely necessary to keep a poet vulgar, in the good sense of the word,—that is, catholic; for it is his proudest office to take his stand, with Homer and Shakespeare, on the highways of life, leaving its byways to those who lack the faculty which elicits the beautiful from common things. Moreover a thought rendered palpable by being embodied in a fact, will thus become connected with a feeling likewise; and feeling is a solvent through the aid of which thought penetrates dull and otherwise inaccessible natures. It is no disparagement of the Imagination to observe that though it can organise a world of order out of a chaos, it cannot create one absolutely out of nothing. All species of truths are the better for mutual fellowship; the breed is the sounder for being crossed; and the humble truth of literal fact is the alloy, which only debases the ideal truth of poetry to make it malleable.

The opinion that a close observation of outward things is unworthy of poetry proceeds, not from too exalted a theory of Art, but from an unworthy estimate of Nature; as if the latter were something merely material, existed but for temporal purposes, and turned up by accident only its various products of good and evil. Truth of fact is worthy of reverence, on the contrary, because Nature itself has been modelled upon a framework of moral truth, while the kindred world of Circumstance is ruled by Providence. The most common events of human life have in them a supernatural element which, if at all times detected,— as it is on those occasions which are especially termed providential, because their seriousness causes them to be especially noted,—would at all times approve itself divine. Among the attributes of the inspired writings is to be noted the power with which they bring home to us high truths, not by a didactic process, but in brief, luminous narrative, flashing forth the truth of the idea, as if by electric touch, from the truth of fact, which is commonly at once its shrine and its veil. So is it with Song—that lower form of inspiration which yields us the poetic rather than the spiritual interpretation of Nature. But it is not to the common eye that Nature reveals this lore. She offers it, indeed, to all; but it is only "a gift of genuine *insight*" which can penetrate her meanings. We see for the most part, not that which exists, but that which we select from the mass of surrounding objects, and combine into a perspective of our own arranging. We select, reject, and combine according to some internal formative principle; and thus a prejudice or a fancy may build up our world. The ordinary condition of men is to have eyes and to see not. It is the prophet who merits the title, of "the man whose eyes are open"; nor do we possess any faculty more exalted or more inspired than that which enables us truly to see what lies around us, and to see that it is good. Among the countless wastes of intellect and power, there are few more deplorable than those committed by poets (and among them are to be found poets of every class except the highest), who, passing Nature by, have expended ability and industry on conventional themes, recommended but by the fashion of the hour; thus painting their frescoes with adulterated colours and on a tottering wall. While their ambitious works have mouldered into dust, how many an unpretending ballad has escaped as if by miracle, and when disinterred like some old coin, has circulated from hand to hand, not in consequence alone of the skill that shaped it, but because it bore the sovereign impress of Nature. To all men of genius who have thus laboured, may be given that praise which an eloquent and original critic has bestowed upon the English professors of a kindred art;[1] "that although frequently with little power and desultory effort, they have yet, in an honest and good heart, received the Word of God from clouds, and leaves, and waves, and kept it." Artists trained in this school work in a region as wide as the universe, and as deep as the heart of man. They, in their degree, preach Nature's Truth which was delivered once for all, and follow its footsteps whithersoever it goes. They are fellow-labourers with all who have received a commission to teach and have not spoken by a usurped authority. Their subjection to Nature has been their true freedom, a thing never connected with an arrogant independence. The human mind must ever rest upon something: and Nature, in tendering her aid to those who add from their own stores as much as they receive from hers, does but substitute the ministry of her

---

[1] *Modern Painters*, by a Graduate of Oxford, second edition, p. 60.

works for the prompting of books. It is from the
union of Nature and the human mind that Art as
well as Science derives its origin and principle of
growth. The products of the imagination, unfecun-
dated by Nature, ever remain barren. Poetry drawn
ultimately from experience flows forth in a rich and
manly vein. Poetry, on the other hand, which testifies
nothing of what the eye has seen and the hand handled,
is innutritious and hard, consisting mainly of *à priori*
thoughts and untested feelings, with no living bond
to connect the two classes.

If poetic reality absolutely requires truth in character and truth of fact, not less does it need that truth
which relates to sentiment and to thought. Thought
without truth is but serious trifling. There is no subject which will not suggest innumerable thoughts to
as many different minds, or to the same mind in its
various moods. Of these thoughts, while many are
perhaps at first equally imposing, nine out of ten will
too probably prove unsound. It is by the inspiration
of genius, and of a right mind, that a poet is drawn
toward the true thought, and warned away from the
rest. One of his chief functions is to vivify the
True, and so to strengthen and cleanse the minds
of men by the inbreathed virtue of the imagination
as to raise them above the Illusory. Our intellectual
strength is in proportion as we realise the true
thoughts. It is a mistake to cram poetry with
many thoughts; for it is not their multitude but their

gravity that makes poetry truly intellectual. It is a still greater mistake to wander in search of originality. Without originality, indeed, there is no true poetry; but where genius exists, it will be found unsought. Originality does not invent, so much as detect the new, revealing to us what lay about our feet, but lay there unobserved, until a beam fell upon it, as on a dewdrop in the grass, or on a stream in a distant landscape. Many of the noblest passages in poetry are truisms; but these truisms are the great truths of Humanity; and he is the true poet who draws them from their fountains in elemental purity, and gives us to drink. People are in the habit of supposing that they believe truths with which their inner mind has never once been in real contact. They are not aware that, in morals, as in physics, few of the objects with which we seem in contact really touch us; nor that it is impossible to determine how small a particle of vital truth will affect us, if it has once been truly incorporated with our internal constitution. The difference between a seeming and a real belief is in religious matters tested by obedience to Duty. In poetry—which is concerned with the Indicative more often than with the Imperative of Truth—it is by the inspired strokes of Genius that we are made to feel how wide is the gulf which separates the eternal verities of Nature from that world of semblance in which our superficial being moves.

At all periods the analogy between moral truth and the truth of poetry has been acknowledged; and the greatest poets have exercised at need, directly or indirectly, a privilege of exhortation and reproof, like that which constituted a part of the prophetic "Burden" of old.   It is one especial province of poetry to assert the cause of virtue and justice, and to rebuke corruption whether exalted in high places, or diffused throughout the body of society.   Chaucer and Dante shot many a Pythian shaft against the iniquities of their day.   Milton spoke, if more briefly, yet with more efficacy in verse than in prose,—though much of his prose was poetry,—against the civil oppressions of his time.   The social allurements of a later date, though intertwined with much of generous promise, have yet been regarded with an undazzled eye, and denounced with an unsparing tongue, by the chief poets of our age.   Its unspirituality in sentiment, its empiricism in philosophy, its covetousness, its restlessness, and its emptiness, have felt the lash, not of splenetic satirists, but of great moral teachers, who, watching with a sleepless heart the progress of the nation, did not fail to remember that progress is impossible without stability, and that even a "stationary state" in morals, not to speak of a retrograde, when contemporary with a rapid economical advance, must end in subversion and overthrow.   Mr. Taylor's estimate of some important characteristics of English society is expressed in the concluding stanzas of the poem entitled "Lago Lugano"—

> Ambition, Envy, Avarice, and Pride—
>   These are the tyrants of our hearts : the laws

Which cherish these in multitudes, and cause
The passions that aforetime lived and died
In palaces, to flourish far and wide
    Throughout a land—(allot them what applause
    We may, for wealth and science that they nurse
And greatness)—seen upon their darker side
    Bear the primeval curse.

Oh! England, "Merry England," styled of yore!
    Where is thy mirth? Thy jocund laughter where?
    The sweat of labour on the brow of care
Makes a mute answer—driven from every door!
The may-pole cheers the village green no more,
    Nor harvest-home, nor Christmas mummers rare.
    The tired mechanic at his lecture sighs;
And of the learned, which, with all his lore,
    Has leisure to be wise?

Civil and moral liberty are twain :
    That truth the careless countenances free
    Of Italy avouched : that truth did we,
On converse grounds and with reluctant pain,
Confess that England proved.   Wash first the stain
    Of worldliness away; when that shall be,
    Us shall "the glorious liberty" befit
Whereof, in other far than earthly strain,
    The Jew of Tarsus writ.

So shall the noble natures of our land
    (Oh! nobler and more deeply founded far
    Than any born beneath a southern star)
Move more at large ; be open, courteous, bland,
Be simple, cordial, not more strong to stand
    Than just to yield,—nor obvious to each jar
    That shakes the proud : for Independence walks
With staid Humility, aye hand in hand,
    Whilst Pride in tremor stalks.

From pride plebeian and from pride high born,
    From pride of knowledge no less vain and weak,
    From overstrained activities that seek
Ends worthiest of indifference or scorn,
From pride of intellect that exalts its horn
    In contumely above the wise and meek,

> Exulting in coarse cruelties of the pen,
> From pride of drudging souls to Mammon sworn,
> Where shall we flee and when?

Here is another remarkable passage in which Thought and Sentiment are enkindled to Passion, and the eloquence of Passion, through Moral Reality. The poets of Queen Anne's time were skilful and sometimes splendid in metrical declamation; but that declamation seldom went beyond rhetoric. True poetic *eloquence* is a higher and rarer thing. A noble specimen of it is Southey's "Ode written during the negotiations for Peace with Buonaparte in 1814." A still finer one is Mr. Taylor's poem "written after the return of Sir Henry Pottinger from China." It thus sums up a vindication of Captain Elliot, Sir Henry's predecessor in the Chinese command—

> What makes a hero?—Not success, not fame,
> Inebriate merchants and the loud acclaim
>   Of glutted avarice,—caps tossed up in the air,
>   Or pen of journalist with flourish fair,
> Bells pealed, stars, ribands, and a titular name,—
>   These, though his rightful tribute, he can spare ;
> His rightful tribute, not his end or aim,
> Or true reward ; for never yet did these
> Refresh the soul or set the heart at ease.
> —What makes a hero?   An heroic mind
>   Expressed in action, in endurance proved :
>   And if there be pre-eminence of right,
>   Derived thro' pain well suffered, to the height
>   Of rank heroic, 'tis to bear unmoved,
> Not toil, not risk, not rage of sea or wind,
> Not the brute fury of barbarians blind,
>   But worse,—ingratitude and poisonous darts
>   Launched by the country he had served and loved :
> This with a free unclouded spirit pure,
> This in the strength of silence to endure,

> A dignity to noble deeds imparts
>   Beyond the gauds and trappings of renown :
>   This is the hero's complement and crown ;
> This missed, one struggle had been wanting still,
> One glorious triumph of the heroic will,
>   One self-approval in his heart of hearts.

Among the strongest forms of poetic Reality is that of genuine Passion. The passion of purely ideal poetry plays in the air with flame that has no heat ; and in poetry of a meaner sort, exaggeration is a common device to hide its absence. Poetic passion is a subject but little understood. The cravings of ungovernable appetite, and the ravings of impotent self-will, expressed in swelling sentences hysterically broken, pass for passion with very inflammable, or with very cold readers. Passion, however, like that Nature from which it springs, is not often in convulsion ; and, like that Truth which is its sanction, does not always speak in a loud voice. He has no eye for passion who can describe only its agonies. There are indeed seasons when it is "perplexed in the extreme," and when, mounting to its height, it descends in ruin. Even then there is in it a retributive strength, and a light that illumes the waste. For the most part, however, it is slow, serious, profound ; soft, yet irresistible ; not killing, but making alive ; no volcanic outbreak, but a genial fire like that from the heart of the world which is revealed only in its benefits, and which, equably diffusing itself, quickens the sacred growth of fruit and flower. There is no subject which poetry can worthily treat without passion, for it is by love only that it penetrates into the life of things, and knows them.

The highest and most passionate sensibility is that which belongs to the cause of truth and justice. That half truth, that

> Most men
> Are cradled into poetry by wrong,
> And what they learn in suffering, teach in song,[1]

is based on the relations between passion and justice. Suffering and wrong, so far as they initiate a soaring spirit into the mysteries of a painful yet purifying reality, are among the wholesome bitters on which the poet feeds. They give him that tender, yet austere and sharp seriousness, without which the imagination cannot work through the dusky sphere which it must penetrate before it issues forth and meets the perfect day. The error, however, into which Mr. Shelley fell, and to a far greater degree Lord Byron (who, as the former tells us, suggested the lines quoted above), was the assumption—an unreasonable and egotistical one—that the poet must himself have been the victim of suffering and wrong. The world is always full of these trials ; and surely, if the poet's sympathies be but large enough, he may kindle into a wise indignation, or "share the passion of a just disdain," though he should have no personal injuries to resist or to revenge. Sympathy is intimately connected with true passion. Egotism, therefore, to a certain degree, must be its antagonist. Yet egotism—even

---

[1] Shelley.

the egotism of the most limited egotist—is often mistaken for passion. Lord Byron would in many poems have been thought cold but for the energetic exhibition of self-love—in some persons the least inconstant form of affection. The same is true of Rousseau, who felt much more for himself than for others, and whose egotism is commonly reflected in that of his readers when not resented by it. Rightly to sympathise, the poet ought to be endowed in equal measure with unselfishness and with sensibility; and poetic passion favours this twofold endowment, for it merges the poet's merely individual being, in proportion as it melts it into that of surrounding things.

Reality of passion, though rooted in the soil of a truthful and poetic heart,—and where the moral ground of poetry is shallow its intellectual growths will ever be stunted,—is in no small degree promoted, as well as guarded, by another species of truth,—truth of style. While the importance of style in prose compositions is universally acknowledged, its equal, if not greater, importance in verse has been too frequently disregarded by modern poets. In Mr. Taylor's it always holds a very high place. With the merely technical rules of style poetry has indeed little concern; just as in its diction it is able (the more apprehensive method of the imagination superseding such aid) to dispense with many particles and copulatives, which are yet necessary in prose as links to

unite the leading parts of speech.   But this very
independence of the lesser matters in style renders
attention to its essential principles yet more obligatory.
Without a pure and masterly style, a poet may be
popular, but he will never become classical.   It is
also that branch of the poetic art in which he meets
with the largest return for his expenditure of care.
His care, however, must be habitual, conscientious,
and temperate; and not the overstrained and morbid
labour which corrects and recorrects until the unity
of the original conception is lost, and all freshness
has been dissipated.   A truthful style is a vigorous style,
which of itself gives individuality to character, vividness to description, weight, purpose, and point to
sentiment and to thought.   A truthful style shows itself
in two different ways, that is, in the logic of poetry and
in its rhetoric.   The logic of poetry is indeed distantly
related, if at all, to the syllogistic logic of the schools;
but it is not the less certain that the imagination
works by a logical method of its own; and that he
only who is impressed by its laws is capable of great
works of sustained imagination.   The logic of poetry
has, however, humbler functions likewise.   A just
principle of division and a sagacious distribution of
the subject-matter are necessary, if poetry is to keep
as well as to take possession of the hearts of men,
which seldom continue permanently divorced from
their intellects; and it is for want of some moderate
appreciation of categories that there are to be found
in many a popular poem passages which, were they

not tricked out in gay apparel, would carry on their very faces the absurdity and incongruity that really belongs to them.

A deficiency of poetic reality proceeding from a lack of truthfulness in style is yet more noticeable in the bad rhetoric than in the false logic of inferior poetry. It displays itself first by a superabundance of figures. A metaphor tells us what things are like, not what they are. In many cases indeed this is all that we can know; and the higher species of symbol, by tracing things apparently diverse to a common law, is unquestionably an organ of philosophy. It is in fact the basis of that analogical argument upon which Bishop Butler has built so stately a fabric, and of that " Philosophia Prima," spoken of by Bacon : as such, too, it is of the same kind with the parable, the great oriental method of instruction, which, in one form or another, has flourished on every soil. Where employed in its place it seems impossible to prescribe a limit to its use : for it is the most concise, the most piercing, and the most luminous method of imparting ideas at once comprehensive and subtle. But figurative writing has passed the limits within which it can minister to the nobly beautiful, as often as it so penetrates the subject intended to be illustrated, as to destroy its palpable solidity, and to leave no quiet surface for the repose of light and shade. Nor do figures, when used out of place, simply fail in effect. They are exposed to a more serious charge. If brought in to make plainer what is already plain, they but confuse the understanding and divert the attention. The result is worse still, if they are introduced but for the purpose of ornament,—for they then betray an insensibility on the part of the poet to that primal beauty of truth, which finds in obtrusive ornament only an incumbrance. Yet there is another form of error more mischievous than mere excess. It is, by incongruous images, and yet more by broken or absolutely false metaphors, that untruthfulness in the rhetoric of poetry is fatally evinced. In many cases there is a coldness about them, which proves that they were but after-thoughts. Another and more common defect in style is the use of quasi-metaphors in its ordinary texture; a tawdriness which, without imparting significance, destroys manly plainness, and produces nothing but what is incoherent and purposeless. Analogous to this defect is that of showy lines, ambitious point, pretentious expressions, which, as it were, admire themselves, and mar the context. When Byron describes the human skull as

> The dome of thought, the palace of the soul,

one neither denies the energy nor the cleverness of the expression; but would Homer or Dante, or Shakespeare, have variegated their poetic robes with such purple patches? These are the sallies of an irregular ambition, catching at applause; and they are as inconsistent with that grave, unrapacious, scarcely conscious desire for sympathy, which ought to be a poet's external stimulus, as with that quietness and confidence which is his internal strength.

Another element in style is that of diction.   Here, also, for reality the first requisite is truth.   Unequivocal words alone carry weight with them.   Energetic truth forbids diffuseness; for it is through brief, select expression that thoughts disclose their characteristic features.   Clearness and intensity are thus found together; and to write with these is to write with force.   Words are frequently called the dress of thought; but they stand to it in a much closer relation, clothing it as the skin covers the body, or as the bark covers the tree.   We think in language: as our thoughts are, our words will be; nor can we think truthfully without rejecting vague constructions, grammatical irregularities or feebleness, and excess in the use of poetical licenses.   There is a mystery in words; and it is impossible to explain the full power which they possess not only in consequence of their defined meaning, and through their associations, but also from those untranslateable ideas which are yet effectually insinuated into us by their harmony and cadence. Very stately processions of words are frequently marshalled with a very prosaic pageantry; and, on the other hand, where but two or three words are found together, the spirit of poetry may be in the midst of them.   It is the singular felicity of our language that, by its two elements, the Latin and the Saxon, two different species of impression are conveyed. Words of a Latin origin address the intellect chiefly, and impart their meaning to it with a peculiar distinctness; but that meaning can only be thus presented to the heart and the moral being as it were through a veil. The Latin element of our language is therefore peculiarly serviceable where dignity is required, and where complex thoughts, not delicate gradations of sentiment, are to be expressed. The Saxon element, on the other hand, is the one in which strength and truth reside. Its brief appeals come home to us immediately, not mediately; address our whole being and not a portion of it; and speak directly to the heart, in its own words of pathos and of power. Neither part of our language should be depreciated: Mr. Taylor enhances the force of each by contrasting it with the other.

There remains a department of poetic truth—that, namely, which relates to the picturesque in landscape. A truthful observation of scenery is a different thing from a passionate love of it. In most modern poetry description occupies a large space (in some instances man becomes but a dot in the landscape); but it is seldom executed with even technical accuracy, and yet more seldom with a higher truth. The poets of antiquity, on the contrary, regarded picturesque Nature as so entirely subordinate to man, that while admirable in the skill with which they touch details, they have hardly left us a single poetic landscape. In Mr. Taylor's poetry also Nature is ever subordinate to man; and he too describes rather particular objects than landscapes. His minor poems especially are enriched by descriptions almost as brief as those

of the ancient poets, and more accurate if less bright.
Here as elsewhere his especial characteristic is Reality.

One test of reality in every work of art is congruity.
What has been truthfully conceived will keep proportions. It has been well pointed out [1] that those early
masters, whose predominant characteristics were aspiration and sanctity, chose, as a fit interpreter for the
saintly forms in the foreground, a sky whose purity
and simplicity should be expressive of the *infinity* of
heaven—the "luminous distance" of evening, with its
pale green, or the morning's "still small voice of level
twilight behind purple hills," so suggestive of "spiritual
hope, of longing and escape." In corroboration of
this remark it will be observed that pictures in which
one artist has painted the figures and another the
landscape, are not often noted for their harmony or
their truth. A closer union has been attempted;
and our National Gallery boasts a great picture in
which a Venetian hand has supplied the colouring
to a Florentine design. If such pictures are among
the wonders of art, they are seldom its best examples.
The colouring of Titian would have sensualised, and
the radiance of Correggio have etherealised the conceptions of Michael Angelo; while the loss of his
sublime strength, thus neutralised, would not have
been compensated by any accession of alien qualities.
Nor more successful, probably, would have been the
experiment, in case those earlier masters, alluded to,
had been able to add the Florentine vigour of design

[1] *Modern Painters*, vol. ii. p. 40.

and variety of composition to their own especial merits
—spiritual elevation and the quietude of pathetic
beauty. The same principle applies to poetry. The
diction which would be prolix in dramatic or narrative
verse may be in perfect harmony in meditative, where
even the slighter shades of thought have a value on
their own account. What would be an excess of the
figurative in philosophical poetry may harmonise with
lyrical. For this reason objections brought against
great works, not on the ground of faults but of deficiencies, are for the most part frivolous and vexatious;
for no excellency is attained except by sacrifice.
Every great poem as well as picture by necessity
includes some high qualities in a greater, and some in
a lesser degree; to be perfect or approach perfection,
it must possess each only in a due proportion. This
proportion is determined, not by external rule, but
inwardly, by that imagination, which conceived the
poem originally, and conceived it as a whole. If this
truth of congruity be wanting, not only will the result
be unsatisfactory, but the work will thus be proved to
have been spurious in its origin; for a work of art, if
it has been genially produced, will be homogeneous
or harmonised. It is impossible for a healthy imagination to beget hybrids or monsters; these are not
natural conceptions: but it is easy for an uninspired
hand to join together a piece of ill-assorted though
splendid patchwork.

It is this note of authenticity which imparts to true
poetry its verisimilitude—a quality without which it

can make no appeal to the heart. Poetry professes to
have witnessed that of which it makes report. If its
witness be true, the sympathies of men will eventually
seal that truth and receive that witness : if its tidings
be but hearsay, its empiricism will be proved by the
inconsistent babbling with which men describe what
they have not known. Let a man's theme be ever so
high or ever so low, he may have seen what he speaks
of, or he may have only wished to see it. Burns,
when he describes a daisy uprooted by the plough, is
scarcely more real than Dante, when Dante sings of
the choirs that rejoice in heaven. The former sees
with true poetic insight that which actually exists ; the
latter with a more creative eye, but with equal truthfulness, sees that which might exist, and which, if it
existed, would appear as it presented itself to him in
definite and authentic vision. It is thus that in
arduous instances of foreshortening, positions of the
human form which could never have been observed,
even in the model, by the outward eye of the painter,
are faithfully exhibited by his inspired guesses.
Dante's unshaken self-possession in the midst of the
marvels around him, is itself a proof that his vision
was poetically real : for had it been false, that excitement, which alone could have sustained the illusion,
would have swept him into the vortices of splendour
and motion which he describes ; and he would have
written with as unsteady a hand as his imitators have
ever done. Self-possession, a thing very different
from unimpassioned sedateness, is a note of mature

greatness in poetry; and it is so noble a resultant of it that Repose itself, which has often been extolled as an ultimate merit in art, may, perhaps, derive no small part of its charm from the fact that it is among the modes by which self-possession is evinced. This is one of the characteristics which mark the analogy between the inspiration of the true poet and that of the true prophet. Without it enthusiasm runs into madness, and passion is self-destructive : without it greatness, instead of rolling onward in an ever ascending wave, perpetually tumbles over like a breaker, and loses itself in foam. Closely allied to self-possession is that rare attribute—poetic Moderation—which excludes such exaggerated admiration of any one especial excellence as must lead to the neglect of others. The highest poetry rests upon a right adjustment of contending claims. Some persons are advocates of the sensuous, and others of what has latterly been called the subjective; but poetry of the first order reconciles both demands,—being of all things the most intellectual in its method and scope, while in its form and imagery it is the largest representation of visible things. Partaking at once the nature both of Science and of Art, it spiritualises the outward world while it embodies the world of Thought. It composes also the warfare between passion and imagination. Though passion frees a man from self, yet it sells him in bondage to outward things,—it clasps the material world like a vine, sucks out and circulates its life-blood, stirs up heroic natures to high achievements; and yet, being itself earth-born and servile in its conditions, it makes the end of their wanderings a blind subjection to Fate. Passion is, therefore, the sanguine life of that tragic poetry which hailed in Bacchus a master, and found its temple in the theatre under the Athenian Acropolis. The imagination, on the other hand, passes through all barriers, and spurns the mountain-tops, taking its pastime on each successive height only till it has gained strength to outsoar it. This is the poetry which sought a patron in Apollo,—the lord of light, deliverance, and healing. Passion by itself would violate the freedom, imagination would transcend the limits of art. Whatever qualities tend to maintain the equipoise between them, to which the innumerable balances of poetry are subordinate, enlarge its sphere and enhance its power. The chief of these qualities is Truth, and especially Truth in the form of Reality.

THE TWO CHIEF SCHOOLS OF ENGLISH POETRY. POETIC VERSATILITY

SHELLEY AND KEATS

A POET is often praised for his versatility, as though it were a gift special to himself, by persons who have not sufficiently observed that it is a quality inherent in all high poetic imagination, although it should doubtless be balanced by a converse quality—viz. intellectual and moral unity. There are two sorts of Versatility. Spurious Versatility is only the exercise of that imitative power which betrays a want of original conception and tenacity of poetic purpose. It is a volatile sympathy with impressions merely external, united with an incapacity of receiving a principle or resting on a conclusion. Genuine Versatility unites mobility of temperament with a large mind and an imagination which takes in all things without absolutely surrendering itself to any, while it can also concentrate itself at will. It is only when the "various talents" are united with "the single mind" that they give their possessors "moral might and mastery o'er mankind." The Hebrew Poet says, "My heart is fixed," and then proceeds, "I will sing." And it is truly when the heart is most fixed that the imagination can afford to be most flexible. It may wave like a pine-tree in the breeze, if, like the pine, it sends its root deep into the soil. On these conditions, the more versatile the genius is, the ampler will be its sweep, and the mightier its resilient power. It is such versatility that enables the poet to apply his own experience, analogically and by imaginative induction, to regions unknown and forms of life untried, at once passing into the being of others and retaining his own. The characters delineated by the greatest poets have therefore been always remarked to possess two great attributes—those of universality and individuality. But they could never unite these two if the corresponding faculties were not united in the versatile imagination, profound moral sense, and accurate observation of the true poet. For want of the first faculty there are men who can produce but a single work of value. Beyond the limit of their individual experience there is for them *nil nisi pontus et aer*, and within that narrow pasture their faculties grow lean. On the other hand, there are too many who, for want of moral depth and tenacity in conjunction with versatility, remain for ever but imitators, and wholly fail to fulfil the promise of their earlier and happier efforts.

To corroborate these opinions it is only needful to observe that the greatest of dramatists not only exhibits the faculty of versatility in its perfection, but proves to us that that gift is consistent with what is most characteristic in genius, and most harmonious in its mode of working.   Shakespeare, it has been said, is but a voice.   If so, it is a voice direct from Nature's heart, not the voice of a mocking bird.   The *affection* which we feel for him is in itself a proof of this.   In poetry, as elsewhere, those who forget themselves are the last to be forgotten by others.   Shakespeare is everywhere present in his poetry, though he may be nowhere distinctly or completely seen.   As the spirit of poetry tacitly pervades all nature,—refreshing, consoling, renewing,—so Shakespeare himself accompanies us through all his works, a potent and friendly genius.   In all his thoughts we recognise one *method* of thought; his own sweet and large nature ever mediates between the natures that he describes, even when they are most discordant ; his manner is familiar to us, and throughout his ample domain we recognise his genial laugh or his doubtful smile—like that of the Dryad evanescent in the branches, or the Nereid descending in the wave.   Does any one need a biography to tell him whether Shakespeare was a kindly man or cold, liberal or niggardly, humble or proud ? whether his faults were faults of infirmity or of malice ? whether there were weeds amid his abundance, or whether his heart was a field protected from them by its barrenness ? whether he was a patriot, or had secluded himself from national sympathies? whether his disposition was to believe or to scoff? *These* questions, at all events, have hitherto furnished no materials for critical battles.

It is of course in dramatic poetry that versatility is most needed; but all genuine poetry is in its spirit dramatic.   It would be a truism to remark, that in narrative poetry there is a dramatic element,—it being, in fact, the soil out of which the drama (but a more concentrated form of narration) grew.   Even in idyllic and in descriptive poetry the dramatic, and therefore the versatile faculty, is also necessary; nay, the humblest object which includes the beautiful, or has ever inspired song, cannot be poetically appreciated by one who is unwilling to forget himself, or unable to pass into other forms of being.   In many an orderly and compact tragedy there is less of dramatic versatility than in Burns's allusion to a worn-out horse, or Dante's description of the bird

> .   .   .   .   who midst the leafy bower
> Has in her nest sat darkling through the night,
> With her sweet brood ; *impatient to descry*
> *Their wished looks*, and to bring home their food.[1]

Such things, it is obvious, cannot be thus described unless they are known—nor thus known except through the imaginative insight of the affections.   Sympathy is, in truth, but versatility of heart; and large sympathies are, therefore, the most powerful auxiliaries of poetic genius.   For the same reason egotism, prejudice,

---

[1] Cary's translation.

a habit of dogmatism, and whatever else locks up our sympathies, are impediments to poetry. On the other hand, among many supposed to be removed from literary influences—among the poor, and especially among children—the very essence of poetry is to be found in the form of prompt and extended sympathies. A versatile imagination is indeed the chief faculty of children. Having as yet hardly realised a self-conscious being of their own, they have the less difficulty in passing into that of others. The consequence is that their life is almost wholly poetical; all that goes on around them is a long drama; a piece of stick with a ribbon tied to it represents a king or a queen; and they can hold dramatic colloquy with men and women impersonated by their fancy alone. Hans Andersen's genius consists mainly in his being persistently a child. It has been often remarked, that with nations also the poetical period is that of early youth. And the reason of this is, that when men have ceased to be pressed down by the selfish wants of savage life, and not yet made selfish by the conventions of material civilisation, the imagination has a versatility, and sympathy a vital power, which at other periods is unknown. It is then that Emotion is strong; in other words, that man has a power of *moving out of himself;* it is then that the most ordinary objects appear to him wonderful, and that nothing wonderful is either extraordinary or incredible; it is then that religion is natural to him, and that Nature is invested with supernatural attributes, and regarded with religious awe. A lively sensibility to grief and joy, to love and to hate, is that through which all outward things acquire for us a real existence, and become objects of interest.   In the absence of these, our nearest domestic concerns would have for us as remote and visionary an existence as spiritual truths possess for the merely secular intelligence ; and in the presence of these, not only the animal races are brought home to our human sympathies—the brooding bird, or the faithful hound—but the inanimate elements become humanised ; waves and clouds live in our life ; if they swell, it is in wrath ; if they fly, it is in fear ; if they pursue, it is in love.   In other words, Nature itself, and all its powers, are dramatised ; and the faculty which makes them rehearse their several parts is that of a versatile imagination.

Versatility changes its character at the different seasons of the poetic growth.   In a young poet it is indeed but a part of his docility.   He will listen, with the susceptive faith of youth, successively to each of the great masters of song ; and the echo which remains in his ear will in some degree modulate his tone.   He will trace every path which the Muse has trod, in the hope of reaching that point from which they diverge ; and it is well that he should try all things, provided he holds fast to that which for him is best.   The infancy of the life poetic, like that of all life, learns much by unconscious imitation ; but it can only so learn when the poet possesses those original faculties which, even when they imitate, seek help only to work out their proper development.   True genius will soon cast aside whatever is alien to its individual nature; while, on the other hand, incorporating into its proper substance all poetic elements that are truly congenial, it will blend them also with each other, and stamp upon them a unity of its own.   The poet will become original when he wields collectively the powers that once were his only alternately; and versatility will then have been exalted into a higher gift,—that of comprehensiveness.

Except at periods of barbarism, of thoroughly corrupt morals, or of utter effeminacy, the poetic instinct will ever assert itself; for the imagination pervades nearly the whole of our nature; and is sure to work its way up into the light, no matter through what obstructions.   If the age be a poetical one, the imagination will embody its sentiment, and illustrate its tendencies.   If it be unpoetical, the imagination will not therefore be repressed.   It will then create a world for itself—or revert to some historic period the memorials of which it will invest with a radiance not their own.   Unquestionably those ages are the most favourable to poetry in which the imagination can pluck the ears of corn as it passes through the field, and is not obliged to seek its food afar.   At those periods in which no political conventions strive to supply the place of valour and wisdom in rulers and of a generous loyalty in subjects, in which the first great triumphs of patriotism are won, and in which temples rise from the ground at the bidding of a zeal which has not learned to economise its efforts,—at such periods it is that poetry is most genial, most real, and most authentic. Such were the periods at which Homer, Dante, and Shakespeare wrote. The heroic age of Greece, the theology and philosophy of mediæval Europe, and the manners and history of England, furnished these men respectively with the main materials of their verse. These are the great *National* poets of the world. They belong indeed to all ages; but they belonged especially each to his own. The materials of each were supplied by the objects surrounding him, or by the traditions which had descended to him by inheritance.

It would, however, be a grave error to suppose that the national is alone the great poet. On the contrary, it is among the results of poetic versatility, as well as of the instincts of the human heart, that there has ever existed in our literature, and, to no small degree, in that of other countries, two great schools of poetry, one only of which can properly be called national. It does not depend on the circumstances of the age alone whether the poet finds his materials in the circle of surrounding things, or seeks them elsewhere: this will in the main be determined by the constitution of his own moral nature, and the preponderance in it of a vivid sympathy with reality on the one hand, or, on the other, of an ardent aspiration after a supreme excellence. In either case the same high gift, the imagination, will lend to him its mediating powers, in the former interpreting the outward world to him, in the latter interpreting his ideal to his fellow-men. Even in the best and healthiest periods of national development the human mind will aspire after a region more exalted and pure than it can ever find on earth; even in the most prosaic it will be able to detect something noble in the world of common things. From this double power arise two converse schools of poetry; the one characterised by its plastic power and its function of embodying the abstractedly great and the ideally beautiful; the other by its reality, its home-bred sympathies, and its affinities with national history, character, and manners. These two schools have existed from the beginning of our literature, and have been reproduced in our own day. The merest outline will illustrate the momentous truth that neither in nations nor in individuals does poetry hold an isolated existence, but that it flourishes or declines in conjunction with that moral, political, and spiritual wellbeing which, when itself sound, it helps to sustain, though by two very different modes of procedure.

Poetry has ever recognised these two great offices, distinct though allied—the one, that of representing the actual world; the other, that of creating an ideal region, into which spirits whom this world has wearied may retire. The former function is chiefly discharged by the *historia spectabilis* of the drama; the latter belongs for the most part to poets lyrical or mythic, who, in the "enchanted islands" of the Fancy, or in the "snowy cloisters" of a more spiritual imagination, have provided retreats in which spirits,

> Assoiled from all encumbrance of the time,

may rest and be thankful. A perfect poet ought to discharge both those great offices of poetry. To a limited extent the greatest have done so; but even in their case the balance has ever preponderated in one direction or the other.

In Greece, as in England, those two species of poetry coexisted; but in the former neither of them connected itself much with materials derived from any foreign country. No region more beautiful than Greece could then be conceived of; and the Greek poet could only forsake the company of its heroes for that of its gods. But in our northern regions, which, on emerging from barbarism, found the ancient literature a perfect work imperfectly explored, the South has always been regarded with feelings akin to those entertained by the Greek for the fabled Hesperia of the West. It was a region of beauty and delight on which the imagination might rest half-way to heaven, —an asylum which combined the solidities of this earth with the ideal perfection of worlds beyond ours. The beauty of the southern countries, their remoteness, and their ancient fame, favoured the illusion; and the imagination of England was further drawn to them by the indirect attraction of those other arts which had been carried to perfection in the South alone. The southern mind, moreover, is more inventive than that of the North, though less thoughtful and imaginative; and, as a consequence, Italian and Spanish "Novelle" supplied a plot to half our British dramas,—a circumstance too commonly ascribed to the single fact that on the revival of letters the literature of the South had earliest sprung into existence. All these influences imparted a character distinctly southern to that school of English Poetry which was inspired rather by the love of the beautiful than by national associations, as both advanced to their development.

It was in Shakespeare and Milton that the two great schools found their chief representatives. The former is the greatest of national poets, though he sometimes forsook the national for the ideal department of song; and Milton is not a national poet, although (his ideal resulting as much from his religious bias as from his imagination) his-poetry derived from the stormy Puritanism of his land and day a reality rare in the ideal school. This distinction between the character of the two poets is illustrated by the different reception their works have met. Shakespeare's sympathies were keenly native; and he has therefore ever been a favourite with the people. He is above their appreciation, indeed, but not beyond their love. His dramas have many planes of interest, which underlie each other like the concentric layers of bark produced by the annual growth of a tree; and while the most philosophic eye cannot penetrate to the inmost, the most superficial is pleased with that which lies outside. Where any love of the drama remains, Shakespeare is enjoyed even by the most homely audience. But if any one were to submit to such an audience a page of the *Paradise Lost*, far from being received like the Rhapsodist of old, the Ballad-singer, or the Methodist Preacher, it would effectually disperse the crowd. The audience which Milton demanded was "fit though few": Shakespeare demanded none; but if people came, he probably thought "the more the merrier." The latter wrote for the stage, but seldom was at the trouble of publishing his plays: the former prescribed for himself a choral audience consisting of grave divines, sage patriots, and virtuous citizens; and when this selected audience hissed him, as occasionally happened, he cursed them to their faces in Hebrew and in Greek—as "asses, apes, and dogs," whose portion ought to be with the schismatics who had "railed at Latona's twin-born progeny!"

It is not, however, its deficient popularity so much as its subject and its form which proves that Milton's great work is not a national poem, high as it ranks among our national triumphs. If that mind had remained with him, which was his when English landscape supplied the scenery of his *Allegro*, and Christian theology inspired the moral teaching of his *Comus*, he would probably have fulfilled his youthful aspiration, and celebrated Britain's mythic hero, Arthur; but instead of the great romance of the North, he wrote its religious epic. Some will affirm that he illustrated in that work his age if not his country. His age, however, gave him an impulse rather than materials. Puritanism became transmuted, as it passed through his capacious and ardent mind,

into a faith Hebraic in its austere spirit,—a faith that
sympathised indeed with the Iconoclastic zeal which
distinguished the anti-Catholic and anti-patristic theology of the age, but held little consent with any of
the complex definitions at that time insisted on as the
symbols of Protestant orthodoxy. Had the Puritan
spirit been as genuine a thing as the spirit of liberty
which accompanied it; had it been such as their
reverence for Milton makes many suppose it to have
been, the mood would not so soon have yielded to
the licentiousness that followed the Restoration.
Milton laboured as a patriot-partizan while a field of
labour was open to him : he then turned again to his
true greatness. The dust of the conflict had fallen;
and the mountain heights shone out once more from
the serene distance : once more he confronted the
mighty works of ancient genius. They pleased him
still, from their severity and their simplicity; but
they did not satisfy him—because they wanted elevation. In his *Paradise Lost* he raised and endeavoured
to spiritualise the antique epic. There are many who
will always regard St. Peter's temple in the air as the
first of architectural monuments. The admirers of
the classic will, however, feel that the amplitude and
height of the wondrous dome are no sufficient substitute for that massive simplicity and breadth of
effect which belong to the Parthenon; while those
who revere our cathedrals will maintain that it lacks
the variety, the mystery, the aspiration, and the infinitude which characterise the Christian architecture of

the North. On analogous grounds the more devoted admirers of Homer and of Shakespeare will ever be dissatisfied with Milton's work, however they may venerate his genius. It is obviously composite in its character—the necessary result of its uniting a Hebraic spirit with a classic form. Dante, like Milton, uses the Greek mythology freely ; considering it, no doubt, as part of that "inheritance of the Heathen," into possession of which Christendom had a right to enter ; but he uses it as a subordinate ornament, and in matters of mere detail. His poem is a Vision, not an Epic, that vision of supernatural truth, of Hell, Purgatory, and Paradise, which passed before the eyes of the mediæval Church as she looked up in nocturnal vigil ; not the mundane circle of life and experience, of action and of passion, exhibited in its completeness, and contemplated with calm satisfaction by a Muse that looks down from heaven. But a mystic subject, open rather to apprehension than comprehension, would not have contented Milton, who, with his classical predilections, had early laid it down as a canon that poetry should be "simple, sensuous, and impassioned," a statement of the utmost importance where justly applicable, but by no means embracing the whole truth. To him the classic model supplied, not the adornment of his poem, but its structure and form. The soul that wielded that mould was, if not exactly the spirit of Christianity, at least a religious spirit—profound, zealous, and self-reverent—as analogous, perhaps, in its temper to the warlike religion of

the Eastern Prophet, as to the traditional Faith of the
second Dispensation.   Such was the mighty fabric
which, aloof and in his native land an exile, Milton
raised; not perfect, not homogeneous, not in any
sense a national work, but the greatest of all those
works which prove that a noble poem may be produced with little aid from local sympathies, and none
from national traditions.

From the earliest period of our literature we have
possessed the two schools, which culminated in
Shakespeare and in Milton.   In Chaucer the national
element greatly preponderated : it reigns almost alone
in many of the Canterbury Tales, especially in the
humorous ; but in several, of which the moral tone is
higher and the execution more delicate, a southern
spirit prevails.   Of these his "Second Nonne's Tale,"
embalming the legend of St. Cecilia, is a beautiful
example, illustrating, as it does, that moral influence
of which the origin eluded the eye, like the invisible
garland of the saint,—that influence which was exhaled
from the life and manners of the first Christians, and
through which, in a large part, their religion was
diffused.   The national element of our poetry, too,
asserted itself almost exclusively in our historical
ballads, that exquisite series, the musical echo of so
much of our history.   Surrey and Wyatt, in no slight
degree, represented that Italian-Gothic school of which
Spenser may be considered as the great representative.
In him the spirit of chivalry elevated the love of the
beautiful ; and both, while often ennobled by a

meditative piety, were enriched by all the gentler associations of classical song. He was a man of a far graver mind than belonged to any of his models ; and we miss in him the buoyant gaiety which animates the poets of the South ; but such deficiencies were amply atoned for by that profoundly contemplative spirit which pervades his poetry. His hymns on " Heavenly Love" and " Heavenly Beauty " are poetic specimens of the Platonic moral philosophy ; and we can nowhere meet an exposition of the Christian Religion in its completeness and proportions, doctrinal, devotional, and practical, more searching while so brief as exists in the tenth canto of his *First Book*, describing the visit of the Red-Cross Knight to the " House of Holiness." In the *Faery Queen*, indeed, we find the essence of the prose romances of the Middle Ages—as we find the essence of their theologians in Dante. Ariosto is neither more various nor more picturesque than the English poet, while in sincerity, tenderness, and elevation, he is immeasurably inferior ; nor is that imaginative love-sentiment which, rather than the passion itself, was the theme of the ideal poets, celebrated with more grace, refinement, and sweetness, in the sonnets of Petrarca than in those of Spenser. Spenser's fairy-land will never be much frequented by those whose sympathies are exclusively with Action, Passion, and Character. But with poetic students of another class, who, if they have advanced less in the lore of life, have wandered less far from the breast of the Muses ; with those by whom ideal beauty, generous sentiment, rich imagery, "fancies chaste and noble," harmonious numbers, and a temperament of poetry steeped in the fountains of pleasure, but irradiating them with its own purity,— with those by whom such qualities are cherished, the poetry of Spenser must ever remain a favourite haunt. It more resembles the Italian Gothic than a classic temple which charms and rests the eye by the perfection of its proportions: yet to it also belongs, in its several parts, a southern definiteness. It is a forest palace,—half natural, half artificial: we wander through groves as regular as galleries: and catch glimpses of openings like stately halls dismantled,— but our foot is ever upon flowers; and the moonlight of the allegory favours the illusion.

From the chivalrous paradise of Spenser's *Faery Queen* to Milton's *Paradise Lost* the two schools of English poetry maintained a friendly rivalry. Both sources of inspiration contended at times in the same author, even when a dramatist. Marlow, in his classical narrative poem "Hero and Leander"; Shakespeare, in his "Rape of Lucrece" and his " Venus and Adonis "; Fletcher, in his "Faithful Shepherdess"; Shirley, in his "Narcissus and Echo," are southern, not only in their subject but in their mode of treating it. In Brown's "Britannia's Pastorals," a poem full of beauty, the classic spirit reigns almost alone. The scenery itself is classical, though the author was probably never out of England; and its "silver streams" and "pleasant meads" are never depressed by the shade of northern mountains or clouds.   The sonnets of Drummond abound in an Italian beauty; as indeed do many of Daniel's, whose other writings are characterised by an English robustness and thoughtfulness.   The exquisite fragments which, in his swift and brief career, were carelessly shaken from Sidney's affluent genius, are as full of the southern inspiration as the morning dew-drops are of light ; and in Lovelace, Suckling, Carew, as well as other lyric poets of their time, we find a terseness and light-hearted grace which are not of northern origin.   In Herrick the southern spirit becomes again the spirit of the antique.   In the very constitution of his imagina-tion he was a Greek ; yet he sang in no falsetto key : his thoughts were instinct with the true classical spirit ; and it was, as it were, by a process of translation that he recast them in English words.   It is to this circumstance that we are to attribute his occasional reprehensible license.

With the exception of Milton, the period that succeeded the Restoration was as fatal to the ideal as to the national school of English poetry.   The religious sentiment had bled wellnigh to death, through the wounds of a society cut up with sects and schisms. The political enthusiasm had burned out.   The sublime had been changed into the ridiculous ; the performance had mocked the conception ; and if Milton's majestic prose treatises had sounded the Prologue, the Epilogue of the Tragi-comedy was furnished by the shrewd and thoroughly English comment of Butler's *Hudibras*. Cromwell passed away; and the strong but gloomy world his shoulders had supported, fell with him. As if the Puritan prophets had but prophesied in somnambulism, as if the nation had but in hypochondria fancied itself a Levitical community, as if their lofty Hebraic aspirations had been but an ethical " renaissance " or " the nympholepsy of some fond despair," the work of their hands melted strangely away before the eyes, and with the seeming consent of the English people !

The cavaliers had again their day ; but their success turned out likewise a failure. The king had been brought back ; but he could not believe in himself— and the ancient loyalty was no more. A less imaginative age had succeeded, and the riot of sense were called in, to supply the place of spiritual illusions dispelled. The degradations of society infected literature. The revel subsided ; but the debauch of the night left the head giddy and the stomach weak in the morning ; and the epicurean had soured into the cynic. That period was succeeded by a still colder one. Its chief political work, the Revolution, was effected in business-like fashion,—but with little on either side of that faith or hope which had elevated the earlier struggle. Its theology held equally in suspicion whatever was passionate and whatever was traditional : its philosophy repudiated abstractions and *à priori* views ; and its arts lacked the fervour alike of ideal conceptions and of home-bred affections. High aspirations and national recollections faded alike ; poetry necessarily became imitative; and the Anglo-Gallican school grew up. The silver age of English poetry was adorned with writers of admirable abilities; of whom Dryden was the greatest in mental power, while Pope has left behind him the most perfect works. Conventional manners, satire, and if not moral philosophy, at least moral disquisition, supplied their cheap materials to that school; and in the absence of a creative spirit or a shaping art, its chief attractions were found in its executive skill, and a style accomplished, masculine, and pointed. It died out soon, however, for it had no root. Its classical illusions, taken at second hand, had never breathed a genuine classical spirit; and its disquisitions gradually degenerated into metrical treatises on botany, hunting, or medicine!

In conjunction with stronger political interests and deeper feelings on moral and religious subjects, Poetry gradually revived. It exhibited from the first a native origin that attested its authenticity, and in time it developed an ideal aim. The former was marked by its fidelity to Nature, and its frequent reference to the rural manners of England. The nature which Thomson describes is living Nature, and the blood flows freely in her veins; but a refined appreciation of the graceful and the poetical he lacked; and the deficiency which makes itself ridiculous in the clumsy handling of his "Musidora" and other narratives, exists also in his delineations of scenery. The landscapes of Thomson, like those of Rubens, are sensual, though in each case we remark that quality less than when the subject treated is a higher one, and in each the want of refinement and spirituality is compensated by a rich combination of less exalted merits. The poet and the painter alike present us, in their landscapes, with the "fat of the land"; their substantial plains and well-watered meads remind us that they were intended to be meat for man and for beast; and whatever they may lack, they are not deficient in reality. With an idyllic a moral poetry rose up. The moral meditations of Young had comprised much vigorous declamation of native English growth. Cowper, a far greater poet, expressed in purer and simpler language thoughts with more of substantial worth, as well as a strain of sentiment, manly, religious, and gravely affectionate. In him, too, we find an admirable fidelity to outward nature in detail; although with her grander forms, unendeared by association, he had little sympathy; while ideal representations of scenery are no more to be found in his poetry than ideal conceptions of character.

If the poetry of Cowper belongs to our national school, that of Burns is yet more racy of the soil. He was more fortunately circumstanced for poetry, though he had more to contend with. The period at which he lived furnished materials sufficiently poetical, when presented to his keen insight and vivid sensibilities; and Burns was luckily without that smattering of learning which often leads men from what surrounds them, without enabling them truly to appreciate the spirit of another age. He felt deeply; and he affected nothing foreign to his genius. Song and ballad, and light tale and humorous dialogue, the forms of composition with which the neighbourhood was familiar,—with these, while he "unlocked his heart" he also interpreted that of his country. Most of those qualities which were distributed among his countrymen met in his larger being, or were embraced by his sympathies. It is not chiefly the romantic side of the Scotch character which was represented in Burns,—its imagination, its patriotism, its zealous affectionateness, its love of the legendary, the marvellous and the ancient,—that part, in fact, which belongs most to the highlands: he was more amply furnished with the stronger lowland qualities,— sense, independence, courageous perseverance, shrewdness, and humour, a retentive heart, and a mind truthful alike when fully expressed or when partially reserved. These qualities were united in his abundant nature; and his poetic temperament freed them from the limitations which belong to every character formed upon a local type. The consequence is that his songs are sung at the hearth and on the mountain-side; his pathos is felt and his humour applauded by the village circle; his sharp descriptions and shrewd questions on grave matters are treated as indulgently by ministers of the "National Assembly," the "Free Kirk," and "orthodox dissenters," as Boccaccio's stories once were by the Italian clergy; and for the lonely traveller from the South the one small volume

which contains his works is the best of guide-
books,—not indeed to noted spots, legendary or
famed for beauty,—but to the manners, the moral
soul, and the heart of the Scotch people. Burns
is emphatically the most national of poets.

This brief retrospect has brought down nearly to
our own times its imperfect sketch of the two main
schools into which our poetic literature may be
divided; and it will be perceived that both these
schools have their origin in the imaginative and social
instincts of man, which occupy themselves alike with
what is above him, and what is around him, and no
less in that special gift of high poetry—viz. versatility,
which enables it to provide food for both of those
two cravings. This truth derives a historical con-
firmation from the fact that both schools became
extinct together, when English poetry had declined
into mere imitation; and that whenever the poetic
genius of England has been most powerfully developed, both have flourished together—united like
the Latin and Saxon elements of our compound
language. The poetic mind of England, on its
revival towards the end of the last century, again, as
of old, manifested itself in the form of two schools
which, with much in common, still represented,
notwithstanding, the northern and southern hemi-
spheres of our literature. Wordsworth and Coleridge
were the chief examples of our national school;
though in Coleridge the national frequently passed
into a mystical inspiration; Shelley and Keats of the

ideal. These were far from being among the popular poets of their time ; but they were the most characteristic, and they have exercised the most enduring influence.

The word School is an inadequate one, but it suffices for the convenience of classification. The growths of the same region, however diverse in detail, have yet characteristic features in common ; and it is thus also with the growths of the mind. In Coleridge's poetry the reasoning faculty is chiefly that of contemplation and intuition ; in Wordsworth's, the meditative and the discursive prevail ; but to both a predominance of the thoughtful is common ; and in that respect both poets not only illustrate the peculiar genius of their country, but are also fit interpreters of the *spirit* of their age, as distinguished from the fashion of the moment, and from its unspiritual and materialistic tendencies. In the poetry of both, little change took place except that of growth. Till their genius had found out its own nature and scope its strength remained undeveloped. In both these poets we find a deep-seated patriotism, a reverence for the hearth, a love of local traditions, an English enjoyment of nature, a humanity, mournful not seldom, and even in its cheerfulness grave—as though cheerfulness were less an instinct than a virtue or a duty. Most of these qualities exist also in the poetry of Southey, in which, with less both of thought and imagination, and a style less pregnant and felicitous, there is more of invention, and a more determined purpose. It is thus that with many and important differences poets whose individuality is complete admit of being classed together. The same fact is true with respect to Shelley, Keats, Landor, and others who might be named, — poets in whom, though their diversities were great, a southern temperament and classical ideal predominated.

It was in temperament chiefly that Shelley belonged to the classical school. In intellect he was metaphysical and abstract, to a degree scarcely compatible with the sensuous character of Greek poetry. His imagination likewise, admirable as it was, differed essentially from that of the classic poets. It was figurative rather than plastic. In place of moulding the subject of a poem as a whole, it scattered itself abroad in the splendour of countless metaphors, seen sometimes one through another, like a taper discerned through a taper. A beautiful image had for him an attraction independently of the thought it illustrated; and, once brought within the sphere of its attraction, his fancy fluttered around it, bewildered and intoxicated.) A thought had for him also a value irrespectively of the place which it held in his poetic theme : he prized it as truth; he prized it yet more as knowledge; and with such thoughts his poetry, at once subtly and expansively intellectual, is charged to a degree almost unprecedented. The lamentable errors which lurked in the first principles upon which he had so recklessly precipitated himself (errors, however, hardly worse and less insidious than many that lurk in grave treatises welcomed with little mistrust at the present day) of course infected his results. The conclusions, however, at which he arrived, were logical; and those who can learn from errors as well as truths, will find a sad instruction in the coherency of his reasonings, and a comparative safety in the audacity with which they are expressed. If, for instance, we adopt the opinion,—which is a suppressed premise in all his speculations—namely, that there exists no moral evil in the nature of man except that which finds its way there accidentally,—it will be hard to avoid conclusions analogous to his, respecting both religion and government. The seed at least of such principles will be planted, and their growth will depend on the ardour of the climate, and the fertility of the soil. It is only with his poetry, however, that we are now concerned. Its abstruse as well as imaginative character would have rendered it almost unintelligible, if he had not possessed, though apparently by nature rather than by study, a singular gift of language. His diction, which was searching, vigorous, various, arranged itself into periods, scholastic in the skill that joined clause on to clause, and the varied melody of which at once discriminated the meaning and enforced the sentiment. The same dialectical precision gave force and dignity to his style, whether he wrote in verse or prose; and imparted to both the utmost clearness which the subject matter, the recondite thought, and the re-dundant imagery allowed of. This faculty was eminently Grecian; and the very sound of that noble language, which was not so much a study to him as a delight, will often be found in his verse. He reminds us of the Greek inspiration chiefly by the skill with which he illustrated the ancient mythology. In his *Prometheus Unbound* his classical vein is too often checked by political or metaphysical disquisitions often inappropriately introduced; but in it, and in the choruses of his " Hellas," there is an Æschylean energy; and many of the classical touches in his " Adonais " are admirably true. It is, however, in his minor poems that he most belongs to the South. His " Hymn of Apollo " and " Hymn of Pan " are full of the musical hilarity of the Greeks; his " Ode to Naples " is a true choral ode of compact structure and concentrated purpose; and his " Arethusa," the metre of which sweeps along like a vernal torrent, and in which the nymph and the element she presides over are with such skill blended and alternated, proves that Shelley's versatile temperament included that Protean power by which the Greeks dramatised Nature and humanised all her forms.

In few writers are we more instructively reminded than in Shelley, of that living bond between the Poet and the Man, without which poetry would hold little inward significance and moral power. His temperament was of the most sensitive order. All temperaments, doubtless, except the phlegmatic, can lend themselves to poetic purposes; but while that one which unites the saturnine with the impassioned produces poetry often, as it were, by disease, poetry is the natural expression of one like his,—sanguine, and organised with the utmost of nervous susceptibility. The former quality is marked by that soaring hope with which he watches the destinies of man, heralding the promise of a future on which he—the professed enemy of Faith—had too credulous a dependence. The second we trace in the childlike wonder with which he regards the daily face of Nature ; all objects, from the far-off peak to the flower at the mountain's base, wearing for him a radiance, as if the glorious apparition of the earth had but just bounded into existence. His disposition also, as it is described by his friends, cordial and full of sweetness, though threatening if assailed,—impetuous, yet shy at intervals, and when shy, opening no more,—makes itself felt throughout his poetry in many a passage, the sentiment of which, if deficient in robustness, is alive with pathetic tenderness.⟩ His personality, too, affected as it was by untoward accidents, stands up in his works conspicuous, for evil and for good. His poetry, in truth, is the embodiment of a social creed, not only dogmatic and exclusive but aggressive. His song is no voice from Nature's recesses, sent forth to indicate the whereabout of sweet and secret passion ; still less is it the orderly array of thought with which the ambitious scholar studiously adorns his theme and commends his name to posterity. It is the chant of the bard, or rather the warnote of the prophet-chief. In the solitudes of the soul, and when most "hidden in the light of thought,"

Shelley was a public man—bent on political designs, such designs as even now convulse the world. His spirit did not, indeed, like Milton's, "sit in the pomp of singing robes," but, to use his own expression, "hovered in verse o'er his accustomed prey." In so estimating himself, he did not mistake either his vocation or his abilities; but he greatly mistook the subject and himself. He taught when he had but begun to think, and before he had begun to learn; and the perverse error which blinded his eyes was a snare also to his feet, and made void one-half of the work of his hands. Seldom have such gifts been so abused. He was strong in zeal, but weak through self-confidence; he rushed into the fight without armour though with boundless courage; and with the weapon of an idle and ignorant scorn he struck, not only at abuses and corruptions, which such as he are sent to plague and to destroy, but at truths older than either science or song, and higher than his highest hopes for man.

The errors of Shelley as regards religion were not such as a true charity either conceals or palliates. The infidelity of the mind has its root oftentimes in the will; and in those cases the gravity and the danger of such error cannot be exaggerated; but few will pronounce on its origin in individual instances; nor do its effects admit of being treated of in a few words. Partly to account for his opinions, and partly in the passion of the hour, vices were imputed to Shelley from which he was remarkably free. To one who appreciates his poetry, such charges could present little of plausibility, since a nature, however darkened, yet neither corrupt nor insincere, must be the basis of works like his. (One of the lessons which we have to learn from Shelley is the insufficiency of moral aspirations or beautiful dispositions alone, and in the absence of religious faith, to realise their highest aims whether in life or in literature. It is with the latter only that we are here concerned.)

With great moral energies he had great moral deficiencies. Few men possessed more than he that high faculty of admiration, through which men learn so much and become so much. He gazed in admiration at all things, whether the triumphs of the human mind or the commonest achievements of mechanic skill; yet in all his poetry we find no trace of his having possessed the kindred, but nobler habit —that of veneration. And yet, to be without veneration is to be shut out from a complete world,—the world moreover which *contains* that in which we live. The spirit of his poetry often looks up in wonder and glances around in love, and flings its gaze far forward in anger or in scorn; but its eyes are never cast reverently downwards,—and therefore, even in its zeal for truth, it overruns the soil in which truth is sown. He had an intellectual defect which corresponded with this moral one. He had no power of suspending his judgment. He could not doubt wisely and provisionally, or believe tentatively. His infidelity itself was in part an inverted faith in certain ethical principles with which he rashly assumed

Christianity to be at war; and in part that undiscriminating hatred "of priestcraft" to which the fanatics of
Free Thought are subject. His mind was extraordinarily keen, but deficient in breadth. Such minds,
especially when irradiated by an imagination neither a
law to itself nor recognising a higher law, admit no twilight of intelligence. All their thoughts stand out as
realities, until eclipsed by rival thoughts. This one-
sidedness of mind accounts in part for the fact, otherwise inexplicable, of his having denied, at an age
when others are at worst but doubters,—and obtruded
rather than confessed his unbelief. His temper also
was impetuous, to a degree which, while it misapplied
his reasonings, deprived his poetry of that perfect
sanity which we find in the great masters. He was
aware that it lacked self-possession and serenity. It
lacked it because his whole nature — constitutional,
intellectual, and moral—was deficient in gravity. He
wrote moreover ambitiously, and with too much effort;
and his genius was to a slight degree sophisticated by
egotism. The ideal of a poet often includes something
of himself; and Shelley's nature, in its militant capacity,
is indicated in two of his chief works, his *Prometheus*
and his *Revolt of Islam*: but his "Alastor,"
"Prince Athanase," and many of his minor poems,
prove that he was fond of dwelling upon it in other
relations, and in a spirit of anatomical scrutiny. We
should err, however, in our estimate of Shelley's genius
if we did not allow for the degree in which its products
were modified by circumstance. Ill-health had preyed

on him till his natural sensibility had been heightened
into nervous irritability. This circumstance, together
with the belief that his time in this world was short,
made him overtask his faculties, which were thus
ever in a hectic state of excitement. The abstract
habit of his mind gave an additional daring to his
conclusions; and that habit was increased by the
fact that between him and his countrymen there was
war. Isolation indeed always intensifies, for good or
for evil, the energies of speculative men ; whose powers
are at once tamed down and enriched when merged
in friendly communion with other minds. In the case
of Shelley it also left his poetic education incomplete.
He had carefully fed his mind on all things beautiful and sublime; nor had the influences of study,
philosophical, scientific, and political, been wanting to
him ; but living remote from practical life, his genius
lacked one species of nourishment, the knowledge that
comes by experience. It had never been disciplined.
     To estimate justly the faults as well as the merits
of great minds is a duty which we owe not only to
truth and to ourselves, but to them. It is only when
we know what hindrances were opposed to their
greatness by the forfeits exacted from their faults, that
we can know to what that greatness might, without
such obstacles, have amounted. We can but guess
what would have been the mature works of such a
mind as Shelley's, when that planet-birth had cooled
down sufficiently to produce healthy growths. The
manhood of human life is still but the boyhood of

the Poet ; yet how much did he not leave behind in his brief span !   There is scarcely·one of his larger works which is not a storehouse of condensed thought and beauty — whatever may be its faults in the way of unreality or exaggeration.   His "Hymn on Intellectual Beauty," his odes to " Liberty," to " Naples," to " The West Wind," his " Cloud," his " Skylark," and many· a choral ode in his Lyrical Dramas, are in themselves a conclusive answer to a charge frequently brought against English poetry, namely, that it has seldom soared into the highest region of lyrical inspiration ; and in his shorter pieces there are numerous snatches of song to which the term "essential poetry" would not be misapplied,—poems not only of magnetic power, but as flawless as the diamond, and in their minuteness as perfect as the berry on the tree or the bubble on the fountain.   Great indeed is the bequest which Shelley has left us : and it is not without some- what of remorseful sorrow that we remember what life gave him in return.   Looking on what is past and gone through the serene medium of distance, all petty details vanish from our view, and a few great realities stand bare.   In sad retrospection we look forth—and we see a man and a life !   A young man, noble in genius, in heart ardent, full of emotion and affection, his whole being expanded to all genial and cheering influences as "a vine-leaf in the sun,"—such a being we behold, endowed richly with the treasured stores of old learning and cherished hopes for future man. With the joy of a strong swimmer he flings himself—

upon the stream of life, and finds himself bleeding and broken on the rocks it covers! To say "it was his own fault" is a mode of disposing of the matter rather compendious than satisfactory. For his errors he is answerable at another tribunal than ours. The age which partakes of and fosters such errors, and others more sordid, may find time to remember his sufferings as well. Through trials not the less severe because not unprovoked, he fought his way, not, alas, in peace of conscience, yet certainly with high courage and quenchless hope. He deemed that he had lived long. But he was only in his twenty-ninth year when the Mediterranean waves closed above his head. A sad career was his. He had his intellectual raptures, and he had friends—few of them worthy of him; several of them deeply indebted to him; one of them fatal to him, because the supplanter of his youthful faith—Godwin.

The genius of Keats was Grecian to a far higher degree than that of Shelley. His sense of beauty was profounder still; and was accompanied by that in which Shelley's poetry was deficient—Repose. Tranquillity is no high merit if it be attained at the expense of ardour; but the two qualities are not incompatible. The ardour of Shelley's nature shows itself in a vehement evolution of thought and succession of imagery,—that of Keats in a still intensity. The former was a fiery enthusiasm, the latter was a profound passion. Rushing through regions of unlimited thought, Shelley could but throw out hints which are often suggestive only. His designs are always outline sketches, and the lines of light in which they are drawn remind us of that "Temple of a Spirit" described by him, the walls of which revealed

A tale of passionate change divinely taught,
Which in their winged dance unconscious Genii wrought.

Truth and action may be thus emblemed; but beauty is a thing of shape and of colour, not of light merely, and rest is essential to it. That delighted rapidity of interwoven thought, in which Shelley exulted, was foreign to the deeper temperament of Keats. One of his canons of poetry was, that "its touches of beauty should never be half-way, thereby making the reader breathless instead of content. The rise, the progress, the setting of imagery, should, like the sun, come naturally to the poet, shine over him, and set soberly, although in magnificence, leaving him in the luxury of twilight." He disliked all poetical surprises, and affirmed that poetry "should strike the reader as a wording of his own highest thoughts, and appear almost a remembrance." Shelley's genius, like the eagle he describes,

Runs down the slanted sunlight of the dawn.

But Beauty moves ever in curved lines, like the celestial bodies, and even in movement simulates rest. Beauty was the adornment of Shelley's poetry; it was the very essence of Keats's. There is in his poetry not only a constant enjoyment of the beautiful, —there is a thirst for it never to be satisfied, of which

we are reminded by his portrait. Shelley admired
the beautiful, Keats was absorbed in it; and admired
it no more than an infant admires the mother at whose
breast he feeds. That deep absorption excluded all
consciousness of self,—nay, every intrusion of alien
thought; and while the genius of Shelley, too often
like a double-reflecting crystal, returned a twofold
image, that poetic vision which day by day grew
clearer before Keats was an image of Beauty only,
whole and unbroken. There is a peculiar significance
in the expression, "A child of song," as applied to
him. Not only his outward susceptibilities retained
throughout the freshness of infancy, but his whole
nature possessed that integrity which belongs but to
childhood, or to the purest and most energetic genius.
When the poetic mood was not on him, though his
heart was full of manly courage, there was much of a
child's waywardness, want of self-command, and inexperienced weakness in his nature. His poetry is
never, like some of Shelley's, *juvenile*. It is either the
stammer of the child or the "large utterance of the
early gods."

Keats possessed eminently the rare gift of invention
—as is proved by his narrative poems. He had also,
though without Shelley's constructive skill as to the
architecture of sentences, a depth, significance, and
power of diction, which even the imitational affecta-
tion to be found in his earliest productions could not
disguise. He instinctively selects the words which
exhibit the more characteristic qualities of the objects

described. The most remarkable property of his poetry, however, is the degree in which it combines the sensuous with the ideal. The sensuousness of Keats's poetry might have degenerated into the sensual, but for the ideality that exalted it, and by the absence of which his imitators have discredited him,—a union which existed in consequence of a connection not less intimate between his sensitive temperament and his wide imagination. Perhaps we have had no other instance of a bodily constitution so poetical. With him all things were more or less sensational; his mental faculties being, as it were, extended throughout the sensitive part of his nature— as the sense of sight, according to the theory of the Mesmerists, is diffused throughout the body on some occasions of abnormal excitement. His body seemed to think; and, on the other hand, he sometimes appears hardly to have known whether he possessed aught but body. His whole nature partook of a sensational character in this respect, namely, that every thought and sentiment came upon him with the suddenness, and appealed to him with the reality of a sensation. It is not the lowest only, but also the loftiest part of our being to which this character of unconsciousness and immediateness belongs. Intuitions and aspirations are spiritual sensations; while the physical perceptions and appetites are bodily intuitions. Instinct itself is but a lower form of inspiration; and the highest virtue advances to a spiritual instinct. It was in the intermediate part of our nature that Keats had but a small part. His mind had little affinity with whatever belonged to the region of the merely probable. To his heart, kindly as he was, everything in the outer world seemed foreign, except that which for the time engrossed it. His nature was Epicurean at one side, Platonist at the other—and both by irresistible instinct. The Aristotelian definition, the Stoical dogma, the Academical disputation, were to him all alike unmeaning. His poetic gift was not a separate faculty which he could exercise or restrain as he pleased, and direct to whatever object he chose. It was when "by predominance of thought oppressed" that there fell on him that still, poetic vision of Truth and Beauty which only thus truly comes. The "burden" of his inspiration came to him *in leni aurâ*, like the visits of the gods; yet his fragile nature bent before it like a reed. It was not shaken or disturbed, but wielded by it wholly.

To the sluggish temperaments of ordinary men excitement is pleasure. The fervour of Keats preyed upon him with a pain from which Shelley was protected by a mercurial mobility; and it was with the languor of rest that he associated the idea of enjoyment. How much is implied in this description of exhaustion! "Pleasure has no show of enticement, and Pain no unbearable frown; neither Poetry, nor Ambition, nor Love have any alertness of countenance; as they pass me by they seem rather like three figures on a Greek vase—two men and a woman, whom no one but myself could distinguish in their disguisement.

This is the *only happiness ;* and is a rare instance of advantage in the body overcoming the mind."[1] A nobler relief was afforded to him by that versatility which made him live in the objects around him. It is thus that he writes: "I scarcely remember counting on any happiness. I look not for it, if it be not in the present hour. Nothing startles me beyond the moment. The setting sun will always set me to rights; or if a sparrow were before my window, I take part in its existence, and pick with it about the gravel."[2] Elsewhere he speaks thus of that form of poetic genius which belonged to him, and which he contrasts with that of the "egotistical sublime." "It has no self. It is everything and nothing—it has no character—it enjoys light and shade—it lives in gusts, be it foul or fair, high or low, rich or poor, mean or elevated—it has as much delight in conceiving an Iago as an Imogen."[3] In this passage, as elsewhere, he seems to confound mental versatility with the absence of personal character. That versatility of imagination is however by no means incompatible with depth of nature and tenacity of purpose as is remarked by Mr. Milnes, whose life of Keats is enriched with many passages of sound criticism. In "Endymion," Keats reminds us of Chaucer and slightly of Spenser ; in "Hyperion" of Milton ; in his "Cap and Bells" of Ariosto ; and in his drama, the last act of which is very fine, of Ford. Mr. Milnes remarks, with reference to the last two works, that Keats's

---

[1] P. 264, vol. i.   [2] P. 67, vol. i.

[3] P. 221, vol. i.

occasional resemblance to other poets, though it proves
that his genius was still in a growing state, in no degree
detracts from his originality: he did not imitate others
so much as emulate them; and no matter whom he
may resemble, he is still always himself.

The character of Keats's intellect corresponded
well with his large imagination and versatile temperament. He had not Shelley's manifold and sleepless
faculties, but he had the larger mind. Keats could
neither form systems nor dispute about them; though
germs of deep and original thought are to be found
scattered in his most careless letters. The two friends
used sometimes to contend as to the relative worth of
truth and of beauty. Beauty is the visible embodiment
of a certain species of truth; and it was with that species
that the mind of Keats, which always worked in and
through the sensibilities, held *conscious* relations. He
fancied that he had no access to philosophy, because
he was averse to definitions and systems, and sometimes saw glimpses of truth in adverse systems. His
mind had itself much of that "negative capability"
which he remarked on as a large part of Shakespeare's
greatness, and which he described as a power "of
being in uncertainties, mysteries, doubts, without any
irritable reaching after fact and reason,"[1]—a capability
perhaps inconceivable to Shelley's militant nature.
There is assuredly such a thing as philosophical doubt,
as well as of philosophical belief: it is the doubt
which belongs to the mind, not to the will; to which

[1] P. 93. vol. i.

we are not drawn by love of singularity, and from which we are not scared by nervous tremors; the doubt which is not the denial of anything, so much as the proving of all things; the doubt of one who would rather walk in mystery than in false lights, who waits that he may win, and who prefers the broken fragments of truth to the imposing completeness of a theory. Such is that uncertainty of a large mind, which a small mind cannot understand; and such no doubt was, in part, that of Keats, who was fond of saying that "every point of thought is the centre of an intellectual world." The passive part of intellect, the powers of susceptibility and appreciation, Keats possessed to an almost infinite degree; but in this respect his mind appears to have been cast in a feminine mould; and that masculine energy which Shakespeare combined with a susceptive temperament unfathomably deep, in him either existed deficiently, or had not had time for its development.

If we turn from the poet to the man, from the works to the life, the retrospect is less painful in the case of Keats than of Shelley. He also suffered from ill-health, and from a temperament which, when its fine edge had to encounter the jars of life, was subject to a morbid despondency; but he had many sources of enjoyment, and his power of enjoyment was extra-ordinary. His disposition, which was not only sweet and simple, but tolerant and kindly, procured and preserved for him many friends. It has been commonly supposed that adverse criticism had wounded him deeply and in an unworthy manner; but the charge receives a complete refutation from a letter written on the occasion referred to. In it he says : "Praise or blame has but a momentary effect on the man whose love of beauty in the abstract makes him a severe critic on his own works. . . . I will write independently. I have written independently *without judgment.* I may write independently, and *with judgment,* hereafter. The Genius of Poetry must work out its own salvation in a man. . . . I was never afraid of failure."

There are, however, trials in the world from which the most imaginative cannot escape ; and which are more real than those which self-love alone can make important to us. Keats's sensibility amounted to disease. "I would reject," he writes, "a Petrarchal coronation—on account of my dying day—and because women have cancers!" A few months later, after visiting the house of Burns, he wrote thus: "His misery is a dead weight on the nimbleness of one's quill: I tried to forget it . . . it won't do. . . . We can see, horribly clear, in the works of such a man, his whole life, as if we were God's spies."[1] It was this extreme sensibility, not less than his ideal tendencies, which made him shrink with prescient fear from the world of actual things. Reality frowned above him like a cliff seen by a man in a nightmare dream. It fell on him at last ! The most interesting of all his letters is that to his brother,[2] in which he, with little anticipation of results, describes his first meeting with the Oriental beauty who soon after became the object of his passion.

<hr>

[1] P. 171.   [2] P. 224, vol. i.

In love he had always been, in one sense ; and personal love was but the devotion to that in a concentrated form which he had previously and more safely yearned towards as a loveliness scattered and diffused.   He loved and he won ; but death cheated him of the prize.   Tragical indeed were his sufferings during the months of his decline.   In leaving life he lost what can never be known by the multitudes who but half live; and poetry at least could assuredly have presented him but in scant measure with the consolations which the mere Epicurean can dispense with most easily, but which are needed most by those whose natures are most spiritual, and whose thirst after immortality is consequently the strongest.   Let us not, however, intrude into what we know not.   In many things we are allowed to rejoice with him.   His life poetic, if not his external life, had been one long revel.   "The open sky," he writes to a friend, "sits upon our senses like a sapphire crown : the air is our robe of state ; the earth is our throne ; and the sea a mighty minstrel playing before it !"   Less a human being than an Imagination embodied, he passed, "like a new-born spirit," over a world that for him ever retained the dew of the morning ; and bathing in all its freshest joys he partook but little of its stain.

Shelley and Keats remained with us only long enough to let us know how much we have lost—

We have beheld these lights but not possessed them.[1]

---

[1] " Mary Tudor."

LANDOR'S POETRY

LANDOR was the earliest of our modern poets specially characterised by their devotion to ideal beauty and to classical associations. With classical literature his name has long been intimately joined, not only by many an "Imaginary Conversation" in which the heroes, poets, and philosophers of antiquity are evoked from the shades, but yet more by his poetry, formed as that was, after a classical model,— his English poetry, not less than that written with such signal merit in the Latin language. That model has its deficiencies as well as its excellences. How great are the latter is attested by the fact, that after the lapse of so many centuries, and the intervention of so many sources of interest, alien or adverse, we still meet both scholars and men of original genius who seem never at home but when they breathe the air of antiquity.

In Landor's earlier dialogue between Southey and Porson, the latter is introduced expressing a preference for ancient above modern poetry. If his opinion, however, was expressed in the passage referred to, it has apparently undergone no change from the publication of *Gebir* to that of the *Hellenics*, a book which cannot be better described than by saying that the name has not been ill chosen. The following promise is made good :—

> I promise ye, as many as are here,
> Ye shall not, while ye tarry with me, taste
> From unrinsed barrel the diluted wine
> Of a low vineyard, or a plant ill-pruned,
> But such as anciently the Ægean isles
> Pour'd in libation at their solemn feasts.

The Hellenics have all the clear outline, the definite grace, and the sunny expansiveness of Greek poetry, and not less its aversion to the mysterious and the spiritual.   Above all, they are classical in their peculiar mode of dealing with outward nature.

The difference between ancient and modern poetry is in some measure analogous to that between the landscape of the South and of the North.   Seen through air of gemlike purity, the former is characterised by its amplitude and its definiteness.   A wider horizon embraces a noble and large field,—a field, notwithstanding, distinctly limited ; for in that clear air the distant mountain cuts the sky with a sharp and marked line.   The landscape of the North is, on the contrary, seen as through a mist ; but that mist harmonises the light and shade, freshens the near thicket with a more various colouring, and diffuses over the retiring distance a shadowy tenderness and pathos.   In the former, the remote mountain looks

like a hill, so clearly is every bush and rock revealed ;
in the latter, the hill hard by is robed in blue, and
from being thus placed at an imaginary distance,
seems a mountain. The southern landscape is more
beautiful to the senses, and lends itself more easily to
the painter's art. In delineating its majestic and
graceful outlines, and its colours,—mellow, and as it
were seasoned, even in that resplendent light, he finds
comparatively little which requires to be idealised.

How little the enchanting landscape of the South
contributed to Poetry in ancient times, has been often
remarked, but the circumstance has been hardly
adequately accounted for. And yet this deficiency
could never have excited surprise if the true character
of ancient poetry had been understood. That mountain scenery should have been distasteful to a Greek
is a fact easily explained. Mountain scenery, like that
found in most parts of Greece, is to none a matter of
indifference. Like music, it is positively repugnant
to those for whom it has not an attraction. Two
characteristics of the Greek imagination indisposed it
to such scenery,—its love of the orderly and the
symmetrical, and its aversion to the unlimited and
the terrible. There is a sort of infinitude about
mountains. The broken precipice and abysmal gulf ;
the ridges, line beyond line, pointing to and stretching
after unattainable distances ; the rocks in their fall
indicating unmeasured force, and where they lie
arrested, eternal repose ; the labyrinthine defiles
drawn out in endless perspective ; the chaos of cliff

and peak in their wild harmony suggestive notwithstanding of a veiled design ; the valley convulsed in
a moment, and the sabbath of the mountain-top,—
these things, nay, the very odours from forest depths,
and the sighings of innumerable pines, include in
them an element of the infinite.   In such scenery the
Greek imagination, possessing no key to its harmonies,
saw nothing to delight it, but much to disquiet, to
discompose, and to abash.

It is less easy to account for the fact that we find
in Greek poetry but few allusions to the *landscape* of
the plain.   The Greeks were a loquacious race, and
what they enjoyed they ever celebrated; and moreover
there are not only countless species of beauty in
Nature's ample domain, but very many different modes
of enjoying the same beauty.   The Greeks, however,
appear to have regarded Nature in a manner at once
too sensuous and too imaginative for the appreciation
of landscape.   For the mere bodily eye landscape
does not exist : the separate objects that compose it
appeal, no doubt, individually to the sense; but to
combine those objects into one harmonious whole, to
follow in thought the stream that flows past homestead
and tower and town, to diffuse one's spirit over a wide
tract, playing with the reeds in the foreground, reposing
in relaxed enjoyment on the gradations of distance,
and wistfully bending over the purple on the horizon,
—in other words, to enjoy the landscape as landscape,
—is an endowment not of sense but of mind and
imagination sustained by associations and affections.

The Greek enjoyed Nature not less than the Moderns, but in an opposite manner. The very vividness with which each natural object, taken separately, thrilled through his delicate organisation, enkindling a child-like admiration and delight, must have proved an obstacle to that calm activity which combines object with object. His imagination also, as well as his sensibilities, acted after a fashion more impulsive and less reflective. He dwelt long on the object close by; then, looking on it as on a marvel that needed inter-pretation, he crowned it with a legend.

Few things are more curious than the connection between Pantheism, the philosophic basis of Greek religion, and that polytheistic worship, apparently its opposite, though in reality but a different stage of its development. The Pantheist believed in no creative God existing independently of Nature. He believed in a Spirit or a Power, diffused throughout all Nature, animating it and sharing its eternity. He looked upon Nature in a double aspect. Its perishable details he regarded with a lofty indulgence, or with an Epicurean sympathy. But on its cyclical and self-renewing revolutions he gazed with wonder and with reverence. The raging torrent or the fertilising stream seemed alike to him an attribute of the one pervading Might, —a function of the one diffused Life. A divinity not representing a prevailing Will, but a pervading Exist-ence, and presented to the Mind rather than to the Moral Sense, was thus worshipped in the natural objects that symbolised its offices. Such a theology will not long remain a religion in the higher sense of the term.   It will not *bind* men, through a spiritual awe, to purity and self-sacrifice.   The balance between the sensuous and the supersensuous may by it be maintained as long, and only as long, as conscience retains a supreme place in the human heart; but in the downward tendency of natural instincts, the heart gradually surrenders its charge to the unsafe keeping of the imagination, a faculty prone to divinities, but less jealous in the vindication of their authority than of its own liberty.   The belief which Fancy simulates for its own contentment fills up, indeed, for a time, the place, and conceals the departure of that Faith to which the soul had once acknowledged a devout allegiance. The sense of religious obligation, however, once dissipated, the great central idea, that of the unity of the all-pervading Divinity, relaxes its grasp; and in the warm atmosphere of a pleasurable credulity, the seal melts from the testament of Faith, the covenant of Duty is abrogated, and the spiritual inheritance is forfeited.   Powers which formerly were venerated as distinct but indivisible attributes of the one universal Divinity, require more and more, in proportion as their common internal support is removed, a sensible type, in order to be realised.   Previously those powers had, as it were, stood around the circle of material existence, symbols of the Divine, but not divinities: in a moment the centre to which they were linked ceases to exist; each of them now lives and moves; emblems become realities, and attributes rise into gods.

At the same period that religion is superseded by art, priests are supplanted by poets. These poets are mythologists; and daily in their hand the worship which consecrates grove and stream acquires a more distinct articulation. Reverence for the Supernatural having passed away, their function is to make relics of the memorials it has left behind, to bind into chaplets the flowers which Proserpine dropt ere she was snatched into the shades, and to elevate Nature without transfiguring it. Marvellously did the Greek intelligence, penetrating at once and plastic, adapt itself to this labour. A profound sympathy with Nature made them familiar with her kindly meanings and half-uttered words. They set the latter to a congenial music; but while interpreting her works, they were careful to add little, and to explain nothing away. They never, like the Indian or Egyptian mythologist, sacrificed beauty to philosophy, or extended the symbol into ungainly allegory. The powers which embodied the different elements continued elemental still. If the nymph emerged from the sea,

> Her mantle showed the yellow samphire pod,
> Her girdle the dove-coloured wave serene.

The Hamadryad, with her labyrinthine hair, her shadowy aspect, and murmuring, scarce organic voice, seemed as native to the boughs from amid which she gleamed, as the bubble is to the fountain. These divinities represented nothing truly divine, because they did not include the idea of Holiness;

but they were next to the divine, for they were human without the burden of mortality. The tutelary powers of hill and dale, if they kept the keys of no temple, opened out at least the "palace of the humanities," and enabled man to behold his own image in every earthly shape—not his Maker's.

The closeness of the elemental divinity to the element it represents is illustrated by Landor's poem called "The Hamadryad." Its merit is enhanced by the art with which the mythological idea is blended with a human interest. A Carian youth gazes wistfully on Gnidos from the mountain-side, while the rural population is thronging to the temple of Venus, to celebrate her festival. His father sends him to help in cutting down an old oak. The Hamadryad reveals herself—

<pre>
                              The youth
        Inclined his ear, afar and warily,
        And cavern'd in his hand. He heard a buzz
        At first, and then the sound grew soft and clear,
        And then divided into what seemed tune,
        And there were words upon it, plaintive words.
        He turned and said, "Echion! do not strike
        That tree : it must be hollow ; for some God
        Speaks from within. Come thyself near." Again
        Both turn'd towards it : and behold ! there sat
        Upon the moss below, with her two palms
        Pressing it, on each side, a maid in form,
        Downcast were her long eyelashes, and pale
        Her cheek, but never mountain-ash display'd
        Berries of colour like her lip so pure,
        Nor were the anemones about her hair
        Soft, smooth, and wavering like the face beneath.[1]
</pre>

---

[1] P. 33.

The youth addresses her—

> Who art thou? whence? why here?
> And whither would'st thou go?   Among the robed
> In white or saffron, or the hue that most
> Resembles dawn or the clear sky, is none
> Array'd as thou art.   What so beautiful
> As that gray robe which clings about thee close,
> Like moss to stones adhering, leaves to trees,
> Yet lets thy bosom rise and fall in turn,
> As, toucht by zephyrs, fall and rise the boughs
> Of graceful platan by the river side.[1]

They become lovers.   Raicos, though he conceals the marvel from his father, persuades him to spare the tree; and the old man's piety receives its reward from the Hamadryad's bounty in a constant tribute of honey and of wax.   For a long time the love of the mortal and the immortal meets with no disturbance; but in an evil hour the Hamadryad devises a means of proving her lover's fidelity—

> Raicos went daily; and the nymph as oft,
> Invisible.   To play at love, she knew,
> Stopping its breathings when it breathes most soft,
> Is sweeter than to play on any pipe.
> She play'd on his : she fed upon his sighs :
> They pleased her when they gently waved her hair,
> Cooling the pulses of her purple veins,
> And when her absence brought them out, they pleased.
> Even among the fondest of them all,
> What mortal or immortal maid is more
> Content with giving happiness than pain?
> One day he was returning from the wood
> Despondently.   She pitied him, and said
> "Come back!" and twined her fingers in the hem
> Above his shoulder.   Then she led his steps
> To a cool rill that ran o'er level sand,

---

[1] P. 34.

> Through lentisk and through oleander, there
> Bathed she his feet, lifting them on her lap
> When bathed, and drying them in both her hands.
>   .   .   .   .   .   .
>   " There is a bee
> Whom I have fed, a bee who knows my thoughts
> And executes my wishes : I will send
> That messager.   If ever thou art false,
> Drawn by another, own it not, but drive
> My bee away : then shall I know my fate,
> And . . . for thou must be wretched . . . weep at thine." [1]

The bee proves a trusty messenger, but not a
skilful negotiator.   One night it buzzes at the ear of
Raicos at the moment when he is perplexed by
impending defeat at a game of draughts.   Rashly and
recklessly the youth raises his hand, and the bee
returns to the oak, bruised and with broken wing.
The legend ends thus—

>   At this sight
> Down fell the languid brow, both hands fell down ;
> A shriek was carried to the ancient hall
> Of Thallinos : he heard it not ; his son
> Heard it, and ran forthwith into the wood.
> No bark was on the tree, no leaf was green,
> The trunk was riven through.   From that day forth
> Nor word nor whisper sooth'd his ear, nor sound
> Even of insect wing : but loud laments,
> The woodmen and the shepherds one long year
> Heard day and night ; for Raicos would not quit
> The solitary place, but moan'd and died. [2]

In the gods, as described by French poets, the
godlike element is left out; while the heroes of
antiquity were during the last century restored to life
as courtiers and fine gentlemen, touchy about their
honour, and admirable in the decorum with which

---

[1] Pp. 40-42.   [2] P. 44.

they carried their wig above peplon or toga. Prior was not unfamiliar with ancient mythology, yet, in his jocular vein, he too frequently degrades his Venuses and Cupids not less than his Chloes and Silvias. Akenside, in his "Hymn to the Naiads," presents us with forms truly antique, but the spirit of life is not in them; and the repast which he lays before us is served up cold. Dryden and Pope, men whose masculine understandings and manifold accomplishments must, despite the caprices that affect public taste, long preserve for them a high place with just thinkers, largely as they translated from the ancient poets never entered into the genius of the ancient mythology. The spirit of Theocritus is not to be found in Dryden's version of his Idyls. In his noble "Ode on St. Cecilia's Day" it has been well remarked that when he makes Bacchus show "his honest face," he wholly misses the mythic idea of the mysterious divinity whom he vulgarises. Pope, in his ode on the same occasion, is still more unfortunate; and although, in his "Tartarus," Proserpine is stern and Orpheus devoted, while Ixion, Sisyphus, and the Furies, "do what they ought to do" with laudable industry, we lack, notwithstanding, both the awfulness and the serenity of the Elysian region.

Nor has ancient mythology fared much better in the hands of most of our recent poets. They have loved it more; but their love has often been as undiscriminating as that of a wood-god for a fugitive nymph. They have not always appreciated the character of divinities, even when exhibited in sculpture before their eyes. Lord Byron, in his " Childe Harold," describing the Venus de Medicis, asks the goddess whether she appeared "in this guise" to Paris, or to "more deeply blessed Anchises," or to Mars more fortunate still ; and then follows a rhapsody about "lava-kisses, melting while they burn." Such a description would befit a Phedra better than the Venus of the Florentine Tribune, that beautiful and passionless impersonation of the morning star. Elaborate blunders in a case of this kind are the less pardonable, because it is especially through the interpretation of Greek art that the several characters of Greek divinities are to be distinguished. We require no allusive attribute, neither quivered shoulder nor crescented brow, to recognise a Dian in those feet, firm and alert, though for the moment arrested, that slender but sinewy form, and, above all, the far-projected Apollonian glance, clear as the beams of the sister luminary embodied. With the form, equally girlish but simply joyous and blameless, of a Hebe or a Grace, such a divinity was almost as strikingly contrasted as with a Pallas, a goddess chaste as the Huntress that outsped the shafts of Love, but chaste from the collected sternness of self-sufficing strength, and from the high wisdom, confederate with virtue, which subdued the presuming with its Gorgon and presided over every industrious art. The character of a Venus was expressed not less plainly, in early ages of art, by the union of perfect beauty with a sacredness which belongs to the maternal relation, and in later times, very differently, by the languishing eye, the drooping lid, the lips wreathed with smiles, the dubious look, the marvellously-moulded form, in which numberless and incalculable curves were lost in one another; and finally by the tread, at once confiding and insecure, apparently accustomed to a more unstable element than earth. The genius of a nation's poetry is exhibited in its other arts, as the latent spirit of its philosophy is disclosed in its laws.

The merit of Landor's poetry consists so much more in the grace of his narratives, and the perfection of their proportions, than in· particular passages, that extracts do it little justice. We meet the beautiful Hamadryad once more in the tale of Acon and Rhodope. On the anniversary of that day so fatal to her and to her lover, the oak is visited by a plighted youth and maid, who exchange love vows beneath its black and blasted branches. The father of Acon is rich, and does not choose that his son should marry without an ample dowry. The youth laments, but submits, and the girl is deserted.

> Rhodope, in her soul's waste solitude,
> Sate mournful by the dull-resounding sea,
> Often not hearing it, and many tears
> Had the cold breezes hardened on her cheek.
> Meanwhile he sauntered in the wood of oaks,
> Nor shunn'd to look upon the hollow stone
> That held the milk and honey, nor to lay
> His plighted hand where recently 'twas laid
> Opposite her's, when finger playfully
> Advanced and pusht back finger, on each side.

> He did not think of this, as she would do
> If she were there alone.[1]

Acon dies, and the hard father

> Had land enough : it held his only son.

Landor's poetry has sometimes been charged with a deficiency of pathos.   It is true that in general he loves rather to exhibit human life in the exhilarating and equable light of day, than tinged with the lights of a low horizon, and clouded with the shadows of eve. His pathos has, notwithstanding, a peculiar depth and tenderness; and though unostentatious, is very far from being infrequent.   The " Death of Artemidora " may serve as a specimen; a longer and still more perfect one, though less adapted to quotation, is " Corythos."

> " Artemidora !   Gods invisible,
> While thou art lying faint along the couch,
> Have tied the sandal to thy slender feet
> And stand beside thee, ready to convey
> Thy weary steps where other rivers flow.
> Refreshing shades will waft thy weariness
> Away, and voices like thy own come near
> And nearer, and solicit an embrace."
> Artemidora sigh'd, and would have prest
> The hand now pressing hers, but was too weak.
> Iris stood over her dark hair unseen,
> While thus Elpenor spake.   He lookt into
> Eyes that had given light and life erewhile
> To those above them, but now dim with tears
> And wakefulness.   Again he spake of joy
> Eternal.   At that word, that sad word, *joy*,
> Faithful and fond, her bosom heav'd once more :
> Her head fell back : and now a loud deep sob
> Swell'd thro' the darken'd chamber ; 'twas not hers.

---

[1] P. 48.   [2] P. 60.

Very different is the terrible, though rather suggested than expressed pathos of that tragic scene entitled the "Madness of Orestes."   It commences thus—

Orestes. Heavy and murderous dreams, O my Electra,
Have dragged me from myself.
                                        Is this Mycenai?
Are we . . . are all who should be . . . in our house?
Living? unhurt? our father here? our mother?
Why that deep gasp? for 'twas not sigh nor groan.
She then . . . 'twas she who fell!   When? how? beware!
No, no, speak out at once, that my full heart
May meet it, and may share with thee in all . . .
In all . . . but that one thing.
                                        It was a dream.
We may share all.   They live? both live?   Oh say it!
  Electra. The Gods have placed them from us, and there
        rolls
Between us that dark river . . .
  Orestes.   Blood! blood! blood!
I see it roll : I see the hand above it,
Imploring ; I see *her.*
                        Hiss me not back,
Ye snake-haired maids!   I will look on ; I will
Hear the words gurgle thro' that cursed stream,
And catch that hand . . . that hand . . . which slew my father!
It cannot be . . . how could it slay my father?
Death to the slave that spoke it! . . . Slay my father!
It tost me up to him to earn a smile,
And was a smile then such a precious boon,
And royal state and proud affection nothing?
Ay, and thee too, Electra, she once taught
To take the sceptre from him at the door.
Not the bath-door, not the bath-door, mind that! . . .
And place it in the vestibule, against
The spear of Pallas, where it used to stand.[1]

Landor's many and great dramatic gifts are seriously marred by one deficiency.   He has not the faculty of devising a plot in which incident not only follows,

---

[1] Pp. 82, 83.

but results from, incident, while each and all, instead of being connected merely by the chain of phenomenal causation, rest also on a moral support, and illustrate character. He is accordingly more successful in his fragmentary dramatic scenes than in his dramas, which, except in parts, have not the same power, either in the delineation of character or of passion, as we find in many of his "Imaginary Conversations"; for instance, in that true prose poem, the dialogue between Tiberius and Vipsania; or that one between Peleus and Thetis, in which a mournful passion is so marvellously introduced into a subject belonging, it might seem, exclusively to the imagination. Among his dramatic fragments is a poem entitled "Luther's Parents," remarkable for its combination of humour with a rich fancy. Martin's mother has seen, in a dream, an infant radiant as the stars, who holds a sword at which "tottering shapes, in purple filagree," tug in vain, and round whom devils with angel faces throng without appalling him. Her ambition is fired. She has hopes that her child may one day be a chorister; and she ruminates the several steps of advance to which so high a beginning might possibly lead, till her more impatient husband— an honest peasant — anticipates the goal of such reveries, and exclaims,—not without some particle of truth—

> Ring all the bells! Martin is Pope, by Jove!

Scattered among Landor's works are to be found

many fine passages of philosophical poetry. The
following lines, the commencement of a poem called
" Regeneration," will serve as specimen :—

> We are what suns and winds and waters make us ;
> The mountains are our sponsors, and the rills
> Fashion and win their nursling with their smiles.
> But where the land is dim from tyranny,
> There tiny pleasures occupy the place
> Of glories and of duties, as the feet
> Of fabled fairies, when the sun goes down,
> Trip o'er the grass where wrestlers strove by day.
> Then Justice, called the Eternal one above,
> Is more inconstant than the buoyant form
> That burst into existence from the froth
> Of ever-varying ocean : what is best
> Then becomes worst ; what loveliest, most deformed.
> The heart is hardest in the softest climes,
> The passions flourish, the affections die.[1]

The longest and most important of his narrative
poems is *Gebir*, the tale of an Iberian chief who, in
vindication of his ancestral claims, undertakes the
conquest of Egypt ; and who, when, smitten by the
charms of Charoba, the young queen of that land, he
has abandoned the enterprise, is slain at the marriage-
feast by the treachery of Dalica, her nurse.   This poem
was originally written in Latin, and as regards sustained
poetical beauty, it has no rival among modern Latin
poems with which it can be compared.   It is in this
poem that we meet most abundantly with instances of
Landor's extraordinary descriptive power.   Charoba,
alarmed at the approach of her unknown enemy, has
resolved to win him by persuasion to terms of
peace—

[1] P. 274.

But Gebir, when he heard of her approach,
Laid by his orbed shield ; his vizor-helm,
His buckler and his corset he laid by,
And bade that none attend him : at his side
Two faithful dogs that urge the silent course,
Shaggy, deep-chested, croucht ; the crocodile
Crying, oft made them raise their flaccid ears
And push their heads within their master's hand.
There was a brightening paleness in his face,
Such as Diana rising o'er the rocks
Shower'd on the lonely Latmian ; on his brow
Sorrow there was, yet nought was there severe.
But when the royal damsel first he saw,
Faint, hanging on her handmaids, and her knees
Tottering, as from the motion of the car,
His eyes lookt earnest on her, and those eyes
Showed, if they had not, that they might have loved,
For there was pity in them at that hour.[1]

The descriptive passages, so thickly scattered over
this poem, frequently remind one of an antique relievo.
Such are the lines describing a procession (Book IV.
line 200) in which we read of

Stubborn goats that eye the mountain top
Askance, and riot with reluctant horn.

Invariably, also, they are characterised by brevity, as
in this picture of moonlight on the sands—

Restless then ran I to the highest ground
To watch her : she was gone ; gone down the tide ;
And the long moonbeam on the hard wet sand
Lay like a jasper column half uprear'd.

Not less in the spirit of antiquity is the following
image :—

And now the chariot of the Sun descends,
The waves rush hurried from his foaming steeds,

---

[1] P 488.

> Smoke issues from their nostrils at the gate,
> Which, when they enter, with huge golden bar
> Atlas and Calpè close across the sea.

The Greek spirit of this poem is nowhere more marked than in a love Idyl which it includes. In the Middle Ages that passion was sometimes elevated by the influence of Christianity and of its offspring, chivalry, into an imaginative worship. The objects of this devotion belonged to an ethereal region of seclusion and mystery, shining with benign virtue on the ways of men, but rather rewarding adoration than reciprocating passion. The love described in modern literature has descended from the firmamental region to that of the clouds; and if it remains loftier in its character than that delineated by the ancients, it walks with a vaguer step. Love, as conceived by the Greeks, was neither ennobled by sentiment nor weakened by sentimentalities. It neither languished in love-sickness nor glimmered like a wandering meteor. It was a plain, honest passion,—ardent, joyous, and earnest; free from all morbid consciousness, and going straight, like a sun-shaft, to its object. As such it is portrayed by Landor. In the person of the sea-nymph who has become enamoured of Tamar, the shepherd brother of Gebir, it is expressed with the wild, spontaneous impulse which belongs to the elemental Powers, touched but by the fleeting shadows of humanity—

> Return me him who won my heart, return
> Him whom my bosom pants for, as the steeds
> In the sun's chariot for the western wave.

In a mortal maiden the same passion is very differently indicated—

> I since have watcht her in each lone retreat,
> Have heard her sigh, and soften out the name;
> Then would she change it for Egyptian sounds
> More sweet, and seem to taste them on her lips,
> Then loathe them; *Gebir, Gebir* still returned.
>
> .   .   .   .   .
>
> Lone in the gardens, on her gathered vest
> How gently would her languid arm recline!
> How often have I seen her kiss a flower,
> And on cool mosses press her glowing cheek!

Among the severer tests of artistic skill in poetry may be included the use or abuse of Episode. In nothing else have the ancient poets shown a finer executive tact. Too often in modern narrative an episode is but an impertinent interruption, swelling its bulk and checking its progress. Among the functions of an episode one is to relieve the graver tenor of a poem by the introduction of an interest subordinate to and yet congenial with its main interest, or at once analogous to it, and contrasted with it. Toward the end of a poem an episode, especially a short one, frequently adds to the reader's interest by the interposition of an obstacle, leading him away from that which he would fain explore, as the parent bird lures the intruder from her nest. In this department of the poetic art Landor is very felicitous. As an instance may be cited the episode of the marriage of Tamar, in the sixth Book. The sea-nymph, the morning after her espousals, desires to

withdraw the thoughts of her mortal bridegroom from
the evil omens which threaten his brother.

> "O, seek not destin'd evils to divine,
> Found out at last too soon ! cease here the search,
> 'Tis vain, 'tis impious, 'tis no gift of mine."

She touches Tamar's eyes, and the wonders of the
watery realm pass before them.

> " Thus we may sport at leisure when we go
> Where, lov'd by Neptune and the Naiad, lov'd
> By pensive Dryad pale, and Oread,
> The sprightly Nymph whom constant Zephyr woos,
> Rhine rolls his beryl-colour'd wave ; than Rhine
> What river from the mountains ever came
> More stately?   Most the simple crown adorns
> Of rushes and of willows intertwined
> With here and there a flower : his lofty brow
> Shaded with vines and misletoe and oak
> He rears, and mystic bards his fame resound.
> Or gliding opposite, th' Illyrian gulph
> Will harbour us from ill."   While thus she spake
> She toucht his eyelashes with libant lip
> And breath'd ambrosial odours, o'er his cheek
> Celestial warmth suffusing : grief disperst,
> And strength and pleasure beam'd upon his brow.
> Then pointed she before him : first arose
> To his astonisht and delighted view
> The sacred isle that shrines the queen of love.
> It stood so near him, so acute each sense,
> That not the symphony of lutes alone,
> Or coo serene, or billing strife of doves,
> But murmurs, whispers, nay, the very sighs
> Which he himself had utter'd once, he heard.
> Next, but long after and far off, appear
> The cloud-like cliffs and thousand towers of Crete,
> And further to the right, the Cyclades ;
> Phœbus had rais'd, and fixt them, to surround
> His native Delos, and aerial fane.
> He saw the land of Pelops, host of Gods ;

> Saw the steep ridge where Corinth after stood
> Beckoning the serious with the smiling Arts
> Into her sun-bright bay.
>
> .　　　.　　　.　　　.　　　.
>
> He heard the voice of rivers : he descried
> Pindan Peneus and the slender nymphs
> That tread his banks, but fear the thundering tide :
> These, and Amphrysos, and Apidanos,
> And poplar-crowned Sperchios, and, reclined
> On restless rocks, Enipeus, where the winds
> Scatter'd above the weeds his hoary hair.[1]

The chief fault of *Gebir* is its occasional obscurity: an obscurity, indeed, of more kinds than one. In several places the story is not distinctly made out. A few lines interposed here and there would be sufficient to clear up all doubt, which indeed, in the Latin version, is precluded by the argument prefixed to each *Book* that excellent invention of times when the interest of a novel was not sought in poetry. The ancients, treating in general themes well known, threw their narrative poems into large masses, and often neglected the connecting link of mere detail by which part is joined to part; influenced no doubt by the same aversion to the trivial and the accessory which made the Greek sculptor abstain from connecting the head of the horse with the hand of the rider by a marble bridle. *Gebir* was reduced before publication to half its original length. In making such large reductions an author does not always observe when the meaning which still stands clear in his own mind, and which was at first impressed with equal clearness on his work, has been

---

[1] Book VI. line 116.

allowed to slip from before the eye of a reader.   It
is not, however, in Landor's narrative only that we
meet obscurity.   It is to be found in several passages
of reflection.   In his minor poems this proceeds
chiefly from an extreme condensation of language,
from a certain degree of mannerism, apparently the
unconscious result of classical associations, and perhaps
from that elaborate refinement which, in adding one
grace more to a fine passage, sometimes sacrifices its
simplicity.   Still more often, no doubt, it is produced
by excessive subtlety, both of thought and of sentiment.
It is in his minor poems that we find most abundantly
that delicacy, propriety, sweetness, and concise precision which remind us of the Greek anthology.
Among many such poems it is difficult to make a
selection.   The following, however, may serve :—

> Ianthe ! you are call'd to cross the sea !
>   A path forbidden *me !*
> Remember, while the Sun his blessing sheds
>   Upon the mountain-heads,
> How often we have watcht him laying down
>   His brow, and dropt our own
> Against each other's, and how faint and short
>   And sliding the support !
> What will succeed it now ?   Mine is unblest,
>   Ianthe ! nor will rest
> But on the very thought that swells with pain.
>   O bid me hope again !
> O give me back what Earth, what (without you),
>   Not Heaven itself can do,
> One of the golden days that we have past ;
>   And let it be my last !
> Or else the gift would be, however sweet,
>   Fragile and incomplete.

Landor seems to turn with aversion from many

forms of composition to which recent poetry has habituated us. A ballad is not to be found among his works; nor a didactic poem; nor a sonnet; nor, we might say, a song, using the term in its stricter sense. The temperament of his poetry, buoyant at once and serene, finds apparently a more suitable form of expression in the Idyl, especially that larger and graver kind for which, in his Latin volume, he claims the title of "Idyllia Heroica"; but he is also attached to the elegiac commemoration, to the brief but pregnant inscription, and to the epigram, especially to the epigram which embodies poetry, not wit, and which can dispense with a sting in the last line. These poems are frequently marked by a playful tenderness, and as often by a tender pathos.

> Mild is the parting year, and sweet
>   The odour of the falling spray ;
> Life passes on more rudely fleet,
>   And balmless is its closing day.
>
> I wait its close, I court its gloom,
>   But mourn that never must there fall,
> Or on my breast or on my tomb,
>   The tear that would have sooth'd it all.

In the following lines there is an Epicurean mournfulness :—

> The place where soon I think to lie,
> In its old creviced nook hard by
>   Rears many a weed :
> If parties bring you there, will you
> Drop slily in a grain or two
>   Of wall-flower seed ?

> I shall not see it, and (too sure)
> I shall not ever hear that your
>   Light step was there :
> But the rich odour some fine day
> Will, what I cannot do, repay
>   That little care.

We find also many examples of the brief Horatian Ode, as· distinguished from the Pindaric triumphant chant, the mythic hymn, or the choral ode, as, for instance, in the graceful stanzas beginning

> To write as your sweet mother does ;

the exquisite lines—

> Fate, I have asked few things of thee ;

and the poem in the *Pericles and Aspasia*, supposed to be addressed by Corinna to her native city, Tanagra.

The unobtrusiveness of true poetry, a quality but infrequently exemplified of late, is among the finer characteristics of Landor's. He is wholly free from exaggeration, and he never transgresses the Delphic precept, $M\eta\delta\grave{\epsilon}\nu$ $\check{\alpha}\gamma\alpha\nu$, "not too much of anything." Nothing is inserted for effect; and his best passages, contented often to lurk in shadow, are never rendered more salient by a sprinkling of "barbaric pearl and gold." In his pages heroism never struts and sorrow never wails. Seldom, indeed, has fine poetry more ascetically renounced finery, or passion more religiously abstained from bluster. This unobtrusiveness has perhaps been a hindrance to his popularity. An object must sparkle to catch attention when seen through the dust of the thoroughfare ; and in the crush of modern literature, the thought which is not forward to claim a place, is likely to wait long without one. The music which is music *only*, without the jar of wood and wire, will be heard but in the still gallery or lonely grove.

Warmly as the admiration of not a few among our first poets as well as scholars has been expressed with regard to Landor's poetry, that sentiment has not, as yet, made its way to the mass. Many readers are repelled from it by its extreme refinement as they are from Coleridge's by its spirituality. Apart, however, from any defect on the part of the reading public, Landor's genius is not of the popular sort. There are two contrasted orders of original genius in the world ; and while one of these remains fixed in isolation, or fastens its regard on some remote period, drawing inspiration thence alone, the other dwells in the present, as in its native home, and in interpreting the present points to the future. Genius, even of the latter sort, will not often be early and fully appreciated ; or rather, it is the attribute of the highest genius as well as of the highest beauty, moral or physical, that it "never can be wholly known"; but it can hardly wait long for a reception to a certain extent in the sympathies of men, since it throws open for many a heart its inmost chamber, and utters for multitudes what they vainly wished to say. Genius in harmony with the age, like that of Shakespeare and Burns, sometimes leaps at once to a nation's heart. Genius of an order more remote and alien is tried by time, is recognised by the few, is passed on to the many, and by them is received in the fulness of days with pride, but less often with cordial enjoyment, as a part of their inheritance.

Do the poets of antiquity obtain the popular sympathies of our countrymen, or must we admit that they lived in the hearts of those only for whom, and among whom, they wrote, and that they delight few save the studious at this distant day? The latter seems to be the truth. Homer is an exception, for his genius, like that of Shakespeare, was universal ; but the other great poets of antiquity, however religiously the "public" may revere them, are yet the objects of a worship in which there is more of fear than of love, and more of tradition than of devotion. We set up their images in the high places of our mind, as in our streets we elevate the statues of great men on the tops of pillars ; but in each case the equivocal compliment renders the features of those thus honoured indistinguishable ; and a passer-by might insinuate that we only desired to put Greatness civilly out of our way. A more charitable interpretation of this fact may, perhaps, lead us to a deeper truth. It may be a lesson, teaching us that poetry is a practical thing, rooted in realities, embodying the complete mind of a nation, and corresponding with the estimate formed by that nation on every important subject,—religion, philosophy, politics, nature, art, science—as well as with its morals and manners. We know how closely allied Greek poetry was to the Greek conception of nature, and to a Pantheistic worship. There is a connection also between that poetry and some other qualities of Greek mind and society.

The main characteristic unquestionably of Greek poetry was its embodiment of Beauty; and the attribute which gave expression to its every gesture was Grace. These merits it united with a plain masculine strength, ever exercised without violent effort. It was lofty without being aspiring, and firmly seated owing to the breadth, not the depth, of its foundation. It ascended into no pinnacles, and descended into no crypts, but raised its structures of stately thought along the plane of ordinary apprehensions, though in proportions so fine that while many recognised the effect, few could trace it to its cause. Absolute perfection in the treatment of its theme was the artistic aim of Greek poetry: for this reason the same historical record or religious mythus afforded a subject to poet after poet. It did not, for the sake of variety, affect a complex intermixture of human interests and sensibilities. From whatever was intricate, evanescent, or shadowy, it revolted as inconsistent with simplicity in all subjects, and with grandeur in subjects of an elevated character. Above all, Greek poetry, except in the case of tragedy, excluded the mysterious. Its nymphlike muse was not to take her stand among the Caryatides; and the Temple's projecting cornice was neither to depress nor to overshadow that face radiant ever in its stillness—

> Fit countenance for the soul of primal truth,
> The bland composure of eternal youth.

The art of Song was part of the Greek's art of Life, and that art turned from all perplexing problems. In shrinking from the painful Greek poetry lost the profound, and in abjuring the mysterious it missed the spiritual likewise. It possesses on the other hand its compensating advantages; the crown of its excellence consisting in that sustained majesty which can only stand palpably out where solidity of material is united with perfect proportions in a monument neither too vast to be comprehended by the eye, nor too complex to be understood by it at a glance.

It is hardly necessary to dwell on the degree in which these characteristics are to be found in the other Greek arts. Greek music, we know, relied mainly upon melody not harmony, the former satisfying the mind by the completeness and symmetrical arrangement of a definite series of sounds, while the latter launches forth into worlds unknown and without limits. Not less was the resemblance between Greek poetry and Greek architecture,—the latter extended its level lines over the solid ground, which the perpendicular Gothic spurns in heavenward aspiration. The same remark has been often made as regards sculpture. The distinguishing characteristics of Greek sculpture—its ideality, its serenity, its unity, its distinct embodiment of a beautiful idea, detached from all accessories, and dependent upon no associations of time or place—belong to Greek poetry no less. They disappeared in the sculpture of the Middle Ages when the latter asserted a native

character of its own.   The paintings of the ancients
were strictly congenial with their sculpture, as we may
infer from the descriptions of them which have come
down to us, as well as from the qualities for which
they were especially admired.   The frescoes disinterred
at Pompeii and elsewhere, though in point of execution very imperfect specimens of ancient painting,
are yet sufficient to exhibit its spirit.   What that art
expressed was Beauty perfect in a finite mould, and a
pleasurable sense of healthful life, sometimes contrasted
with, but more often united to that majestic forbear-
ance and chaste reserve which the Graces themselves
ordain.   Greek painting illustrated but the simpler of
the affections, forcibly and delicately as it illustrated
these.   Its compass was narrow; and neither in
sentiment nor in composition did it seek after various
or ample combinations.   It differed from sculpture
but little except in its superior vivacity.   In other
respects, comparing the livelier with the austerer art,
one might have imagined that the notes of some lyre,
potent as that of Amphion, had dissolved the im-
movability of the marble, and commanded the still
Relief to float along the frescoed wall or enwreathe
the encaustic vase.   How opposite in character is the
painting of the middle ages, so devoutly domiciled
in a region of spiritual aspirations and spiritualised
affections!   When the latter fell from its first estate, and
imitated the antique, how seldom did it catch the
Greek spirit!   There is but one complete exception.
In the Idyl pictures of Nicolo Poussin we find the

true genius of antiquity,—the exuberant life, the beauty not lost even in Bacchanal riot, the vehement appetite, oppressed by no "dishonest shame," but unelevated by the "seriousness of passion"; while, amid the rout, a blameless and buoyant Humanity steps lightly, like a new-born goddess, over the subject waves of the revelry,—unparticipant of, and not desiring, the gift and burden of a spiritual life.

The analogy between Greek poetry and the other Greek arts is scarcely more intimate than that between the same poetry and the metaphysics and politics of Greece. One of our best scholars[1] has subtly remarked upon the difference between our philosophic term "understanding," and the corresponding Greek word $\epsilon\pi\iota\sigma\tau\eta\mu\eta$, the first syllable of which means, not *under*, but *upon*. It is thus, he indicates, that modern intelligence confesses that the region of its knowledge is above it; while the Greek mind looks down, as it were, upon a world of conquered thought. This intellectual habit corresponded with the character of Greek poetry, which treated of nothing that it could not master, and owed half its grace to the fact that, like children, it never felt the weight of its own body—which seldom wandered into any scenes but those it could contemplate as from a height—and rested in no region shadowed by that faculty which "looks before and after." The whole of the Greek mythology bears the same character of limitation united with congruity and

---

[1] See *Guesses at Truth.*

systematic beauty. It accounts, like Greek science, for all things by one great hypothesis, embracing in its interwoven cycles and epicycles a single centre of thought, though the largest, probably, and the most complete that ever issued, there or elsewhere, from uninspired humanity. Once more: it has been noticed that Greek poetry, in its delineation of character and manners, was averse to the merely individual, tending to the generic, and seldom condescending to those minuter details of heart and hearth by which the peculiarities of personal character are marked. In these habits it corresponded with the polity of ancient communities, in which the individual was willingly merged in the State, liberty meaning rather national independence than personal freedom. The largest affection which a Greek felt was that for his country; and the fortress-crowned acropolis which represented it was perhaps his most truly religious idea. He had heard of no "abiding country" beyond his native soil, and of no "city" of which all mankind are citizens. Neither had his personal nature been exalted by a Faith which, in making each man, even the humblest, the representative of a redeemed race, communicates to the individual being, and to those domestic relations in which eternal ties are emblemed, a worth otherwise not theirs.

It is, however, in the department of Greek ethics and morals that we shall discover the most authentic analogies to Greek poetry. The noblest moral conception of the Greek mind was that of Justice.

Justice, accordingly, in the form of just Retribution, was the great idea which inspired Greek tragedy. No corresponding conception then existed of a Mercy and Love, strong as Justice itself, and neither mastered by nor superseding it. The moral poetry of the Greeks, for this reason, is marked by a character of hardness. . Their Elysian fields are more remote than the kingdom which Rhadamanthus judges; and even in them the shade of Achilles rejects homage as a mockery, and declares that it is better to labour as a slave in the upper air "than rule, the sceptred monarch of the dead." The practical idea of Virtue with the Greeks consisted mainly in the becoming, the seemly, the fit; the το ἀγαθον meant the το καλον and the το πρεπον; and the moral taste, rather than the conscience, was the arbiter of it. In harmony with such sentiments was the fine balance of their poetry, which admitted nothing overstrained or disorderly. That Moderation so highly extolled in the Grecian philosophy presided with them over every art: and, as in Plato's "Banquet" the guests begin by discussing whether they are to drink to intoxication or for the sake of pleasure, so in every intellectual feast likewise the "law of not too much" was deemed the limit of rational enjoyment. Against excess, even of the noblest sort, their canons of taste were inflexibly severe; and Æschylus narrowly escaped banishment because one of his tragedies had excited the feelings of the spectators over-vehemently.

How different from such a conception of Virtue

was that high idea, of a maturer time, which, though
including, yet superseded it! How many of those
attributes illustrated in the pictures and the chivalrous
and religious poetry of the Middle Ages could possibly
have been rendered even intelligible to a Greek?
What, for instance, would he have thought of religious
Zeal, and of the enterprise of the missionary? Not
believing in any revelation of divine truth, he could
hardly—however useful and auspicious religious worship
might have seemed to him—have regarded it as a duty
to maintain and to propagate a Faith. To the sceptic,
indifferentism must necessarily have seemed to be
both charity and common sense; and the heroism of
the chiefs who sailed in search of the Golden Fleece
far more commendable than the self-devotion of St.
Augustine and St. Paulinus voyaging in search of a
barbarous race, and boldly claiming "not theirs, but
them." Again, what would a Greek have thought of
Obedience as a law of life? If he did not brand it
as a want of spirit only worthy of Orientals and slaves,
assuredly he would have seen little dignity in it. As
incomprehensible to him would Humility have been.
Wisdom is not likely to be humble in the absence of
Revelation; for all its knowledge has been found in
its own stores, or gleaned by its own hands; and
Virtue must needs walk proudly where, except the
strength that is in itself, it sees none. The Homeric
heroes always praise themselves; and the whole Greek
race vaunted, not only of its achievements as a race,
but of man's physical position in creation; boasting

that it was "articulate-speaking," and "horse-taming,"
and that it compelled the earth, though a goddess,
to give us her fruits. Revelation, meantime, like the
Copernican System of the Universe, has translated
man from a finite to an infinite region. It has shown
him at once his actual littleness and his potential
greatness, and accordingly taught him that true magnanimity consists not in self-assertion, but in self-
renunciation and self-oblivion. Heroism, in ancient
song, commonly sought and found a present reward of
praise, if not of success. Men were called "godlike"
where God was not known. Glory itself does not
necessarily minister to pride : it may unite, not separate, rendering greatness not *dis*tinguished, but *con*-
spicuous. In the great Christian poem of the middle
ages a thousand crusading Spirits form but a single
halo, projected, in shape a cross, against that ruddy
sphere,—their celestial home. Fifteen hundred years
had passed away before a modified Tragedy revived,
and man was again bidden to gaze in unqualified
admiration upon individual man.

The Greek estimate of human Well-being accorded
justly with such an idea of Virtue. The celebrated
adage, *Mens sana in corpore sano*, might well
describe it. Such an estimate necessarily repudiates
the austerity of self-denial as much as the lawless
gratification of the passions. It does not aspire to
bring the body under; it wishes, simply, that body
and soul should live amicably together, neither of
them a tyrant, and neither of them subjugated. It

does not believe that by renouncing the lower gratifi-
cations, which a fallen nature can seldom use largely
without abusing, an ampler participation may be ob-
tained of higher joys.   Mortification it counts an Indian
Fakir's folly; and vigil it leaves to the priestess of
Diana, solitary beneath the stars, in her rock-built
tower.   Regarding the body not as the temple of a
spirit, but as the most beautiful and vigorous of
instruments, it places a proportionate value upon
wealth; and even the religious Pindar, extolling the
objects of his respect, celebrates them as "good and
rich,"—a mark of their being dear to the gods.
Greek poetry corresponded, by necessity, with Pagan,
not Christian, beatitudes.   It never recorded the
blessedness of those who mourn, the inward abundance
of the poor, or the large fruition of terrestrial things
extended, by Nature as well as by Grace, to those
meek spirits who can enjoy without possessing.   It
commemorated sometimes the constancy of the martyr,
but its martyrs were patriots who sacrificed their lives
for their country, and whose reward was Fame.   It
flung upon the grave the chaplets of a pensive fancy;
but the grave returned no vernal symbols of immortality with which the shrines of religion were to be
decked.   Yet it did what it could.   It embalmed the
memory of the brave; and in its breeze of martial
music it carried the patriot band to the frontier.   It
harmonised the rural dance and added order to the
village festival.   It caused a sad hour to be forgotten
an hour sooner than it would otherwise have been,

and a glad moment to be remembered an age later. Its matutinal feet were hurried by no attraction to the angel-haunted tomb; but it polished the funeral urn, and it encompassed the sarcophagus with laughing nymphs.

As Greek religion consisted chiefly in the worship of visible Nature embodied in human forms, and generally in the deification of Humanity, so in Greek ethics Inhumanity was the chief, if not the only, grave offence. Whatever sprang from that root the Greeks abhorred. Cruelty and tyranny they would have no dealings with: sins of another sort they regarded with an indulgent eye. For this reason, in the intercourse of daily life, though they affected not the magnanimous urbanity of the aristocratic Romans, a friendly address and graceful bearing were regarded as a part of good morals. The same character belongs to all their arts. Their poetry is by nothing more characterised than by its cordiality, its communicativeness, and its pleasant aspect. It recoils from the rude, the boisterous, and the insolent, as from a species of blasphemy; and satire it leaves to Thersites. But what if a poet born later—he, let us suppose, who saw the Triple Vision —could have conversed with a brother bard of Greece, and spoken to him of a Divine awe compared with which all human respect is dwarfed and brought low? What if he had told him that the temple gates all over the world had been shaken open in one night, and that the people had been bidden to enter where once the priest only stood? What if he had spoken of virtues in conformity with an elevation at once so high and so perilous,—of a revealed infinitude of light and of darkness, of bliss and bale,—of such duties as Contemplation and Purity, Aspiration and Compunction,—of eloquent lips sealed close, and of curiosity repressed? The Greek bard would have called his companion a Visionary, and advised him to exchange Eleusis for Epidaurus as a place of sojourn. In other words, he would have been repelled by the "Divina Commedia." The principles and instincts which consigned him to a moral system concerned rather with outward acts, than with affections and motives, would have attached him to a poetry material if not epicurean. Of the merits which belong to a more spiritual poetry he must, with all his keen insight and various knowledge, have remained "invincibly ignorant." The converse of this must prove equally true. As little can classical poetry be expected to come home to the popular sympathies of a later age.

Is the change to be regretted? Are we, it may be demanded, whose lot has been cast in the fulness of the times, to return to our morning dreams? Should we prefer to the choral vesper chant of creation the early and slender trill of a bird but half awakened? Ministered to by the powers of the unseen world, must we wander in retrograde imagination to groves and fountains haunted by divinities which the objectless heart created "after its own image"? Encompassed with the more excellent glory of an abiding vision, which embraces our little sphere of space and time as with a spiritual zodiac, must we search for that herb which opened the eyes of Glaucus, and sigh for the credulities which saw wonders in every floating cloud or misty rock? Begirt by, nay, a part of, Realities which, if seen in the clear light vouchsafed to the pure in heart, outshine all poetic conceptions, and might be expected, by their awfulness, to quell the poetic spirit, shall we endeavour, with idle industry, to shut out great things by decorated trifles, and to hide behind a veil of radiant fancies the countenances of Life and Death? What part have we with gods and goddesses? What commerce can there be between Paganism and the race of the Baptized?—It would be as dull as wrong to make light of the momentous truth involved in such questions. But that truth has another side to it. It was doubtless the indirect influence of Christianity chiefly which, widening and elevating the moral nature of man, introduced into his imagination a spirit antagonistic to Pagan conceptions, and laid the foundation of mediæval arts and life. This large change in public sentiment was inevitable, having been involved in the destruction of those associations which are the conductors of popular and poetic sympathies; but it does not follow, therefore, that the continued alienation of popular sympathies from classical themes proceeds from the same high cause by which it was originally produced. The Arts of the middle ages soared above Paganism: the Imaginative Mind of modern times stands for the most part aloof from it; but it often stands aloof from Christianity also. Secularity is its prevailing character; while even in Paganism there was a spiritual element. We may not, without a risk of insincerity and presumption, indulge in either an exultation or a regret higher than corresponds with our low position. Can we with truth say that the portion of our modern literature which reverts to ancient mythology is less religious than the rest? Is it not, in the case of some authors, the only portion which has any relations, even through type or symbol, with religious ideas? Would Danté, would even Milton, have found more to sympathise with in the average of modern literature than in Homer or in Sophocles, in Wordsworth's "Laodamia," or Keats's "Hymn to Pan"? What proportion of our late poetry is Christian either in spirit or in subject,—nay, in traditions and associations? Admirable as much of it is, it is not for its spiritual tendencies that it can be commended. Commonly it shares the material character of our age, and smells of the earth; at other times, recoiling from the sordid, it flies into the fantastic. As our modern metaphysics, with no character of its own, hunts up the trails of innumerable philosophies gone by, like a dog questing after its master, so much of our poetry has sought wild adventure and strange experience in the spirit rather of the *ennuié* than of the knight-errant, but has seldom lighted on any authentic image of the heroic or the religious. It is our life which is to be blamed: our poetry has been but the reflection of that life. The dust of worldly business, like the ashes of worldly pleasures, is not holier in

Christian than in Pagan times. It is not the least
religious of our poets who exclaims—

> I'd rather be
> A pagan suckled in a creed outworn,
> So might I, standing on this pleasant lea,
> Have glimpses that would make me less forlorn ;
> Have sight of Proteus rising o'er the sea,
> Or hear old Triton blow his wreathed horn.

The sentiment is true, whether in verse or prose. It
affirms but that Triton is better than Plutus; that the
imagination has more of the spiritual about it than
self-interest has; that the shepherd, watching the
distant foam from his green pasture, is likely to be
greeted with higher visitations than the merchant who
hurries to the seaside but to inspect his bill of lading.

Nor can it with truth be asserted that Greek poetry
was only an art intended to minister to enjoyment.
Nothing with so low an aim would conduce to the
permanent enjoyment of a rational and moral being.
Founded, as has been observed, on the idea of Justice,
and faithfully adhering to the rule of the " Fit," Greek
poetry might almost claim to have celebrated, if not
the " beauty of holiness," at least the beauty of virtue ;
for the nobler beauty which it embodied shone ever in
the light of purity, and whatever corrupts or depraves
fell from it as raindrops from the myrtle leaf. It
reverenced the affections, and chiefly the parental,
friendship, the rites of hospitality, the white head of
age, the claims of country, the sanctions of religion.
In Andromache it saw every domestic tie imaged and
united in the central bond of marriage ; in Iphigenia

it sacrificed life to duty and a parent's will; in Antigonè
it was faithful to the dead, and revered the law of conscience more than the laws of men.   In Homer it
expanded itself in genial sympathy with all human and
social relations : in Sophocles and Pindar it elevated
those relations, venerating a holier sanctuary than
Colonos, and pointing to an Olympic course of which
gods not men were the spectators.   Even in its lighter
mood, inspired, as might seem, simply with the joy of
life itself, it was not more the voice of gladness than,
if rightly interpreted, the acclaim of gratitude, singing
in the ear of Nature her own ceaseless praises, and
thanking her, not amiss, for her liberal grace.   Greek
poetry could not have included in it so high a character
if Greek religion and Greek philosophy had not contained, implicitly or explicitly, an element of greatness
and truth.   Such was the fact.   The Platonic philosophy was, be it remembered, the chief secondary cause
of the diffusion of Christianity, doing for it more than
the favour of Constantine could ever have done; and if
Plato expelled the poets from his ideal commonwealth,
—a commonwealth very different from that which he
would have attempted to realise,—it was because
he himself, the "greatest fabler of the State," could
tolerate for the discipline of youth no song that Urania
herself had not inspired.   Truth, yet more elevated,
lurked under the symbolic veil of the Greek legend.
It was the father of Inductive philosophy who, in his
Wisdom of the Ancients, set forth the hidden meaning
of mythological fable, and asserted that it contained,

although but in broken fragments scattered abroad "like unto the limbs of Orpheus," no small portion of moral, political, and even of religious truth; thus inheriting at once and vindicating the ancient opinion that the gentile world had not been left wholly without inspiration,—that it was visited by streams, running long under ground, but derived from sacred sources, —that some beams of a better light were refracted, before sunrise, into its murkier air.

Hardly, indeed, could it have been otherwise. If that Fall which depraved the Will, and subverted the order of man's moral being, had left behind it no *mens divinior*, dimmed, not obliterated, there would have remained no faculty by which the better light, when vouchsafed, could have been recognised, and no hand by which the priceless gift could have been received. That *mens divinior* is the great inspirer of poetry. True poetry has ever a substratum of Religion in it, either pointing towards a Faith not yet revealed, or surviving it and flourishing with wild luxuriance on the soil in which that Faith has been interred. Poetry is the vital religion of Nature, and as such, though it may walk in devious ways, its eyes, at least, must often be raised to something above Nature. Nature itself was the first revelation made to man, and was necessarily made congruous with that higher revelation destined from the first not to supersede, but to redeem, to harmonise, and to complete it. Where, as in Greece, there existed most of that insight which fathoms Nature's meanings, and of that creative mind which interprets hints, man caught most frequent glimpses of that higher scheme of thought and life, proportioned to Nature as the building is proportioned to the foundation. Such as the heart of man was, such were the songs that lifted it up ; and it is as such that they retain a moral significance for all time. An adequate estimate of the Natural must ever raise our conception of that Supernatural which consummates and crowns it. We should not indeed "divide the crown" between Cecilia and old Timotheus ; yet we may reflect that the instrument which in later times shook the Christian temples with awe, or thrilled with the secret of a hushed and subdued pathos the sanctuary itself, bore yet in its glorious aspect and manifold organisation no small analogy to the simple reed-pipe of the Arcadian divinity as well as of the shepherd watching his flock by night.

The analogy between the Greek mythology and the true religion which in interpreting it abolished it, as Judaism was abolished by its own fulfilment, seems implied in a legend, which may be new to some readers, though perhaps not less authentic than many traditions which belong apparently to the same age : "That voice which, crying aloud unto Thammus, the Greek pilot (when on the night of our Lord's most bitter passion, He voyaged past the island of Paxo), bewailed that 'the great God Pan is dead,' did not more plainly declare the dissolution of Paynim darkness than did the vision of Parmenio, priest of Lycian Apollo, when Polycarp sat yet at Smyrna.

For Parmenio, after his conversion, did confess that as, after sacrifice, he slumbered in the temple (which was a wonder of the world), the pillar against which his head leaned waxed ever taller, and also slenderer as it rose. And, he gazing around, the other pillars waxed in. height likewise, and in thinness became as reeds; and many of them stood together for support. And the wall also ascended, as the cloud that riseth past the cliff; and the roof was lifted up; and the stone that stretcheth from pillar to pillar, and the stone that compasseth the building, raised themselves up in arches, like unto the hands of the priest when he lifteth them in prayer, and did sustain the roof. Moreover, the heads of the pillars, adorned with Asian phantasies, did sprout, like the rod of Aaron, and ran along the roof in traceries as a vine. The temple also grew longer than an Egyptian colonnade; and in the walls thereof there opened out great grots and caves, wherein stood in trance, kings, and prophets, and virgins, and martyrs incarnadine with the blood of their passion, and holding, every one, lily or palm. And from the altar went forth thunderings and lightnings which burned to ashes the chaplets and the offerings, and the statue of Oracular Apollo. And by four gates there entered into that temple, from the four corners of the earth, an innumerable company; and with their psalm which they sang the temple was shaken as it would ascend into heaven. And Parmenio heard a loud cry of Spirits, which wept in the words of the sad poet, Virgilius Maro (that

descended to the Shades), and said, 'We truly did
build, but not for ourselves:' and another voice
answered to them again, and said, 'Since God hath
destroyed your work.'"—For the word "destroyed,"
in the last sentence, might not the word "assumed"
be substituted, without injury to faith or morals?

THE SUBJECTIVE DIFFICULTIES IN RELIGION:

DOES UNBELIEF COME FROM SOMETHING IN RELIGION OR IN THE UNBELIEVER?[1]

IN these later days we hear much about the difficulties connected with Christianity, and even with Theism itself, of which Christianity is daily more and more found to be the sole effectual shield. Those who dwell upon them, whether with a morbid satisfaction or a needless alarm, would do well to reflect on a remark of Cardinal Newman's, to this effect—viz. that a hundred difficulties need not produce a single doubt. Nature is full of difficulties, and most men, except those who would stumble at a straw, know how to pursue their way notwithstanding. We have heard of "an apology for the Bible"; but Nature makes no apology. She says, "Learn of me, and you

---

[1] The following remarks, as they reply to but popular objections, do not profess scientific exactitude of expression.

shall have bread; ignore me, and you shall starve." There are subjects higher than Nature, the very greatness of which would make a true intelligence anticipate that with them many difficulties must be intertwined; while the thoughtless alone could have expected, or even desired, the absence of such. A superficial age fancies that the wonderful is the incredible, and that the great ideas which for ages have awed or charmed mankind can be pushed aside by "points" cleverly manipulated, or by a "rough and ready" cross-questioning,—one, impertinent if directed against an ancient philosophy, and one which apparently assumes that the religion it interrogates is a "character well known to the police." It is after a different fashion that the difficulties found or fancied in serious matters of belief have to be dealt with. They imply defect, doubtless; but there remains the question whether that defect exists in the creed or in the intelligence challenged by that creed. It is certain that the first teachers of that creed acknowledged the difficulties connected with belief, for they went further, and affirmed that it is impossible for the natural man, without Divine aid, to accept, or, at least, "spiritually to discern," Truths Divine. It is equally certain, on the other hand, that they regarded those difficulties as arising both from the blameless limitations of man's intellect and also, too frequently, from a defective moral condition; for they asserted that there is such a thing as "an evil heart of unbelief"; that it is "with the heart man believes";

and that the believing heart is under the influence of a grace descending from Him who is the Supreme Truth—a grace that belongs especially to the humble and the pure, one that may be intercepted by even a single serious and unrepented sin, and that may, after having been possessed, be forfeited when trifled with or abused.

But this is not all. They affirmed not only that Faith—a faith not superseding reason but strengthening and directing it—was possible to man, and was his deepest necessity, but much more—viz. that it was his great initiatory spiritual gift. On that hypothesis, as the optic nerve expands into the retina, so faith is but the nearer and rudimental part, exercised on earth, of a power destined to be expanded after a glorified fashion in heaven, and there passing into Beatific Vision. Such a power could neither have been regarded as a thing inconsiderable, nor as one but accidentally connected with man's appreciation of Truth Revealed. It is a thing dishonestly unreasonable, while dealing with Revelation, to ignore the hypothesis on which it rests. On that hypothesis Faith is a transcendent spiritual power crowning our intellectual being, as our intellect crowns our animal being ; and where it has its perfect work, religion shows itself so plainly to reason thus enlightened and emancipated that not to believe seems a thing self-willed and unreasonable. Such a claim was a strong one, doubtless ; but its "right divine" was attested by its victory. The Faith conquered the world ; and the world, thus conquered, bore the yoke of truth as lightly as a garland. A civilisation such as the old empires, which had degraded the moral more than they exalted the political status of man, never dreamed of, planted pure feet on the earth, and placed it in connection with higher worlds. Divine Truth seemed to have become part of man's natural heritage, and "arts unknown before" passed centuries in singing its praise and picturing its calendars.

For ages, though heresies sprang up, as had been predicted, respecting the definitions of truth, yet doubt as to the Divine claims of religion, natural and revealed, would have been regarded as a pitiable blindness. Men lived in the midst of a great light, its own sufficing evidence; and to turn from it would then have appeared a thing as witless as we should now regard the repudiation of inductive science with all its splendid results. But this could not last for ever. It was forbidden by the very greatness of a religion which, while ruling man, had remembered that he who rules should be as he who serves, and which, while directing, had also liberated the human faculties, and thus consciously prepared for Truth a militant condition, and a series of trials different from those of the early persecutions but not less severe. Religion, apart from the special blessings she had conferred, had also, with an ungrudging wisdom, preserved and transmitted gifts which, though immeasurably humbler, were yet a part of man's inheritance—viz. the ancient languages, with their noblest intellectual monuments. The highest inspirations of classic genius were by her exalted to an office of which they had not dreamed. Her schoolmen completed what the Fathers had begun. Aristotle conversed with St. Thomas Aquinas, and Virgil passed the golden branch on to Dante's hand. It was not all gain. Had such bequests never come to be abused, the Christian estimate of fallen human nature would thus have been proved a fallacious one. It was certain from the first that the arts of the "Juventas Mundi," though grafted on the Christian stock, would endeavour once more to "wanton in youthful prime," and on a pagan soil. The same thing was certain as regards the old world's dialectic science. The little bird was sure, when the eagle on whose back it had mounted had reached her utmost elevation, to take its little flight and twitter a span or two higher.

Another nursling of authentic religion was likely to turn against her after a time, though for a time only —that is, material science, or rather the rash award of those who occasionally take her name in vain. The connection between Faith and Science is not the less certain because indirect; truth is akin to truth, though they have their "family quarrels"; and the most spiritual of religions has proved far more auspicious to the knowledge of material things than any of those pagan religions which, while preserving many truths derived from patriarchal times and the primeval revelation, grew corrupted through material instincts. Unlike them, Christianity sustained the sacred and original doctrine of a Creator. The visible universe was proclaimed not to have existed eternally. It was not an emanation from the Divine, nor the Protean clothing of elemental divinities. It was a creation, and the creation of One Whose action was ever orderly, and Who was known to man as the Supreme Lawgiver. A Christian intelligence could hardly doubt that God's material universe must so far resemble His moral universe as to be grounded upon laws, the general permanence of which was attested, not contested, by the exceptional occurrence of miracles vouchsafed only when required by His Creation's moral ends. The Christian instinct believed also that God, who rewards the strenuous use of His gifts, not the hiding away of them in a napkin, had included in the heritage of man that knowledge of the material creation which, in whatever degree it truly enlarges his intellect, must increase his appreciation of the Creator's greatness, and of the creature's comparative insignificance. But here again, on the Christian hypothesis, the enlargement of man's intellectual sphere might well have been expected to introduce him into enlarged regions of intellectual probation, since physical discoveries, apparently though not really at war with some doctrines of the Faith, could not but present difficulties likely to vanish before physical knowledge more advanced, and theological teaching more defined. In the meantime it is only in a serious and entirely candid spirit that such difficulties can be rightly met. But our theme is a different one; we are concerned with the subjective difficulties men make for themselves, not the objective difficulties they find.

The former class are numerous and clamorous. To many students, as to many statesmen, religion has changed into the "Religious Difficulty." It has become a controversy. And here it must be remarked that the conditions of controversy, however inevitable, are by necessity less favourable to the elucidation of truth on the subject of religion than on subjects of less moment and less dignity. The objector is free to put forward the whole of what he deems his case; the defender of religion, while replying to objections, has often to leave unnoticed a large part of what he knows to be deepest and highest in the truth he defends, lest he should seem either to preach where he should argue, or, in arguing, to assume what, however certain, his adversary is not yet logically bound to concede. The laws of discussion compel him also to address almost exclusively the logical faculty in his opponent; yet he knows that the office of logic, in such subject-matter of thought, though a high, is a subordinate one—rather that of detecting sophisms and methodising inquiry than that of demonstrating truths—and consequently, that when he has confuted his opponent's errors logically, he has not necessarily a claim on his full assent, though, in proportion as that opponent has a candid temper and a philosophic mind, the "sensation of positiveness," which is sometimes strongest where faith is weakest, may have diminished, and the sceptic may have learned an excellent lesson—viz. to be sceptical *as to scepticism*. The logical faculty is but a part of man's understanding, which is but a part of his intellect, itself a part only of his total being; notwithstanding, it is to this logical faculty that controversy mainly addresses itself; while, on the other hand, it is the total being of man, intellectual, moral, and spiritual, not a fragment of his mind, that receives the sacred challenge of Divine Truth. Intuitive Reason sits in a higher court than the "faculty judging according to sense," and pronounces with certainty — *securus judicat*—on matters of which the inferior faculty takes a limited cognisance, dealing, in fact, but with their superficial phenomena. It would be absurd if in studying geometry a student were to demand mathematical demonstration on condition of confining himself to diagram and compass, and of discarding the intuitive part of man's intellect, acknowledging none of those axioms and postulates which admit of no argument because they underlie all demonstration, and are certain without it. Equally unphilosophical must it be to exclude the intuitive when grappling with the problem of a God. Yet this is, in a great part, required in argumentative discussion by the essential nature of controversy. The highest truth in matters theological belongs to a region above the polemical, as Theology has ever been the first to confess. This may also be said of the highest scientific truth; but in another important respect these two orders of truth materially differ. If the intuitions of geometry do not admit of argument, neither do they require it, for they address the reason alone. But the intuitive element in religion belongs both to man's reason and also to that *moral mind* which includes the co-operation of the Will. To demand, therefore, as controversy does, not only such a demonstration of religion as yields certainty to reason at once moral and speculative, and brings peace to "men of good-will," but proof that forcibly excludes all alternative "views" open to man's free-will and insurgent fancy —this is, in a great part, surreptitiously to remove the theme of discussion from its higher grounds of thought and place it on lower grounds. The unbelievers say, sometimes perhaps unconsciously, of the believers, " Their gods are gods of the hill country, but our gods are gods of the plain :"—they demand battle on the lower level ; and in accepting their challenge the defenders of religion fight at disadvantage. All admit that it would be unfair to demand an exclusively logical demonstration as to the existence of Conscience, *i.e.* proof forbidding all appeal to interior emotion, since conscience is, *ex hypothesi*, a moral power, addressing our whole moral nature with all its aspirations and sympathies, its hopes and fears, though it is by no means confined to the region of sentiment, and does not reject the witness derived from experience and expediency. It cannot surely be less unjust to deal after this narrow and arbitrary fashion with religion, which ever proclaims that, although in its relations with man's reason it is bound to respect the rules of logic, so far as they admit of a just application, its empire is coextensive with, and its demonstration addressed to, the total nature of man.

Let us take another illustration. The material beauty of the earth, apart from all her utilitarian helps and appliances, witnesses to a Creator, because it reveals that law of loveliness to which He has subjected creation. But beauty is discerned through the imagination; and thus a faculty which is deficient in many, and which, when existing in excess, is often signally opposed to Religion, has, notwithstanding, a grave office in attestation of her claims. Again, unhelped by the affections, it would be impossible for man to grasp the ideas of honour or patriotism. How much higher, then, must not be the place in connection with religion assigned to the affections of man! Apart from their sacred insight, even human things cannot be understood. The nobler a character is, the less can it be interpreted by a coldly critical observation—

> You must love him ere to you
> He will seem worthy of your love.[1]

A great poet describes a beautiful character as "one that never can be wholly known," and the loftiest have often been those most subject to misinterpretation. How quickly the eye of love detects the need that cannot be expressed! How often sympathy does what genius without it could never

[1] Wordsworth.

do! To apply this remark:—still more powerful than either the imagination or the affections is the moral being of man in sharpening that eye which deals with the super-sensuous. Long before those memorable words had been uttered, "If any man will do God's will, he shall know of the doctrine whether it be of God," the best pagan teachers had proclaimed loudly that it was to the pure heart and the righteous life that the vision of Truth was accorded. It is easy to suggest that such assertions respecting those indirect but vital relations which subsist between man's intellect and his imagination, affections, and moral instincts, are but an attempt on the part of religious apologists to elude the tests of philosophy. The converse is the truth. The assertion is the assertion of philosophy. Nay, and this is remarkable, such a statement may be advanced even respecting man's appreciation of mere material nature, and will then be unchallenged by those who forget how much more eminently it must apply to that which lies beyond nature. Mr. Carlyle maintains, with no less truth than eloquence, that nature has no meaning to the *mere* physical or even to the *mere* intellectual observer. He writes thus:—

Without hands a man might have feet, and could still walk : but, consider it—without morality intellect were impossible for him : a thoroughly immoral man could not know anything at all ! To know a thing, what we call knowing, a man must first *love* the thing, sympathise with it : that is, be *virtuously* related with it. If he have not the justice to put down his own selfishness at every turn, the courage to stand by the dangerous-true at every turn, how shall he know? His virtues, *all of them*, lie recorded in his knowledge. *Nature*, with her truth, remains to the bad, to the selfish, and the pusillanimous, for ever a sealed book : what such can know of Nature is mean, superficial, small ; for the uses of the day merely. But does not the very fox know something of Nature? Exactly so : it knows where the geese lodge.[1]

If Nature requires for her right interpretation "all" a man's virtues, the supernatural may certainly claim, as it has ever done, that of humility. It must require, however, many others also—the "single eye" of the Gospel, since neither moral nor Divine Truth has a meaning for the sophisticated nature ; zeal and perseverance, since the search is often arduous ; purity, since it is the "clean of heart" that "see God" ; reverence, or else the inquirer will overrun and trample down truth in his quest after knowledge. Above all, it requires a devout heart ; for as a heart seduced from the right leads the intellect into error, so a heart faithful to the right leads it to truth. Men sometimes imagine that such statements apply only to revealed religion. They are true not less in relation to Theism. To suppose that this principle applies to human knowledge on all moral subjects, and even on the highest and fairest material subjects, and yet that when cited in connection with man's appreciation of religion, whether natural or revealed, it is but a pretence and a pretext, this is to declaim, not to reason ;—for there is a mental as well as a verbal form of declamation.

It is the whole vast and manifold being of man—

----

[1] Carlyle's *Hero-Worship*, p. 99.

his mind and his heart, his conscience and his practical judgment, his soul and his spirit—that Divine Truth challenges. The sceptic, when proud of his scepticism, insists upon the mighty and manifold problem being presented to his logical faculty alone, and wonders why he can make so little of it. In place of dilating his being to embrace the largest of Truths, he contracts it to a lance's point, and pushes it forth in oppugnancy. He does not perceive that this mental attitude is one that violates not merely the philosophic conditions under which alone the knowledge he seeks could become his, but those under which only it professes to be cognisable. He makes this demand because he insists on gaining his knowledge of things divine in no degree by way of gift, but exclusively as his own discovery: that is, not as religion but as science. He assumes that because religion, like nature, *has* its science, it therefore *is* science, and is nothing more. As well might he assume that nature is nothing more than natural philosophy. If he came forth to the threshold of his house, he would be bathed in the sunbeams. He has another way of ascertaining whether a sun exists. He retires to the smallest and darkest chamber in his house, closes the shutter, and peers through a chink.

The indevout inquirer too often forgets also that even if it were to a single intellectual faculty that divine truth presents itself, still the aspect which it wears when thus seen would depend largely upon the percipient himself. Without any fault in itself it might to him

appear either repulsive or uninteresting. The anatomical plate from which the ordinary eye turns with
dislike is beautiful to the eye of the scientist. This
is because his point of view is that of science. Now,
a man's point of view, when he contemplates the great
religious problem, is predetermined by all the antece-
dents of his life, by all its accidents, and much more
by all its acts, evil or good, remembered or forgotten.
To the mind of man in all the best ages religion has
been a matter of piercing significance. To that of
some particular individual it may present but a blank
or a distortion. More strange still, it may have no
interest for him. He is therefore bound in reason to
inquire where lies the cause of this condition. May
it not be connected with something either morally
wrong or deeply defective in his will, a part of his
being both higher and more responsible than his
understanding! A great philosophical writer has
borne witness on this subject. Coleridge thus sets forth
the results of his long and profound meditations :—

I became convinced that religion, as both the corner-stone
and the keystone of morality, must have a moral origin ; so far
at least that the evidence of its doctrines could not, like the truths
of abstract science, be wholly independent of the will. It were
therefore to be expected that its fundamental truth (he speaks of
Theism) would be such as might be denied, though only by the
fool, and even by the fool from the madness of the *heart*
alone ! . . . The understanding meantime suggests, the analogy
of experience facilitates the belief. Nature excites and recalls it
as by a perpetual revelation. Our feelings almost necessitate it ;
and the law of conscience peremptorily commands it. The
arguments that at all apply to it are in its favour ; and there is
nothing against it but its own sublimity. It could not be
intellectually more evident without becoming morally less

effective ; without counteracting its own end by sacrificing the life of Faith to the cold mechanism of a worthless, because compulsory, assent.[1]

If Coleridge believed that Theism did not admit of a strict demonstration through that " sciential reason the objects of which are purely *theoretical*," apart from the inquirer's " good-will," and in spite of his hostile temper, this was, in his estimate, but because religion stands above such demonstrations. " I believe," he says, that "the notion of God is *essential* to the human mind ; that it is called forth into distinct consciousness principally by the conscience, and auxiliarily by the manifest adaptation of means to ends in the outward creation." [2]

By some this is now stigmatised as " mysticism." Why should men feel aggrieved by all that constitutes the greatness of humanity ? Those who object to mysteries in religion, whether natural or revealed, object to religion's belonging to the infinite, or else to man's being permitted to have any dealings with the infinite. The finite intelligence is of course not able to *comprehend* in its fulness the infinite. Is it, then, an injury to man that he is raised high enough to *apprehend*, at least in a fragmentary way, such portions of it as are nearest to him and most needful ? If such knowledge sometimes strikes upon difficulties, is that strange ? Where the finite and the infinite intersect there must needs be apparent contradictions—that is, there must be truths so large that, as Coleridge remarks,

---

[1] *Biographia Literaria*, part ii. p. 208.
[2] *Literary Remains*, vol. i. pp. 390, 391.

to our petty intelligence they can only express themselves approximately and in the form of converse
statements mutually supplemental, notwithstanding
what at first sight seems mutual opposition.   What
mysteries prove is that man's mind has, by God's aid,
been lifted to its highest, and that God is higher still.
The philosopher who thinks that to him there should
be no mysteries does not think that there should be
none to the peasant.   Yet surely the intellectual difference between man and man must be small compared
with that between man and God.

Those who demand definitions on all occasions,
after that "stand and deliver" fashion more common
among peremptory than profound thinkers, forget that
it is far more often through careful description than
through definition that the most vital, and the most
practical, part of our knowledge reaches us.   If our
knowledge of things divine remained, even when at
its highest, restricted within the limit of exact definitions, a new charge would be brought against it, viz.
that it was not a divine truth revealed to us, so far as
our smallness can receive it, but merely one of the many
petty systems shaped by the human understanding—
its creation and its plaything.   Were it no more than
this, it would include of course nothing that defies an
exhaustive analysis.   It is a special "note" of divine
truth, that although, when presented to man, it does
not contradict the higher reason, yet it transcends that
inferior faculty which exults only in the work of its
own hands.   Religion is given to us as our help, not

our boast. It can raise us, but we cannot bring it down. It is a Truth immeasurably above us, with which we are allowed to have relations :—we cannot therefore inspect it as if it were a map outspread beneath us. We are surely little tempted to complain merely because we are allowed glimpses of more than we can measure, and yet not permitted to see, as a whole, a truth which professes to show us but its utmost parts — those immediately needful for us. Such complaints do not proceed from reason, which, just because it expects proportion in all things, does not expect authentic religion to be without difficulties to a finite intelligence. They proceed rather from petty conceptions of things the largest man deals with, and an exaggerated estimate of man's present faculties.

It is the lawless in man, not the soaring, the purblind, not the clear-sighted, which revolts from mystery. Mystery implies obedience in the form of docility. That is just what a true religion might have been expected to demand. It is the claim which Nature makes. So far as our natural life is cast in a divine mould, as distinguished from that portion of it which is artificial and conventional, it makes upon us, in its initiatory stages, the same demand made by religion. It is through a sympathetic and joyous docility that we learn to walk, to speak, to exercise and direct our first affections, to reach out to the rudiments of all wisdom. The process is one from faith to knowledge. It is but mechanical and technical knowledge that is won on other conditions. Sciolists quarrel with religion for being in analogy with Nature, and for eternalising the youth of our heart. This is a temper the more childish the less it is childlike—one that reaches decrepitude before it reaches intellectual manhood; one that never attains that heroic strength which copes resolutely with the great acts and sufferings of life and death.

Reason knows that man becomes dwarfed the moment he loses hold of God, and that the bond between him and God—religion—ceases to be religion if it discards its sovereign attributes. If it declines from doctrinal Truth and becomes but literature, philosophy, or art, it can do nothing more for man. It can serve him only on condition of ruling him; and it can rule him only through the "obedience of faith," which accepts mysteries because, though it sees, it yet knows that in the present preparatory stage of man's existence, it has to see "as through a glass darkly." Reason perceives that it must be the function of religion to challenge what is deepest in man at once with a potent voice, and a gentle one, thus eliciting a belief which would be barren if it did not work through love. Reason sees that if religion included no mystery it would inspire no reverence; that in the absence of reverence all its truths would for man shrivel up like withered leaves or be sharpened into polemical disputations; that pride would be inflamed, the heart hardened, and a wider gulf than Nature's set between God and man. Reason acknowledges that it is worthy of God that, in His dealings with man, whether through natural religion or revelation, He should both show

Himself and shroud Himself—disclose Himself to men of good-will, who can walk humbly and bravely in His light, and veil Himself from those to whom the revelation abused would prove but a woe.   God shows Himself, and He shrouds Himself, alike in His Word and in His Works.   "The heavens are His garment;" and it is the office of a garment both to indicate and to conceal what it invests.

Reason knows her own limits.   When the subject-matter lies wholly within those limits, as in science, truth is proved *by* Reason; in matters capable of man's apprehension in part, and yet partially beyond those limits, it is proved *to* Reason.   In the former case Reason asserts; in the latter she confesses: in the former case she judges alone; in the latter she sits among assessors.   When reaching her conclusions on revealed religion, she listens without jealousy to the whisper of Faith, remembering that, of all God's creatures on earth, one alone is capable of receiving a challenge so high—His *reasonable* creature, man. When forming her judgment on the great Theistic problem, Reason does not decline as irrelevant the witness of conscience.   She knows that while con-science affirms a law, and therefore a lawgiver, it is yet so far from asserting its own divine sufficiency that it acknowledges it cannot give man strength faithfully to obey that law.   It calls itself but a voice—a voice "cry-ing in a wilderness"; and its power and its weakness alike point to One greater than itself.   Reason knows that it is but declamation to set up morality in place of religion. Gratitude, loyalty, honour, prudence, benevolence, the sympathies alike and the aspirations of humanity, all these have a place in morality ; and, like conscience, they declare that they possess interests in the question whether man has a Creator, a Redeemer, and a Judge. If he has, then man's moral duties must be all of them duties to Him. It is not Reason that refuses to take counsel with such advisers. While bowing to faith in what is beyond her ken, but yet congruous with all her holiest instincts, Reason offers up her " reasonable sacrifice," and receives her reward. That reward is that she is herself received as a subject and citizen into the luminous and measureless kingdom of Theism ; all the verities of that kingdom, the existence of God, His unity, wisdom, love, justice, His providence, omnipresence, and omnipotence, all His attributes, as numerous as the faculties of all creatures capable of knowing Him, becoming thenceforth a portion of her heritage, and having their place in her teaching. Theism having become practical—*i.e.* devotional—the true Theist learns that, from the first, Christianity was implied in it ; and that the doctrine of a Providence ever prophesied an Incarnation.

Reason detects at once the unreasonableness of the charges most commonly brought against Faith. She sees nothing unreasonable in the belief that an endowment or power should exist, as distinct from the mathematical faculty as the latter is from the experimental, one able, not when obliterating the inferior faculties, but when supplementing and raising them, to elicit a new and spiritual "discernment," a power august and helpful to man when meditating on supernatural things and eternal interests. Such a gift would seem a most appropriate reward for inferior faculties rightly used and never abused. The denial that this faculty exists, whether on grounds purely *à priori*, or from prejudice, is among the paradoxical notes of a time when many proclaim, on the flimsiest evidence, the existence of faculties by which we can recognise material objects without aid from the senses, or converse with Souls that revisit earth to play tricks under tables. For some persons the supernatural retains its charm, only provided it can be dissociated from the glory of God and the good of man.

Reason has no sympathy with a common allegation alarming to men at once proud and easily frightened —viz. that Faith means belief on compulsion. A man may profess, but obviously cannot exercise Faith on compulsion ; and, if he simulates it, religion inexorably esteems him but as one who adds hypocrisy to unbelief. To exercise Faith is to believe Divine Truth not only with as great a freedom as reason uses in other matters, but with freedom of a more absolute order. When reason believes, on the testimony of sense, in the material objects around us, the mind is chiefly passive, and exercises little more freedom than a mirror that reflects them. When a higher faculty deals with a geometric problem, the intellect is, no doubt, active ; but, if it discerns the truth at all, it does so by intuition, and must needs accept it. In neither of these cases is there either merit or demerit, for whether the truth be discerned or remains undiscerned, the confession or denial of it is alike involuntary. But when man believes Divine Truth, on Divine Faith, he believes voluntarily as well as reasonably, and therefore meritoriously. It is the special dignity of God's *rational* creature that that union with his Creator for which he was made is effected neither passively on his part nor involuntarily, but through a personal co-operation with grace, which, though the humblest, is also the highest exercise of his most Godlike power—free-will. In mere intellect there is often, as in the animal part of our being, something that resembles mechanism—witness our involuntary "association of ideas." In our ordinary and worldly life there is also an element of bondage, for we act, though only within certain limits, under the suasion of downward-tending inclinations, and with a preference determined in part by the balance of earthly interests. But Soul remains free; and the Will, the spiritual within us, when it is a "good-will" becomes the highest expression of our freedom, lifting the reason into its loftiest sphere, and delivering the heart from the thraldom of inferior motives. The obedience of this nobler Will to grace is the "fiat" which unites man with God; and faith, the light of the soul, is the child of that union. The Creator's primal *Fiat lux* was an act of supreme authority; the Creature's *Fiat voluntas tua* is an act of humility, and irradiates the world within.

Faith, so far from being belief on compulsion, is, in the highest sense, a spiritual *act*, and an eminently reasonable act, though also more than reasonable. There is no difficulty in recognising this truth except to those who have been entangled by sophisms, and cannot discern what is divinely simple. The unbeliever unconsciously assumes that the frank acceptance of a creed is much the same sort of thing whether that creed be true or false. He thus implicitly implies that truth does not exist; for if it exists it cannot but wield a discriminating power. Religion affirms the contrary—viz. that objective truth does exist, and that God's *reasonable* creature was created in a dignity so high, and after his Fall was renewed by a grace so admirable, that his well-being consists in communion with Truth, whose claim he has been made capable of recognising :—" Deus, qui humanæ substantiæ *dignitatem* mirabiliter condidisti, et mirabilius reformasti." The creature challenged by the Truth is also a creature formed "in the image of God"; and therefore to that challenge he responds, "This is flesh of my flesh and bone of my bone." Enough has come to him in the way of evidence, not to make any creed, but to make a true creed, credible : —belief is consequently reasonable; but the mind is not therefore compelled to believe : a moral motive is presented to a man "of good-will," and Faith, which is morally bound to crown Reason, supervenes upon it because the will is in vital sympathy with the true, and is not held back by "invincible" hindrances. It is plainly illogical to say that this, religion's statement respecting the nature and genesis of Faith, is unsound, merely because false creeds or creeds that mix error with truth are sometimes accepted. Such creeds are accepted, not by Divine Faith, but, at best, by mere human faith; and creeds wholly corrupt are accepted by that blind and depraved credulity which "believes a lie." True Faith is not the less true because it is imitated by false faith, just as Virtue is not abolished because hypocrisy is common. The perfect freedom of Divine Faith is a fundamental hypothesis of theology; faith would otherwise lose all that nobility which authentic religion has ever claimed for it; while unbelief, nay, Atheism itself, would involve no more responsibility than erroneous judgments on scientific or historical subjects. A man may esteem Cæsar a bad general, and yet be only mistaken; but if he repudiates the laws of Conscience, he obviously stands guilty unless he has the excuse of an ignorance not connected with the will. If moral faith be thus a duty, and yet be free, why should religious faith be branded as compulsory merely because it is a duty? Is this a just judgment or a calumny?

Reason does not sanction another charge brought against religion—viz. that it is a spiritual "bribery and corruption," and that its votaries believe only to gain enjoyment, or shun suffering, in a future life. This is at best a misconception, and sometimes not without a touch of the spiteful. Religion does not reserve her rewards for the next world exclusively;

or, rather, those who dwell in the temporal world dwell also in the eternal, eternity not being a prolongation of time, but a vaster sphere clasping a smaller one, and reaching with its penetrating influences to creatures enclosed at once within both. It is a commonplace of theology that the Christian seeks the Cross, and commonly finds it; while yet the consolations of religion not only exist for those who dwell upon earth, but are granted in their higher degrees to those who have most of earthly suffering. Moreover, the desire of heaven is not a spiritual form of selfishness. On the contrary, it is the only effectual cure for selfishness. The selfish man makes himself the centre of his universe, loving little besides, except so far as the love of others can minister to self-love : but heaven is not an earth improved for the help of specious baseness; it is the " Beatific Vision " which draws the beholder into Itself, renewing the creature after the Divine Image, while it also makes him realise that merely relative and dependent character which belongs to all merely creaturely existence. In that Vision individual self-love is lost, while true Personality, far from being even merged, is developed to the utmost. The desire of heaven, that is, the love of God and the belief that the highest good must consist in the fruition of the Uncreated Good, is not founded on any calculation of interests, but is a primary spiritual instinct. The converse fear is also a primary instinct of our spiritual being, and one of which the animalised nature seems incapable. It is the fear of an eternal

exile from the supreme Good and the supreme Love
—an exile self-inflicted by an eternal hate.

If it be objected that the promised reward of
righteousness, in the present or a future life, destroys
the disinterestedness of religion, it suffices to reply
that the cavil might be raised equally against virtue,
since "virtue is its own reward," and against disinterestedness itself, since disinterestedness is man's
sole protection from many of his heaviest trials.
Who would affirm that filial love means but the
child's selfish desire for parental protection, and that
parental love is but the parent's intention to enjoy his
children's reverence, or their aid in his old age?
Fame and power are among the rewards of good
actions done for man's behoof; yet it is not true that
those actions are done only, or chiefly, or need be
done at all, "for pay." Those who look only at the
wrong side of the tapestry can see nothing save the
stuck-out ends of threads; but they are not philosophers on that account. A world in which there
existed no connection between happiness and excellence would be a world in which happiness must
chiefly spring from, and gravitate towards, evil—a
belief which would *implicitly* deny the existence of a
Creator Himself at once all-blessed and all-good.
The aspiration after a love for God wholly disinterested
has seldom been expressed with such ardour as in the
celebrated Hymn of St. Francis Xavier, who, notwithstanding, believed the Saviour's promise that the
humblest good action shall "not lack its reward";

and those who disclaim all religious fear, on the ground that "perfect love casteth out fear," are claiming for themselves perfection—where it is least likely to exist.

Another popular charge against religion, while one that reason repudiates as sophistic, is one which vanity and weakness are especially intimidated by— viz. the charge that Faith is feebleness. Reason perceives that if Faith exists at all, it must, on the contrary, be a strenuous energy. To it belongs not only the gift of spiritual discernment, but that of daring. It is the great spiritual venture, launching forth "in search of new worlds beyond the deep." Like virtue, it is a virile gift. One of the failings which chiefly produces lack of Faith is lack of courage. Faith is a power ; and as, in history, it has wrestled with all the powers of this world, so, in the history of a soul, it wrestles with Powers unseen. Man, even subsequent to the Fall, is, except where a second Fall has drawn him down beneath the level of fallen nature, a religious being—one who has the strength that endures long kneeling, as well as the power of sitting or lying still. He has a soul, as well as a mind and a body. Religion is a strong soul's commerce with God, as scientific thought is the strong mind's commerce with scientific truth, and bodily labour is the strong hand's commerce with nature. That sacred commerce belongs to the soul at once through the submission and the dauntless energy of Faith. The entire and final loss of that Faith is to the soul what imbecility is to our mental, and torpor to our animal being. In its last stage, it is the barrenness of a soul that has not "strength to bring forth" truth. It is no error of strength: it is either the restless feebleness of the world's premature senility, or a malady perhaps but temporary.

Whenever, yielding thus to spiritual weakness, man has relaxed his grasp upon Truth once his, he has commonly been soon after found running upon the downward trails of the old pagan philosophies—a circumstance full of significance. The most irrational of these was the theory which accounted for the universe in its present form by a "fortuitous concurrence of atoms." It would be absurd to impute such a theory to all those who believe in Evolution, for that theory fully admits that, outside what it accounts for, there remain three problems wholly unsolved —viz. the origin of the first matter, of life, and of law, including the laws connected with Evolution. To the theistic evolutionist these three problems are solved by that which "Evolution," if it does not teach, yet does not deny—viz. the existence of a Divine Creator. Matter cannot be eternal; but God, if a man takes in the idea at all, cannot be thought of as other than eternal. He who is the Eternal Existence has created the first matter; He who has life in Himself has created life; and He who is the Supreme Lawgiver has subjected matter and life to the laws they obey. But all evolutionists are not theists; and the atheistic form of Evolution, abjuring the support which a philosophic evolution derives, as some maintain, from

Theism, involves in a more pretentious form an absurdity quite as great as a fortuitous concurrence of atoms—viz. the dogma that a Matter self-subsisting, and quickened by a Life never imparted, obeys a Law never imposed upon it. Again, the most abject of the ancient philosophies was the cynical, which selected the tub for its temple. But not less cynical is that modern materialism (Carlyle would have called it "hog-wash") which, disbelieving in the existence of soul, makes man a mere animal, and educes whatever he thinks or feels out of a perishable material organisation. If man were indeed but the most intellectual of animals, he would be the worst, since he would be the only animal that sins. Among the forms of modern cynicism the chief is that of "Agnosticism," which does not deny that a God may exist, but affirms that, even on that supposition, man must remain ignorant of His existence, adding that knowledge on that subject, or the kindred subject of man's immortality, is needless, such themes being amongst those respecting which a healthy mind will feel little curiosity and no distress. The diseased limb feels no distress when the period of mortification has set in, and that of dissolution is imminent ; and yet mortification is not thought a healthy condition. The paganism of old times, till its season of mortification had arrived, would have despised a contented Agnosticism; for with the hopes and the yearnings derived from a belief in immortality was interwoven whatever was great in the arts or acts of antiquity. The child is no

Agnostic; like the peasant, he is ignorant of many things irrelevant; but he "delightedly believes" in things divine. "Agnostic" is a Greek word, signifying much the same as a time-honoured one derived from the Latin—viz. "Ignoramus"; and one hardly sees why the invention of this new term should be considered as so great a flight of modern philosophy. Contemporaneously with these metaphysical systems there have too often been put forward ethical theories which it would be unjust to charge upon any large school of thought, but which notwithstanding carry with them unequivocal warnings to several schools. They have vindicated suicide, infanticide, the putting to death of persons in hopeless disease, and much besides of a character worse still, which painfully recalls the lowest ages of paganism. The books propounding them have been publicly sold in the streets, and defended in the courts of justice. A boastful age is not without cause for misgivings, and may one day find cause to be grateful for humiliations !

One would have thought that the primary mathematical truths at least must ever occupy an unassailable place; but those who are old-fashioned enough still to believe in the universal and absolute character of geometry are now named as the followers of a special "intuitional school" by persons who ascribe, astonishing as this may seem, our knowledge of abstract, not less than of physical science, to experience, not to reason, and who affirm that in other planets a larger experience may contradict the assertions which it makes in ours, such as that two and two must invariably amount to the same as three and one, and that the angles of a triangle must in every case be equal to two right angles! Once more, personal identity might be supposed proof against cavil; but passages [1] may be found in recent books, which mean—if they possess a meaning—that man's moral existence is but an on-flowing stream of sensations, thoughts, and purposes, not ruled by any independent and personal will, but necessarily winding in the channel moulded for them by irresistible motive and external circumstance.

Scarcely less strange are the conclusions of a certain new philosophy, "Positism," which regards itself as the high-water mark of all systems. It informs us that it was but an extravagance of the human race, in its childhood, which made man turn his attention to things *above* us; that the same race, only a little wiser in its youth, had then indulged in the study of things *within* us, ethics and metaphysics; but that, mature at last, it has now discovered that the one proper object of investigation lies *around* us, viz. material nature. This materialism it calls "Good Sense." Fraudulent nomenclature is one of those fine arts in which false science is an adept. It deserves a sterner censure than most errors, though one confined to those who invented it, and not extended to those who, themselves ensnared, use it unwittingly. It has its alluring side. It praises

---

[1] Several such passages are quoted in Mr. Kirkman's *Philosophy without Assumptions.*

"truth," but truth in its tongue means but truth scientifically discovered—a small portion of what it means elsewhere. It praises the love of truth; but it loves truth so little that it prefers the search after truth to the possession and use of truth, alleging often that the very claim to Revealed Truth is an unworthy one, because it implies a restriction on inquiry. It praises "culture"; but the term, in its cant sense, excludes most thinkers of our time, though highest in art, science, and letters, who have remained believers in the Bible, and includes in its brevet promotion all who believe in the latest theory of Biblical criticism. It boasts its "freethought"; but the "thought" thus lauded is not deep; and the "freedom" does not include a freedom from that presumption which most impedes sound thought, or even from that cowardice which trembles at the charge of "obscurantism." Fraudulent nomenclature has also its cautious side. Working its way through books and journals read by believers as well as by unbelievers, it is skilful not to shock: besides its strong meat for men, it has milk for those who are still but babes in unbelief, draws distinctions between atheism and "dogmatic atheism," and asserts that to admit a God is not to admit a personal God, but only a Force that may exist impersonally, like the law of gravitation. Theists, of course, ascribe to God, but in a transcendent sense as well as degree, attributes such as love, wisdom, justice, holiness, power, which, in a sense and degree immeasurably lower, exist in man also simply because man was made in God's image :—the new nomenclature, inverting the truth, has the assurance to stigmatise such an ascription, in the absence of which the term God could represent no idea and make no appeal either to the moral reason or the human heart, as man's creation of a God after *his* own image, and nicknames it "anthropomorphism." "Positism" has carried this new nomenclature to its utmost extreme. It does not deny a "Grand Etre"; it only denies that he is God. The "Grand Etre" is Humanity: the individuals of the human race perish and vanish, but Humanity remains : it is to be worshipped; and an elaborate system of rites and festivals has been instituted for that worship! This system is certainly original, for it combines atheism with idolatry—viz. worship, the highest it has to give, of that which is not God; and it unites both with a practice as anomalous in the eye of reason as of faith—viz. the adoration of that which has no actual existence; since, apart from the individuals it supposes to pass into nothingness, Humanity is but a collective name.

A word on the ideal end of this philosophy. Assuming its eventual prevalence and the success of its aims, man would have finally put aside all hope of attaining knowledge respecting things divine, and also all belief in the soul's immortality. On the other hand, he would have perfected his knowledge of nature, and his mastery over the material universe. Let us assume also that he had banished diseases, greatly improved civil government, and lengthened

human life.   What does the triumph amount to?
The narrowing of man's being by the extinction of its
spiritual part and the enlarged possession of all those
things which, apart from things spiritual, are nothings!
The human affections, as distinguished from animal
instincts, if we believed that the objects of them must
moulder for ever in the dust, would eventually, and
after a piteous struggle, either shrivel up and wither
away, or survive but to mock us; and we should
envy the animal races among which affections are, as
for such they should be, evanescent.   Unfountained
from above, the higher moral virtues would clothe
themselves with decay for lack of a meaning; and the
imaginative arts would dwindle in sympathy with that
decline.   Our perfected knowledge of physical science,
when nothing connected with it remained to be known,
would waken neither our energies nor our admiration;
nay, possibly, when we had learned how to "put a
girdle round the earth in forty minutes," our last
discovery might be that we had changed our planet
to an asteroid and our palace to a prison.   If a
human aspiration remained, the victories of material
knowledge would but intensify our grief at the invincible barrier placed by Fate between us and all spiritual
knowledge.   Barbaric races live in a twilight region
of intellect, clasped by a boundless horizon of twilight
hope:—the "perfected" conditions of the false philosophy and the foolish philanthropy would abide in a
blinding glare of knowledge respecting matters barren
to the soul and to the heart, encompassed by the very

blackness of darkness respecting all those which are precious whether to the human and moral affections or to the spirit. The contrast would make the loss intolerable. Man would walk upon an earth all ashes, and under a heaven all iron. The ideal of the Positivist philosophy would be the nearest definition of that hell which Christian philosophy, by no means bound to interpret *literally* Scriptural expressions one of which is obviously metaphorical, has found it difficult hitherto to define. And yet this immeasurable despair would be but a misplaced, stunted, and vitiated fragment of that boundless Christian Hope, which includes in its heaven, not lost in a Divine Fruition mightier yet, the perfection of every knowledge separated from the error mixed with earthly knowledge, and graduated aright amid the hierarchy of the knowledges; and which includes not less the perfection of every high and pure affection, cleansed from mortal dross, separated from what was temporary in its purpose, and exalted, not lowered by just subordination in the hierarchy of love.

At a time when " Progress " is the cry, and " We will charge you with reaction " is the threat, it may be well to remark that there is such a thing as progress neither upward nor onward, but downward, and such a thing as reaction in favour practically of ages both remoter and blinder than those traduced by the aspersion that they were " dark ages." In defence of such progress is raised another popular cry, " Beware of tradition," " Beware of prepossessions." This is also a cry to which reason can give but a limited consent. Whatever knowledge has been attained, or will ever be attained, must needs be transmitted by parents to their children, and therefore must reach remote generations largely as a tradition, without on that account forfeiting the benefit of that evidence, whether external or internal, by which it is authenticated. Humanity itself is a tradition, and cannot separate itself from the conditions of an historical existence ; and though philosophy, no less than religion, protests against "traditions *of men*," it condemns by that term only those local and partial traditions of the clique, the school, or the nation, which make void a larger truth at once attested by reason, and brought home, by the universal consent of men, as part of the human heritage to individual man at a period when he is as yet too young adequately to test, though yet he feels, its reasonableness. Moral prepossessions we must have, because the best thoughts of the best ages, when sifted by time, mould our beings from the first, and because, if we had not moral prepossessions, we should have immoral. Should "Agnosticism" last long enough to become a tradition, the child born in that sect will start with prepossessions, such as that "truth" is "what each of us troweth," and that "liberty" consists in our having always an equal and undisputed choice between alternatives, not in our willingly and gladly, and by no means on compulsion, believing the true and doing the right. If we discarded "prepossessions," we should enter on the study of morals without the admission of any responsibility

on our part, and to that of history without any preference for the just ruler above the tyrant. Man could
never have made a beginning of natural philosophy if
he had not come to it with that high prepossession,
the idea of Law; and, as Bacon reminds us, the *pru-
dens interrogatio* is necessary if we would elicit from
Nature more than the fool's answer. If prepossessions
are thus preconditions for natural and for moral
philosophy, are they intrusive in a religion which has
lasted for centuries, and moulded a world?

As superficial is another allegation often made—viz.
"Religion but solves the riddles of existence by
resolving them into another riddle as inexplicable."
Were it true that it only resolved the many into one, it
would so far have followed the aspiration of philosophy,
which is to resolve phenomena into laws, and laws into a
single law, and which knows that the ultimate ground
of all must remain inexplicable to science,—the craving of which is limitless, and to which an "ultimate"
would be defeat, not triumph. But this is the least
part of the sophism. Religion does not substitute
riddles for riddles. She answers a thousand painful
riddles, each of them a sphinx ready to devour us, by
lifting them into a higher region; and she resolves
them, as has been well said by Auguste Nicolas,[1] into
one sunlike Mystery, which, if itself too bright to be
scanned with undazzled eyes, yet irradiates the whole
world besides. The ages and nations bear witness to
that mystery; it is the mystery of power and of healing,

---

[1] *Etudes Philosophiques.*

of life and of love. The knowledge that God exists ratifies conscience and enlightens it; consecrates reason yet humbles it; sets the will free by teaching it to substitute for the thraldom of petty motives a glad submission to a sacred law. It is the mother of progressive wisdom and of spiritual civilisation; it gives man the power to act righteously and to bear patiently; it changes an anarchy of warring passions into a royal commonwealth of graduated powers. For ages it has dried the eyes of the widow and guided the orphan's feet. Yet these are but its lesser gifts, for its higher boast is that it creates an inner world of sanctity and peace, a "hidden life" of the creature with the Creator, the pledge of a glorified life with Him. The spleen of an ungrateful and hasty time may fancy that it can sweep such gifts away; but a true philosophy will rebuke a revolt so self-destructive and so dishonourable. Whatever the theorist may affirm or deny, Christianity professes to be essentially a *life*, the life of individual man, and of social man; and, despite the scandals bequeathed by those who have but taken religion's name in vain, experience has attested her claim. We live in an experimental age: a contented sceptic would do well to become an experimentalist, and test religion by *living it*. Amid his inquiries he should include a careful one as to whether he has been a sincere and a reverent inquirer. We have been told, and not untruly, that "honest doubt" has in it much of faith. But doubt is not honest when it is proud, when it is reckless, when it is as confident

as if resolved negation were solid conviction, or as
apathetic as if Divine Truth would be less of a gain
than the "struggles that elicit strength." We have
been told, in disparagement of creeds, that Life is
Action; but it is in the light, not the darkness, that
brave and sane men act and struggle. It is the Christian Faith that brings that light; and it was the Christian Life that first claimed to be a noble warfare. The
warrior must have solid ground beneath his feet.

And yet the defender of religion must ever end
with a confession. If all who believe had but been
true to their trust, religion must in every age have
shone abroad with a light that would long since and
finally have conquered the world to itself. It is an
eye keener than ours that sees how far each man has
used his wealth of faith rightly, or come by his poverty
honestly. If in many a case unbelief means a defective, perhaps an evil will, in how many is it not the
malady of a bewildered time? How many a one who is
tossed from doubt to doubt may yet, in the depths of
his being, resemble St. Augustine when he was drawing nigh to the truth, and knew it not! God alone
knew that in him the love of the good and of the true
had never ceased, and that, however dry and barren
might be the surface of his soul, there still remained,
far down, the dews of past grace—and the tears of
Monica. Almost to the last in what strange confusions
did not that great soul remain, reserved as it was for
a career so arduous and an expiation so noble from
the moment that peace of heart had fitted him for the

militant life of the Christian, that the darkness which paralyses strength had been chased, and that a divine light had "given the battle to his hands." His conversion came quickly at last. Yet the process had been slow. He had learned that the enemies of religion disputed chiefly with the creations of their own fancy; that their difficulties were but those found no less abundantly throughout the course of nature than in the lore supernatural; that *their* warfare was one against the heart of man, with all its hopes and its aspirations—all that can give security to joy and a meaning to pain. Yet still he wavered. Few things earthly helped more to his conversion than the philosophy of Plato; yet just before that conversion he seemed on the point of committing his life in despair to that of Epicurus. So strongly does man's pride contend against man's greatness; so perseveringly does his ingenuity evade his good! But the happy hour came, and the ages have found cause to rejoice. In becoming a Christian, St. Augustine became also a true Theist—that is, one who not only believes in God, but loves Him and adores; for love, like humility and faith, is learned at the foot of the Cross.

A SAINT[1]

THIS work, the first in a new series of Lives of the Saints, is as delightful as it is unpretending. Its great charm is that which it derives from the character of the Saint it records—a character which it illustrates with a skill shown frequently in wise and deep reflections, and everywhere in the felicity with which the most characteristic incidents of a career as beautiful as it was brief are selected and commemorated. That character suggests a few remarks, all of them connected with a single line of thought, and therefore by no means exhausting the subject, which tend to illustrate at least the Veneration of the Saints,—to illustrate only, as more is impossible without entering the thorny and commonly barren region of polemical controversy.

Sanctity is at once the simplest and the most "many-sided" of all things. The characters of the Apostles, even after Pentecost, remained distinct one

[1] *The Life of St. Aloysius Gonzaga.* Edited by E. H. Thompson. London : Burns and Oates.

from another—a proof in itself, as has been remarked, of the truthfulness which belongs to the chief source whence we derive our knowledge of them. From the corresponding distinctness in the character of different Saints, a similar inference may be drawn as to the authenticity of their "Lives." The gifts of grace are diverse, and in the supernatural order as in the natural we find the most distinctive types of characteristic excellence. Saint is, so to speak, supplemental to Saint; and from the harmonised dissimilitude of its several members, Religion becomes thoroughly equipped with all which it needs for ministration or example. It is true no less that among all Saints are to be found those great generic features which belong to the Household of Sanctity; and that from any one of them the main characteristics of holiness may be illustrated. But where resemblance exists, diversity sometimes teaches us to appreciate it the more; and from a life like that of St. Aloysius we learn many lessons that relate to both.

The author of this biography well remarks: "Perfection is set before all as the object of their aim, but not the same perfection;"[1] and an analogous statement is made in the preface: "Every man has his especial call; and the grace that accompanies it corresponds to the idea of him in the Divine Mind, as elected from all eternity to a certain conformity to the image of His Son—a purpose which the awful privilege of freewill enables the soul to ratify or

---

[1] P. 371.

to defeat."[1] The Saints are those who completely ratify that purpose: the consequence is that those elements of character which, in the case of ordinary Christians remain a confused mass, in their case clear both into distinctness and brightness. They have the diamond's sharpness and definiteness of outline, as well as its splendour. If the uninitiated does not see that distinctness, it is in part because his dazzled eye does not note the lineaments for the radiance which invests them, and partly because he does not take that interest in the subject which alone appreciates individuality. A man without an interest in nature hardly discriminates between tree and tree, while the shepherd's dog knows every sheep in the flock by face. To the man of the world, the lives of the Saints are all alike. For the man "whose eyes are open" they include an infinite variety. In variety, the marvels of natural history are probably small compared with those which belong to the supernatural.

The careless observer often sees distinctness in characters marked by some malformation which he identifies with individuality. Yet even he must see that to an eye which passes his own in discernment, individuality may be marked in a different way. It may be evidenced not through the ruling passion, but through the predominant virtue; not by some picturesque moral disproportion, but by some variety among types, all of which alike have perfection of proportion. The diversity among material forms, all of them

[1] P. viii.

imperfectly proportioned, is not greater than that which, in the vast range of ideal art, is reconciled with perfect proportion. The Saints of God are divine works of art: they are the living monuments of supernatural grace, wrought out, touch by touch and line by line, by that Sanctifying Spirit who is *Digitus Paternæ Dexteræ.* The "Lives" of the Saints constitute the gallery in which those monuments are stored.

Indifference to these triumphs of grace, a deadness which too often proceeds from an exaggerated interest in things devoid of all moral significance, entails even a greater loss than might have been expected. It is not only of *their* examples that we are deprived; but the Supreme Exemplar of perfection is thus also to a large degree hidden from us. The Saints of Christ are mirrors of Christ. In their manifold and derivative perfections, that perfection, one and infinite, which belongs but to the King of Saints is brought down to our poor intelligence, and revealed to us in parts. In the character of Christ all perfections are blended in that ineffable Sanctity which exists but in a human nature assumed by a Divine Person; in the Saints those perfections remain the attributes of beings exclusively human, though their human nature has been grafted into the Divine Humanity of Christ. In Christ we have the white light of Sanctity; in the Saints the coloured beam of this or that virtue, especially imparted to one in particular. In one it is charity, in another humility; in one it is devotion to the Will of God, in another the contemplation of His Being. In all it is Christ; and in proportion as the eye becomes purified by resting upon those manifold but inferior semblances of Christ, the knowledge of Him who unites all perfections becomes more defined, and sinks with a more vital beam into the devout soul. To imagine that the spiritual eye requires little training, or that the Spirit Who alone gives it "discernment," employs no subordinate instrumentalities for that end, would be a grave error. The mere human eye is trained by degrees; and the scientific eye is assisted by numberless instrumentalities which no serious student would discard. The Saints are lenses that accommodate to dim eyes the vision of a virtue higher than such can see. What we know of the Saints we know through a familiarity with the details of their lives. Each is a being in himself; and to make each what he is has required the whole world of God's Providence, and the whole world of His Grace. In no two of them do the virtues that bear the same names in mortal tongue imply altogether the same thing. In one, faith specially implies courage; in another insight; in one love specially implies zeal, in another patience. The relations of these virtues one to another, their progression, their combinations, their modes of joint or separate working —in all these things there is at once an infinite variety and an absolute order. Amid the manifold and the inexplicable there are traces of a mystic unity: and again and again throughout that spiritual universe which they constitute we come upon the same foot-prints of the one Creator. It is as among the Alps, where the Infinite seems to look forth from the finite with aspect at once elevating and overawing,—where the mountain lines—diverging or converging—now shooting past each other, now bearing far away in long oblique angle, and pointing toward measureless distance —seem to reveal, or at least to announce, some dread mathesis that belongs to a vaster world than ours—a world which to our narrow intelligence appears less a world than a chaos, yet where, amid the labyrinth of marble ravine and glacier-river, Nature indicates a method which she will not wholly disclose. Without an initiatory knowledge of Christ we have no key to the character of His Saints; but on the other hand, without a detailed knowledge of them and their ways, our knowledge of their Lord is but stunted.

In this last particular Christian philosophy might have anticipated the lesson which Christian history records. If the Saints are fragmentary images of that illimitable perfection expressed in the Divine Human-ity, so "the Word made Flesh" is Himself to us a picture of Him whom no eye can see. We know Him dimly in Attributes which amid their vastness seem to us opposed to each other, and which to our littleness present no *definite* image. The lines of that incommunicable Countenance change before us like lightning; and voices which mortal ear may not harmonise — the inorganic sound of some infinite universe, infinitely remote—seem to lie beyond all such music as we can grasp and mete. In the Creator become a Creature the formless submits to form. Man had always felt that justice was a divine attribute, and that love was a divine attribute; but how to envisage the two in union he knew not. Their union is to our finite apprehension shadowed forth in Him who denounced eternal woe against impenitent sin, and yet wept over one whom He was about to raise from the dead. In God there is an Infinite Wisdom and an Infinite Power, both of which might seem to suffer contradiction while sin and sorrow riot amid the world He has made. In the Saviour who "opened not his mouth," and suffered because He willed to suffer, we have an image of this dread long-suffering of God. In Christ, who knew all things, and yet, "grew in wisdom and in stature," we have an image of the Unbeholden One, who abides in endless rest, and yet is an Energy and an Act perpetually creating the universe. Between the mode in which Christ images the Father to us and that in which His Saints image Christ, there are analogies. In Christ are made visible not only those attributes which belong to His Father, but others also which could not belong to Divinity except in hypostatic union with humanity; so in the Saints who share, and as it were dilate, their Lord's glorified humanity, we find not only the traits of that humanity, but others beside which He could not possess Who did not share man's fall—penitence, for instance. Again, as without a belief in God it would be impossible for us to recognise His image in "God made man," so without a knowledge of Christ, our great example, it would be impossible to profit by the examples He gives us in His images, the Saints. Once more, as they who from pride and hardness of heart renounce Christ, thereby cut themselves off from the Father, to whom He is the appointed "Way," and thus lose hold at once of a living Theism, and of that Christianity which for us is the only authentic and practical Theism, so those who willingly reject all serious thought of His Saints to a calamitous degree make dim the mirrors in which they ought to see that Incarnate God, in part distorting the idea of His character, in part divesting it of reality.

The diversity of character observable in the Saints results, not merely from the diversity of supernatural gifts, but also from those differences in natural constitution which grace always respects while it directs and harmonises them. That region of human life which perhaps most attracts the thoughtful eye is the horizon line where the natural and the supernatural meet, and where the colouring from above allows itself to be modified by the configuration of its earthly support. In biographies taken, like the one before us, from authentic records, we ever see the man in the Saint, and learn in part how the time, place, and circumstances of his outward life co-operated with that interior grace which shaped him to a definite type of perfection. Some of the traits special to St. Aloysius result from his having belonged to the still surviving feudalism of North Italy at the close of the sixteenth century. We must bear in mind that though he died young, he did not die immaturely. He was a Saint; and therefore all the processes which form character had in him been perfected, though with an extraordinary rapidity.

The foundations of his character seem to have been laid in the intensity which belonged to his realisation of divine things, a gift conspicuous in him when he was yet but a child. "His head lady-nurse, Camilla Maynardi, often told her mistress that when she took the little Prince Aluigi in her arms, she experienced a thrill of devotion."[1] Much must also be attributed to the natural influence on a being of lofty and delicate dispositions of a mother whose earliest desire for him was that he should be a Saint, and who had taught him to lisp the names of Jesus and Mary before those of Father and Mother. Other children learn of heavenly things from earthly. The children of saintly parents begin with the higher, and interpret the lower by them. That lofty, *a priori* estimate of things which is sometimes learned as a branch of the Platonic philosophy by one whose moral habits have already grown hard, and whose lower instincts have perhaps developed themselves according to the maxims of Epicurus, becomes under happier circumstances the living law of a being still plastic and fresh—of one in whom the passions have not yet been awakened,

[1] P. 11.

and in whom experience, far from checking the spiritual aspirations, is contented to walk humbly in their footsteps up the hills of truth. We marvel that some few Christian children should thus start clear, and hold their own. Had we lived when the Gospel first brought to men the tidings of a regenerate humanity, should we not rather have expected that such would have been the usual franchise of the Christian child? There are consequences of grace which may be called natural in the supernatural order. Ordinary persons realise earthly things intensely; while, as a consequence, spiritual things remain un-realised by them, and, though acknowledged as truths, hang in visionary distance like a far cloud on the horizon of their thought. In both respects the converse held good with St. Aloysius. In his daily walks he observed hardly any of the objects which he passed. He took no hold of worldly things, nor they of him; and even when the love of them seemed to have been sown in his youthful heart, it turned out that the seed had fallen "on stony places," and the springing plant withered of itself. A few years after the Turkish naval power had been broken at the great battle of Lepanto, the father of the Saint went in command of 3000 Milanese to defend Tunis, which then belonged to Spain, against the Sultan Selim II. He took his little son with him; and the child was delighted with the military movements, and of course became the delight of the rough soldiers. But strong as was the aptitude he showed for all manly exercises, their attraction faded away, just as the religious impressions of early childhood so often fade away. In all things a law of compensation prevails. Had the future Saint been alike devoted to earthly glory and to the praise of God, it would have been much more wonderful than that he should have valued the latter exclusively.[1]

It is the more remarkable that many should find it difficult to believe in the spiritual gifts which have belonged to Saints, even in childhood, considering the animation with which they record the gifts of another sort often found in the world's favourites. Mozart had so fine an ear that when a child he could detect in every chance sound some latent musical note, and wept if his ear was hurt by the slightest discord. Is not this as wonderful as the spiritual sensibility of St. Aloysius of whom we read,[2] "The first time he presented himself at the tribunal of penance, he was so overcome with reverence, shame, and confusion, that he fainted at the good father's feet." Before Pascal had heard of Euclid he had proposed to himself multitudes of mathematical problems, drawing diagrams on the wall and inventing names of his own for angles and curves. Why should one who believes in some child who can multiply nine figures by nine in his head, or play a game of chess without seeing the board, be staggered when told of a corresponding power

---

[1] A most amusing account of the child-warrior's exploits in his brief campaign, one of which nearly cost him his life, is given in p. 15.

[2] P. 25.

of abstractedness in a youthful Aloysius who prayed for half a day without wanderings of thought? The Saints are in religion what men of extraordinary genius or energy are in the world. At seven years old St. Aloysius refused to use a cushion when kneeling. Some of his austerities were such as to a child must have been needless as a protection against temptation. The smile with which a wise man reads of such fancied dangers has nothing in it either of the sceptical or the scornful.

What we call "genius" has its extravagances and its eccentricities, and is far from running at a regular pace in the harness of conventionalities. It too has much that is worthy rather of admiration than imitation, and much that without demanding either, is the natural result of extraordinary aspirations under peculiar conditions. Perfect regularity and proportion should be looked for only in a Saint perfected—that is a Saint in heaven. It is incompatible with our militant condition. Bacon remarks that when the child's limbs knit quickly, and include no disproportion, it is a sign that he will reach no considerable growth. The Saints are those who have had large spiritual growth in them. We should remember, too, that there is a lower, as well as a higher proportionateness, and that some persons attain it, not by making their nature wholly spiritual, but by eliminating all but what is animal in it. To unite Body and Soul—a regenerate with an earthly life—a mortal lot with an immortal destiny—this is man's condition, and it is certainly to blend very antagonistic forces. Taking all things into account, merely to be born is, it must be owned, to "get into a great scrape," and by no means leads to an easy peace. Much more difficult must it be, then, to make a good thing of our contradictory life, and avoid worse charges than that of eccentricity. The "strangeness" the world complains of in the Saints is but what might have been complained of in ordinary human beings by the merry Wood-Gods and Satyrs that glanced at them from the forest nooks, and re-joiced that they had not themselves to sustain the burthen of a responsible being!

We should bear in mind also that much which to us seems unreasonable in a Saint was probably to him a special inspiration guarding him against some special danger. He who makes His ministers "flames of fire" commonly gives to His Saints a peculiar ardour of nature—an ardour which might have worked itself out either in the sphere of their intellectual or their material being, and which makes them Saints only on condition of its being limited, directed, and forced to develop itself chiefly in the spiritual being. Such are the gifts of Him who gave to men the true Celestial Fire—

> And He tamed fire which, like some beast of prey,
> Most terrible but lovely, played beneath
> The frown of man.[1]

Respectable people sometimes descant on the temptations of the Saints, and affirm that no such trials

[1] *Prometheus Unbound* (Shelley).

assail them.   Perhaps the reason is that they are respectable people but not Saints, and that they are spared what they could not resist.   Perhaps it is that the Tempter deems pettier temptations more suited to their mediocrity—is contented with their self-content —and does not wish to wake them out of their dream of security.   Sometimes they fancy that they meet no temptations because they never resist those temptations, —as the flying leaf does not feel the gale that splinters the tree.   It is certain that the Saints have been marked by a timidity, as the world would call it, as wonderful as their courage, and have guarded the outward senses far more than those who have, compared with them, no inward power of resistance.   Theirs is the timidity that springs from that humility on which alone can be built the virtue which attains a great elevation.   The Saint has no belief whatever in his own strength ; and that Divine Strength which lives within him is a gift which, as he knows, may easily be subverted through a single movement of pride.

Excess in things lawful is to ordinary men often a greater temptation than they are exposed to from things unlawful : by parity of reasoning we see how slight participation in things lawful, but yet incongruous with a higher vocation, may be a snare to the future Saint.   Aloysius was constantly renouncing even what was innocent in human ties : such renunciation might have been dangerous to others, but it gave to him that perfect detachment without which he could never have reached his marvellous gift of prayer.   This is well

illustrated in some of the many thoughtful passages
with which the Saint's life is here recorded. "Solicitude
and desire—these are the great foes of all prayer;
but much more of contemplation. It may be possible
to repeat vocal prayers with a certain degree of attention
where they are not entirely banished; but with prayer
of a higher order they are simply incompatible." [1] . . .
"Here was the secret of all. His lifelong study
had been to pray much, to pray well, to pray
always; and so convinced was he that prayer is the
great lever in spiritual things, that he used to say that
it was wellnigh impossible for any but a man of
prayer and recollection to acquire full dominion over
himself."

This wonderful confidence in prayer, so invariable
an attribute of the Saints, is the natural consequence
of their realising the supernatural world. Prayer is
that which, moving Him Who is omnipotent, has a
derived omnipotence of its own; while it is also the
only earthly power that is not in part illusory. If,
then, those who realise the supernatural world give
themselves for half their time to prayer, like the members of Contemplative Orders, they are but doing,
mutatis mutandis, what the wise worldling does in
his way. He too shuns much that, measured by a
purely worldly and materialistic standard, might fairly
claim to be innocent though not laudable. He passes,
perhaps, not half his time, but the greater part of it,
in applying means to ends, that is, in using those instru-

---

[1] P. 175.

mentalities which are to the natural world what prayer is to the supernatural. The social and the material worlds have, he knows, their laws ; to move them he must put those laws in motion ; and to do this he must conform himself to those laws. He subjects himself therefore loyally to Nature ; and his reward is this, that he gains from Nature a genuine insight into her ways, and such control over them as she gladly bestows on *her* ascetics. This is what is done by the Saint in the supernatural sphere. Prayers, and all those ministrations, in heaven and on earth, which are connected with prayer—these constitute the Living Laws by which the spiritual world is swayed ; and to these he trusts as the engineer trusts to those laws which, at his bidding, call the sea-mole from the mountain quarry, or fling the bridge across the strait. The distance to which the modern intelligence is falling from faith is by nothing more marked than by the narrower limits within which its appreciation of prayer daily shrinks. It began by inveighing against those who prayed constantly, stigmatising the highest spiritual Action as idleness. It now attaches hardly any other efficacy to prayer than that which results from a reaction of the mind on itself. A man who prays can, it admits, warm himself by that exercise ; but he had better not include outward things in his prayer. A prayer really answered it does not believe in. It can excuse much that it cannot accept, and can play with the graceful shadows of devotion when it would be offended by the repulsive hardness of the substance. It revolts from

St. Aloysius's belief in prayer, while it thinks it is only scandalised by his miracles. It says that prayer should be not so much a special act as a general habit of mind ; one of those plausible statements which are true at their affirmative side, but untrue at the negative. From the lives of the Saints we learn that the habit is most constant where the act is most intense. We read of St. Aloysius, "During the ordinary occupations of the day his soul was visited by God with marvellous consolations, and these not passing touches or short elevations of spirit, but overflowing torrents of joy." [1] His humblest duties were consecrated by being discharged in the spirit of prayer, a grace which was rendered easier to him by the habit of seeing in everything a symbol of higher things than itself. "When engaged in preparing for the repast he would say, ' Let us go and lay the cloth for our Lord, or for the Madonna.' " [2]

The root of St. Aloysius's sanctity is to be found in his humility. "I am a crooked piece of iron, and am come into religion to be made straight by the hammer of mortification and penance "—such was his estimate of himself. While studying at the Roman College, he hardly ventured to lift his eyes when conversing even with the lay-brothers and seculars in authority. A more beautiful picture of youthful modesty can hardly be imagined than that which we owe to the graphic touch of his latest biographer. The youthful Prince "Would wander into the country through the

[1] P. 178. [2] P. 246.

Porta Comasina, always selecting Thursday for this stroll ; and, after bidding his attendants remain behind, he might have been seen loitering on the way, now reading, now picking violets, as though to while away the time, like one who is watching and waiting for some expected meeting. By and by in the distance might be descried the black figures of the Fathers approaching. They were returning from Chisolfa, a villa which they possessed about a mile and a half from the town, and where every week they spent some hours of recreation on that day. Lewis would now stand close to their path : he had watched for the joy of that moment to salute them courteously and reverentially as they passed : he would then follow softly on their steps, leaving such discreet interval as should remove him from their company, but keeping his eyes intently fixed on their retreating forms, as if he beheld so many blessed angels defiling from the gates of Paradise." [1] If St. Gertrude conversed with our Lord habitually in the elevations of vision and rapture, so to St. Aloysius the closest union with Him would seem to have been accorded in the lowliest acts of obedience. In this supernatural grace we may trace, perhaps, the workings of a natural law also. Those who know best how to rule, know best also how to obey : and Aloysius, to whom princely sway was a birthright, seems, when he had renounced it, to have been drawn by a special instinct to the converse yet analogous duties which belong to obedience. "He would often beg permission

---

[1] P. 107.

to go about Rome in a tattered habit, with a bag on his shoulder, to solicit alms."[1]

To the same class of virtues we should, doubtless, refer the Saint's unappeasable love of mortifications, whether physical or mental. The sensitiveness of his nature made him shrink when publicly reproved; and therefore "He earnestly and frequently begged to be reprehended before all. This pain, moreover, was entirely voluntary on his part;—owing to the complete mastery which he possessed over his imagination, he might with the utmost facility have distracted his mind from what was going on, so that, hearing, he would have been as one that did not hear; but this he would have considered as defrauding holy obedience of its claims, and himself of its merits; he compelled himself, therefore, to taste as well as drink the cup presented to him."[2]

The tenderness and refinement which belonged to St. Aloysius, whether they resulted from an organisation of unusually delicate fibre, or from the habits of a palace, assumed, like all his qualities, a spiritual character. The pain he felt at any allusion to the worldly greatness he had relinquished showed itself in the blush which displaced the habitual pallor of his face. If any one spoke with feeling of divine mysteries, his colour went and came, his breath became short, and his slight frame was shaken so vehemently by the palpitation of his heart that his superiors sometimes interdicted or limited his devotions. The boy was shy and shrinking

1 P. 163.   2 P. 166.

as a girl; yet he selected the most afflicted in the
hospital as the special objects of his care. He shrank
back in humiliation when an aged ecclesiastic demanded his blessing; yet his lowliness never degenerated into weakness. The instrument was more perfect
because the wood of which it was made had a delicate
grain; but it yielded martial as well as solemn
harmonies—although its "songs of war" were those
that "sound like songs of love." He had the pro-
foundest sense of filial duty; yet year after year he
bore up with humble heroism against his father's
opposition to his vocation. He saved at a crisis of
danger the brother who had owed him a throne; yet
on entering his novitiate, he left "The home and the
friends of his youth without shedding a tear, and
scarcely addressed three words to that brother during
the last brief hours which possibly they were ever to
spend together." Most men are so drawn to self that,
if a few are but moderately true to the *natural* objects
of human affections, the world counts such fidelity to
them as a religious merit. To him the natural ties
were so "full of light" that they became transparent,
and revealed those heavenly relations of which earthly
ties are the types. The aspirations of others had
become his sympathies. His gravitation was upward;
and, as the author of this biography forcibly expresses
it, his soul tended to God "as the falling stone seeks
the earth."[1]

The most sensitive natures are sometimes driven

[1] P. 179.

by a noble necessity upon the most absolute self-mastery, and therefore on the most intense repose. It was so with St. Aloysius. When asked whether he did not pine for those he had left, he answered that "He never recollected them save when he recommended them to God," adding that "By God's grace he was so entirely master over his thoughts that he never reflected upon anything but what he desired."[1] For him, though not for others, it was needful to reach this state or to abandon contemplation. The author well remarks, "Just as an image is broken into fragments when the breeze passes over the surface of the stream, so it is with the soul when any earthly solicitude or desire sweeps over it while it is striving to receive the image of God into its placid depths."[2] It is true no less that, as water which a breath can ruffle yields us, in its stillness, a more vivid image of tranquillity than the solid earth beside it, so the serenity reached by a nature as sensitive as that of St. Aloysius affords to us the most perfect image of peace. To this interior stillness was doubtless owing, not only the Saint's power of contemplating God, but another gift—viz. the power of looking through his own being as if it were that of another. "When by a close scrutiny he had satisfied his mind, so as to enable him to make a true confession, *he gave himself no further anxiety;* for, like St. Teresa, he confessed that his garden naturally produced only briars and thorns. 'Forgive me, Lord,' he would say, 'and

[1] P. 155.   [2] P. 176

grant me grace not to do so again:' after which he was perfectly tranquil, and made his confession briefly, clearly, unembarrassed by a shade of scrupulosity."[1]

The absence of agitation and scrupulosity is not wonderful, where it results from the absence of self-knowledge, and from a forgetfulness of the Divine Justice. It is where the spiritual being has reached a lofty stature that this serenity is as wonderful as if the tall tree stood unshaken in the storm. Such a condition would be impossible, doubtless, but for the special aids afforded by Confession, which alone render habitual self-knowledge compatible with the absence of morbidness. Where self-knowledge rejects in pride the aids which Religion has thus provided for it, unhealthy feelings attach themselves to it so closely that modern philosophy, advancing a step farther on the downward way, recommends as a remedy what it calls self-forgetfulness, meaning thereby self-ignorance and indifference to the soul's health. But neither this life nor the next accepts the burning of the bill as the payment of the debt.

Among the characteristics of the Saints is that mysterious influence which they diffuse around them unconsciously, like a spiritual magnetism. As soon as St. Aloysius had entered on his novitiate at Rome all around him began to be the better for it.

Few weeks had passed before a palpable change came over the Roman College. The flame of divine love seemed to dart

---

[1] P. 163.

from one bosom to another, and even the coldest felt its warmth, and began to kindle like the rest ; so that Cepari himself, the witness of what he describes, when in summer time he contemplated 200 students scattered through the garden in parties of three and four at the recreation hour, could feel well assured, from his knowledge of all, that there was but one subject of discourse among them, as they sat or wandered at will, like so many angels communing together amongst the trees of Paradise.[1]

Nor was his influence confined to his equals ; it was felt no less by his superiors.   In a discourse, delivered in 1608, Bellarmine spoke thus—

When I gave the spiritual exercises of St. Ignatius to Aluigi, I discovered in him such abundance of divine light, that I must confess that, at my advanced age, I learned from this youth how to meditate.[2]

It is not strange that, as his biographer relates—

When raised to the Cardinalate, the venerable prelate not only continued his yearly practice of repairing to the College Church of the Company to venerate the tomb of Aloysius on his anniversary, but used to make a devout visit to the room whence he had taken his flight to Heaven, and there would shed tears of tenderness in memory of their last parting.

A polemical age loses, in dealing with this question, many advantages which an age truly philosophical would possess.   Catholic controversialists have by necessity been thrown so much upon answers to negations relative to the veneration of the Saints that they have not always been able to insist as strongly as they might otherwise have done on the great philosophical principles and moral ideas involved in such veneration, and the practical loss incurred by communities deprived of it.   What the Catholic believes is, of course,

---

[1] P. 208.   [2] P. 305.

not merely that the practice is no remnant of Pagan idolatry, but that it is the Christian's especial preservation against the unconscious revival of that idolatry either in the form of nature-worship, of hero-worship, or of self-worship.   He believes also that not to venerate the Saints is to cut off many channels of communication between the humbler part of Christ's kingdom and its nobler part.   It is to forsake our spiritual Highlands, as men decried the English mountains during the last century.

It is when we study the lives of the Saints that we regard this vast subject, as it were *from within,* and see how closely it bears on our Sanctification.   Children learn to speak mainly through sympathy and imitation, and they exercise those instincts because they associate frankly with those who know how to speak.   The earlier instincts both of honour and of conscience are developed under similar conditions, and are often therefore not formed, or most imperfectly formed, in the hearts of castaways brought up among the courts and alleys of great cities.   Among these last, even when removed at a later time to healthier spots, the higher instincts sometimes will not grow, because, again and again, some rude shock used to break the finer tendrils of their roots just when they were beginning to knit themselves in the soil.   Habitudes are not to be formed out of maxims; and long before the passions of the child have begun to prove a temptation to him his moral sense may have become irrevocably stultified because he has lived among those who regard right and wrong indifferently. At a later period he may receive moral, as he receives intellectual instruction; but it is communicated to him after a barren fashion, as when we teach mathematics to a child in whom the scientific faculty is not yet developed, and who has to measure the diagram with a pair of compasses before he perceives whether the sides and angles are equal. Now the same danger which all recognise as regards our moral training, assails also our spiritual being; and our protection against it is of a corresponding sort. In spiritual matters those who belong to the Church Militant are but children; and like other children they are intended to learn from their elders and betters—that is to say, from the citizens of the Church Triumphant. The two portions of the one great city are not separated, save by the "barricades" of an "emeute." A portion of it sits on the hills amid the purer airs and the brighter lights; and another portion of it—the dark and narrow *Ghetto* within which we live while on earth—occupies the lower region; but there exists a divinely-appointed order of ministrations between the two. The inhabitants of the lower region communicate with those in the higher, and the children borrow insensibly from the elders. It is through the habits developed in that heavenly yet familiar intercourse that they learn to lisp the living language of Sanctity which those amerced of such aids learn as a dead tongue. The supernatural standard of Christian perfection is sustained before their eyes in steadfast elevation; and they believe in it, both as a thing divine and as a thing practicable. Others often have standards though imposing yet far below the Christian ideal; but for them that supernatural ideal is ever the chief of Realities, and lives on both in their heart and their hope. They approach it, though on earth they may not reach it; and their shortcomings deepen their humility.

The blindness of a presumptuous mind on such subjects is "night immersed in night"—the darkness of the natural man, wrapped around by a second cloud of inherited prejudice. A traveller drives into an Italian or Spanish village, bright with flowers, and banners, and lights, and resounding with music. The processions wind along the heights—the fireworks blaze in the market-place, and round the cathedral the crowds swell and surge. In the scene there is much that is ennobling, and something that is quaint. The enlightened "man of culture" can see but the latter when he learns that all this popular enthusiasm is the celebration of the Patron Saint's Festa. He can appreciate the greatness of some statesman whose speech he has lately heard, or some warrior whose anniversary feast he has attended. But the villagers whom he despises have retained a knowledge worth more than all that he knows. Their minds too are haunted by the idea of greatness; but they have never forgotten that primary truth without which the imagination can but pour forth for us the *Vinum Demonum*—the lesson that the truest *Greatness* is *Goodness*. Their Saint is their hero, because he was pre-eminently good; and he was pre-eminently good, not because he fought hard for the world's esteem, but because he sought the lowest place. They are proud of their Saint; and in praising him they praise God, whose praise alone he desired to set forth. He brought them the Faith, perhaps 1500 years ago, and they still rejoice as if a siege had been raised, and their city delivered from destruction, an hour before! Time and its centuries have not made them forget their benefactor; the world with its illusions has not taught them to prefer false glory to true. What discernment, what fidelity, what generosity, what an exalted and authentic standard of all that man should venerate and imitate! To what do the peasants owe these gifts? To the circumstance that they have remained "on speaking terms" with God's Saints! The world, in ceasing to have a loving zeal for these, falls to a distance from them,—a distance that tends ever to increase. First, men cease to aspire after heroic sanctity; next they cease to believe in it; at last the very idea of it departs from their mind, as some ideal of poetry or architecture gradually vanishes from the world. The imagination of society renounces its baptism, and becomes "reconverted to the world."

There can here be no neutral position. The saintly ideal was that which expelled the Pagan ideal native to man's heart—that ideal in which sense and pride combined to dress out the beautiful. Nothing could have effected this miracle but a frank and fearless Christianity—a Christianity which conquers an animalised

by a spiritualised humanity. Pentecost was a beam
from that celestial light which ever lives beyond
the *flammantia mœnia* of mortal life ; and as the sunshine puts out the fire, so this beam from afar extinguished the flame that played on the Pagan hearth.
Among the sects, and in the world, the Pagan
imagination repossesses itself of its abandoned seat.
This is proved by the fact that to the diseased modern
intelligence the Saints wear the aspect of demi-gods,
and the veneration of them seems a new mythology,
though one to them unwelcome.   It is strange !   A
Newton can see the analogy between diamond and a
bit of black charcoal ; but prejudice is unable to see
a difference between gold and any worthless bauble
that glitters.   Equally incompetent seems a paganised
intelligence to discriminate between Christian Saints
and Pagan Gods.   No wonder that others should
advance a step farther, and reject Christ, on account of
some fancied resemblance to Budha.   And yet the
Christian and the Pagan ideals are not only unlike, but
are opposites, and that whether we regard Christ or His
Saints.   History bears witness to this truth.   It was
not till the latest remembrances and desires of Paganism had been " with sighing sent " from their old
homes, that their abandoned shrines in the human
heart had been once more lustrated and made pure,
and that, by the reiterated definitions of councils, the
doctrines of the Trinity and the Incarnation had
ascended to unquestioned thrones in the zenith of
theological science,—it was not till then that the vener-

ation of Christ's Saints became fully developed. At an earlier period it might have been dangerous, or at least misunderstood. Had the Saints but embodied a new sort of mystified mythology, then, as the reverence for these false Gods advanced, that paid to Christ, *as God*, must have receded. Christ would Himself have been regarded only as one of the Saints,—nay, in time all prayers to Him might have been condemned as idolatrous, or condoned as but pious ejaculations.

All who claim the name of Christians would feel insulted by a laboured argument to show that the Character revealed to us in our Divine Lord, if the term may be used, so far from resembling the Pagan ideal of a divinity, is the opposite of it, whether we regard its measureless height of sanctity, or that abysmal humility and love of suffering which marked its condescension. How come they not to see that the character expressed in His Saints is no less the opposite of the Pagan ideal? To be godly, and to affect the Godlike—these are plainly opposite things. The former is to kneel always; the latter is a perpetual strut. To assert *inherent* might in every movement—

Neither to change, nor flatter, nor repent,[1]

was the differentia of an ideal cast in the imagination of pride. To have undergone the greatest of all changes, putting off the old man in regeneration ; to live a life that had renounced Self, the false centre, and

[1] Shelley.

which was an eternal adoration of Him Who is the true
centre; to repent of every act, or thought, or idle
moment, which wilfully warred against, or suspended,
that perpetual adoration for which the created spirit
was formed—this was to be the Saint. Rhetoric,
always dangerous, is fatal in theology.

Let us look farther into this. It was Christianity,
we must remember, which not only brought to man
the doctrine of the Incarnation, but brought back to
him with it that of a Creation. These are the truths
that slay idolatry. Lost in its pantheistic dream,
Paganism did not know that the world was created;
and for this reason every instinct of adoration or of
wonder pushed it upon a sensuous idolatry. Nature
had indeed lost its true elevation, which belongs to it
only as the work and the expression of the one all-holy
and infinite God; but even this very loss imparted to
it a counter wonderfulness of its own, and taught it to
wear the mask of a something divine in which holiness
claimed no place. The next stage was that in which
pantheism became mythology. The mere material
image of the Infinite fatigues and overpowers—this
image soon broke itself up into fragments, which
assumed a separate vitality; and from clear wave and
shadowy bough, divinities—at heart but nature still—
looked forth in the form of Nereid or Dryad. It was
a worship without awe; a poetry that had substituted
itself for religion, and taken its name; one that gave a
luminous projection to man's thoughts, and preserved
the relics of precious truths lost; but one that glorified

no less low passions and base appetites. It was a poetry which ever "gilt that whereon it gazed," but which, whilst it exulted in admiration for all things, could never rise even to the idea of a true adoration, because the supernatural, which is the object of adoration, cannot exist where the thought of a Personal God abides no more. But man, though deluded by a false religion, was not satisfied by it. The God whom conscience demanded was something more than the easy divinities whom Fancy had decorated with her wreaths; and a Parnassus, the radiant beauty of which was but the mellowed and painless reflex of man, and man's life, left man—the self-worshipper—to pine away with the fate of Narcissus. Nature herself made confession that she was both more and less than her worshippers had supposed, and hinted that the gulf between the sphere of finite things and an infinite Creator could not always remain impassable. Man cherished a "fearful hope" that behind the veil of the sense there remained divine realities. These realities at last came to him through a religion that addresses the spirit of man, not the sense, and which addresses it, not through the pride of the imagination, but through Faith. Christ was "the Desire of the Nations" —not the least significant of His titles. In all those legends which typified an Incarnation, and pre-eminently in the Rite of Sacrifice, even the Pagan religions had preserved a memory of the primal prophecy. It had beheld the "Woman" and the "Seed" who was to bruise the head of the serpent.

After the "Desire of the Nations" had come, —when "the Word was made flesh and dwelt among us,"—that thirst which had created idolatry, tormented the human race no more. The World, not the sensualised imagination, became then the chief snare. It was then announced to us that "covetousness is idolatry,"—nay, that those who prefer human to heavenly ties are idolators; and warning was given of an age in which human ties, thus illicitly exalted, should be as ungratefully dishonoured,—one in which each man should worship his own self, installing that idol above both natural and supernatural objects of love. It is the "arch-mock" of the old Spirit of Delusion, when he persuades a world which for eighteen centuries has been lifted up to a plane of higher lights and of darker shades,—of richer graces and of more insidious temptations,—to arm its vigilance against those snares which beset its infancy, and to ignore those which ensnare its maturity and corrupt its decline.

For man's Heart as well as man's Imagination the coming of Him, the "Desire of the Nations" appeased that craving which had led to idolatry, because it awakened that Heart's deepest sympathies. The God-Man had died for man; and the Crucifix was incomparably more often looked upon than the fairest picture of the Babe on His mother's knee. The infinite had entered within bounds; but at the moment of the Annunciation, He who is life itself had subjected Himself to death. All that followed, from the crib to the Cross, and from Calvary to the

Ascension, was included as in a germ in this divine act of obedience to the Father's Will. In the character of Christ is pictured forth the unseen Father; and that character means the infinitude of elevation in the infinitude of condescension. If in the Saints we see the image of Christ, the likeness consists mainly in a measureless humility tending to a measureless elevation. If the obedience of Christ cannot become the object of our thought except when we grasp also the thought of that Father to Whom He was obedient; so the humility of the Saints can find no access to our mind without the correlative thought of Him in Whom alone His members have their being, Whose merits alone give them merit, and in Whose grace alone they are strong. Saints are, of all men, those who have least of the demi-god about them. We may forget the *dependence* of an ordinary man; but that of a Saint is the essence of his character. In other words, the Saint, in place of resembling the Pagan conception of a God, is a living protest against it.

Let us look at this more nearly. In proportion as the idea of God, the "Creator of heaven and earth," stands distinctly before us, we must needs see with a growing clearness that all creaturely perfection consists in dependence, not in a Godlike and self-asserting might. In recent times, wherever Pantheism has been superseding a belief in a creative God, the Pagan ideal of human character has been reasserting itself; and what has the consequence been?—an

avowed and boastful Hero-worship! Men who
refused to yield "honour where honour is due," and
to reverence God's Saints, have expiated their
irreverence by becoming "a servant of servants"—by
rendering a servile adulation to those false Gods of
this world who perhaps in their day had themselves
been the most servile to human opinion. The
doctrine of a Creation is included in Theism, and as
such it was revealed to the Patriarchal Church,
though for us it hardly exists except in connection
with Christianity, in which it is re-revealed. To a
true Theist, God is the Living One, the Personal, the
All-Holy: to believe in Him means to worship Him;
and the only relation which even the imagination can
attribute to the creature in connection with his
Creator is that of a kneeling adoration. Suns and
systems are but as transient motes that sparkle in his
beam. The creature lives but in proportion as he is
united with that Creator: that union can only exist
as the union of dependence; and the closer it is, the
less can the creature claim anything of a separate
light. As the rainbow hangs suspended on the
luminous mist, so that glory of His Saints which
evermore surrounds the King of Saints rests evermore
upon the bosom and breath of His glory. Not only
it cannot exist, but it cannot be conceived of, except
as the reflection of that glory inherent, after His
resurrection, in the triumphant Humanity of Him
who has given to those who serve Him that they
should sit with Him "in His throne judging the

twelve tribes of Israel." How can the nature of such a greatness be misapprehended? Is there a peasant who does not know that what the Saints are, they are through their extraordinary gifts of *grace*, and through their submission to grace? Now grace obviously means dependence; he who possesses it most is but the most conspicuous sign that points to Him from whom it comes.

The humility of the Saint is not merely, like that of the ordinary Christian—a deep sense of his own sins or shortcomings,—it is the intense appreciation of the essential *nothingness* which belongs to the creature, as such. For this reason it increases as sinfulness diminishes and sanctity advances. "I am that which is," our Lord said to a Saint in vision, "and thou art that which seemeth to be." If this, the highest form of Humility, were not their protection, the most advanced Saints might at once be subverted by that pride which smites most, like lightning, the loftiest summits; and their fall would be, like that of the Apostate angels, the sin of a moment and a sin of thought. Their sense of nothingness comes from that piercing insight with which they contemplate God's greatness, in comparison with which all created things are infinitesimal —His Absolute Being, in comparison with which all finite things are but relative—and His everlasting might, in comparison with which the forces of creation are but things seeming, except so far as they are instrumentalities put into motion by His Divine

Energy.   But as God's Providence always co-operates
with His Grace, that sense of their own nothingness
is for the most part externally guarded by the humiliations, afflictions, or temptations which are sent or
permitted to the Saints that their purification may be
the more rapid, and no less by the obscurity which
commonly enshrouds them while on earth.

THE HUMAN AFFECTIONS IN THE EARLY CHRISTIAN TIME; Or

THE EREMITE AMBROSIUS HIS EPISTLE UNTO MARCELLA, A.D. 410

KNEW I not, O Virgin, or ever thy messenger had arrived, how it fared with thee? For nine years (which is thy life half-told) thy feet failed not, following the precept of thy Mother, to climb, well-nigh daily, these crags. Now and again hath the sunrise greeted me first from thy white garment. When thou camest not, I said, "One from the valley hath found her, and detained her in the path of flowers." The snows also on yonder ridge, burn they not twice in the day with celestial roses? O roses of earth, on you, too, descend the dews of heaven! To you also hath God given a breath of sweetness; and in the yearly renewing of your beauty Time pleaseth himself with an image of Eternity. In your fruitful bosoms Immortality is quickened—but not the Rest of Immortality.

Thy letter is spread before me on the rock, and in it thou desirest of me the continuance of my prayers, and ghostly counsel how thou, a maid and a child, shalt walk well and trip not in the novel regions of womanhood and terrestrial life: and " Is this lower ?" thou inquirest.   And again, thou demandest, as in an afterthought, is it superstition to give ear unto thy old nurse, now blind, when she prattleth of a certain flower, which, being gathered before sunrise, hath virtue to preserve unto a woman the love of her husband for ever?   " For ah," thou sayest, " how many women were loved well that are not loved !   Is this a punishment because they loved earth, or a discipline to raise their hearts unto heaven?   Or is it the seasonable work of Nature, despoiling them, before she lulleth them asleep, of things most precious, even as she despoileth them of youth and the wingéd step, and the magic of winning grace ?"

For my prayers, thou hast not mine only, but the prayers of all to whom piety and innocence are dear, and the youthful aspiration which, even if it lengtheneth its way, misseth not its goal.   " Is this lower?" thou demandest.   Blessed is the tender scruple that feareth to have offended.   Though it were lower, yet were it not low.   Who knoweth if it be lower?   None hath ascended and touched with his hand the summit of Contemplation: none hath descended, and touched with his foot the utmost depth of Human Love. On all sides Infinitude doth gird us in ; and all virtues are infinite. By nature the terrestrial life is the lower ; but grace consecrateth nature, and raiseth the low. He that came from on high came in perfect Humanity. No bridal was His : yet at a bridal feast was He a guest ; and there He wrought His first miracle. At the saying of her who was both perfect Purity and perfect Charity, he changed the water into wine, signifying that by His Presence the elements of lower earth were thenceforth elevated into the sacraments of the Life Divine. The excellence of that which thou *leavest* be unto thee the measure of the excellence of that whereunto thou attainest. The single life doth emblem, in a mystery, the Unity and Integrity of God : the marriage bond of Christians showeth forth the union of the soul with her Maker, and not less of the Church with her Lord. Grace raiseth us above terrestrial things, and again, grace sanctifieth terrestrial things. Religion buildeth new temples ; and again, religion subdueth to a blissful rite the temples of the idols. Faith keepeth vigil on the mountain ; and again, in the valley Faith lieth down and taketh her rest, because the Lord sustaineth her. From innocence thou goest, but unto innocence. Thou advancest from virtue to virtue—from the virginal honours to the matronly—from the heart placid within its zone, to the heart that compasseth a world as large as the earth—from the straiter commune with God, to the wider commune with God. Singleness, with penetrating beam, shineth as a star: marriage dispenseth a more various light, coloureth all things, quickeneth the world, reneweth it. In Eden marriage was ordained : in the world marriage was abused : in the second Eden marriage was ordained and restrained, that it might be in elevation sustained.

If then thou demandest how thou shalt walk well and trip not, remember that, as the marriage of this world would be to thee as nothing, so the marriage of that first Eden is now to thee, and to all, impossible. But in the second Eden, which is the Church, there is a lower depth, and there is a higher height : and in it affections, by their nature perishable, are kept alive only by that which raiseth them unto imperishable ends. Children's voices amid its bowers keep note with voices in heaven. The ties of mortal life image the ties of the life immortal—for what else mean we when we say that God is our Father, and Christ our Brother? If they be thus entertained, the bonds which should otherwise have subjected us to this earth, being transferred, do bind us unto the supernal sphere. It was then not by a chain, but by a new dignity imparted to it, that marriage was restrained in the second Eden. "The time is short : henceforth let him that hath a wife be as he that hath none." And why restrained? Because in a world where evil hath a part, there too must sacrifice have a part. Without sacrifice there can be no sacrament. Without sacrifice aspiration offendeth through pride, and fainteth anon through weakness.

At first, and that the perfect life might be known beside every hearth, the mercy of God added unto the Church persecutions ; and not hard seemed it to " have all things as though one had them not," when at the frown of the Prætor, all things might in a moment vanish, except the axe and the stake. Truly when eternity was ever at hand, easy was it to feel that time was short.   But the Church conquered the world, and was, in part, conquered by that which she overcame. Arduous appeared it then to see in power but service, in wealth but opportunity, in wife and child and sister but things immortal in a sweet disguise.   At that time, not in scorn but in reverence of human ties, there was added to man's life the vow monastic : yea, as the birds of the air have leave to build in the eaves of the temple, even so, through a converse charity, it was beneath holy roofs and beside hearths made pure that conventual aspirations first felt the breath of heaven come in under their wings. Then arose convents, like rock-built citadels of ancient virtue, surviving in a region reconquered by a savage race. Yet not to all who had conventual aspirations was accorded the conventual vocation, since thus the Life domestic would have been robbed of its best. If all had fled from the world, Christ must have died out of the world.   In it then there remained not alone the worldly, but those also by whom God was willing to keep the world from corruption.   Still do those children of eternity mingle with the children of time : and theirs is a twofold vow ; the marriage vow in deed and in truth ; the monastic vow in spirit. For them self-sacrifice doeth what persecution did of old ; and possessing all things yea, and they alone possess them—they abide by all things mortal unpossessed. They walk as a spirit, while yet in the body, above the waves of mortal change : they walk and sink not. She that is of their number cleaveth unto her husband without equal or second, in all love, loyalty, and service ; and yet, keeping ever the first commandment, which is the root of all, preferreth infinitely the Creator to the creature, and holdeth by Him as one nearer by far.

Wouldest thou, O Virgin, that the love between you should last? Let it make large your hearts. Let the chief of human ties lead you far on into the bosom of the humanities. It was given unto men to break down the prison of self-love. If the heart grow, then shall that love which is in the heart grow also. When it ceaseth to grow, then beginneth it to decay : then slackeneth its grasp daily; yea, though it clutch fiercely what is little and near. Affections wither when they fulfil not their appointed tasks. For the sake of that love ye bear each other, love all that bears the divine image : for the love ye bear your children, love the poor as your children : for the love ye bear the Church of God, love also your country, which cometh next to her in sacred claims. There is a love that maketh large the heart : and there is a love that maketh it small. The love that enlargeth it cometh from God, and rendereth us benign to all : the love that contracteth it cometh from self, and returneth to self. An evil gift to him that is beloved is this love.

See also that the heart which is large be strong also; for together ye carry one Cross up the heavenly hills. Virtuous labours and noble cares make it strong; and then it is not a rose-leaf rolled up that can ruffle it, nor the sting of every insect that can inflame it. They that live but for each other love amiss; and, even if their love abide, yet the gladsomeness of love is gone. Rejoice rather than lament that the petty cares of mortal life rebuke its petty delights, and force the spirit upon its freedom. If thou strikest a root into time, let it enter deep enough to pass through time into eternity.

Love thou thy husband, not for that in him which flattereth thy choice, but for his virtue, and in that he is thy husband. Yet forget not in thy reverence that thou art the helpmate of his soul. Thou must either be the weight that retardeth him, or the Angel that goeth before him, shedding light on his paths. Henceforth thou voyagest no more alone. Be careful of a slender bark that holdeth twain. Inseparably are ye united, whether in presence or in absence; for your union, which is in God, is of the heart, and of the will, and of the vow. More near shall ye be drawn by sorrow than by joy, by trial and by proving;—most near by Death.

And thus, O Bride, shalt thou find, while seeking after a gift more exalted, that talisman also which conserveth affection.   How shall that husband surcease from rejoicing in his wife who findeth in her, not a conspirer with worldly temptations, but the health of his soul, the strength of his life, the glory and the peace of his house, the music that reawakeneth their youth in his nobler thoughts? That gift wherein female youth exulteth the Christian Wife less loseth than imparts and shares. How shall the dust gather upon her who, bathing perpetually in fresh fountains of grace, exulteth, lily-like, each morning as in the dews of a new baptism? Inexhaustible is she whose spirit is wedded unto things incorruptible and eternal. As soon shall spirits forget to love in heaven, as such spirits to love and be loved on earth.

Such was Saint Cecilia, whose husband, Valerian by name, when he had wondered at her long, received at last such grace that, his eyes being opened, he discerned that garland of angel-tended flowers which from her brows did ever disperse celestial odours through his palace. At that sight, being instantly converted to the Galilean Disesteemed (and his brother with him), he so persevered that ere long, with the Saint, he was honoured with a most happy martyrdom, and retaineth by merit the suffrages of all the churches. The youth that taketh thee to wife serveth not the false gods, so thou writest unto me, but serveth the one God, and goeth forth unto the command that he holdeth, accompanied by thee. So accompany him that benediction may accompany both! What is good make better; for the nest that thou raisest, the same shall sustain thee on high; and the nest that thou warmest, the same shall keep thee warm. Where most is to be gained, there also is most to be lost. Ah me, how great is that loss! A bewildered light leadeth on into the marsh, and vanisheth. The foot sinketh in what is soft. In sloth is sought content. Aspirations wither and drop as plumes of a moulting wing. Perforce the sympathies cling to what is near. In self-defence, the soul forgetteth what it prized of old. The larger charities it banisheth: the loftier hope it rebuketh. Such is the way downward; yet, through God's high mercy, no step is there on that downward way, beside which there goeth not forth that narrow path which leadeth again into the perfect way.

While fall the ruins of the Empire daily, and the Barbarians lay waste even the Holy City, thus have I written unto thee, less as worthy to instruct than as willing to detain thee. For so, on that first morning when thy Mother led thy childish steps up to this cloister of lonely Apennine, didst thou stand with dark devout eyes in attention raised, nor thinking to withdraw them till all was said. Such remembrances haunt age. Now writeth my hand no more — not chilled by age alone, but also by the evening wind that sigheth past the rocky summits. So passeth life as a sigh. But cast thou thy wings thereon, and lightly shall it bear thee aloft! The sun sinketh, and Soractè, as a dial, flingeth its shadow far across the plain. Swan of the mountain-lake, that didst in

solitariness stem the black water under the granite
peak, float thou never upon yellow Tiber; for Clitum-
nus leadeth also most placid and pure waters through
the peaceful mead; and beside it grazeth the milk-
white steer, and the bird singeth, and man doth build.
—Farewell!

RECOLLECTIONS OF WORDSWORTH

IT was about eight years before his death that I made acquaintance with Wordsworth. During the next four years I saw a great deal of him, chiefly among his own mountains; and, besides many delightful walks with him, I had the great honour of passing some days under his roof. The strongest of my impressions respecting him was that made by the manly simplicity and lofty rectitude which characterised him. In one of his later sonnets he writes of himself thus: "As a true man who long had served the lyre;" it was because he was a *true* man that he was a true poet; and it was impossible to know him without being reminded of this. In any case he must have been recognised as a man of original and energetic genius; but it was his strong and truthful moral nature, his intellectual sincerity, the abiding conscientiousness of his imagination, so to speak, which enabled that genius to do its great work, and bequeath to the England of the future the most solid mass of deep-hearted and authentic poetry which has been bestowed on her by any poet since the Elizabethan age. There was in his nature a veracity which, had it not been combined with an idealising imagination not less remarkable, would to many have appeared prosaic; yet, had he not possessed that characteristic, the products of his imagination would have lacked reality. They might still have enunciated a deep and sound philosophy; but they would have been divested of that human interest which belongs to them in a yet higher degree. All the little incidents of the neighbourhood were to him important.

The veracity and the ideality which are so signally combined in Wordsworth's poetic descriptions of Nature made themselves at least as much felt whenever Nature was the theme of his discourse. In his intense reverence for Nature he regarded all poetical delineations of her with an exacting severity; and if those descriptions were not true, and true in a twofold sense, the more skilfully executed they were the more was his indignation roused by what he deemed a pretence and a deceit. An untrue description of Nature was to him a profaneness, a heavenly message sophisticated and falsely delivered. He expatiated much to me one day, as we walked among the hills above Grasmere, on the mode in which Nature had been described by one of the most justly popular of England's modern poets—one for whom he preserved a high and affectionate respect. "He took pains," Wordsworth said; "he went out with his pencil and notebook, and jotted

down whatever struck him most—a river rippling over
the sands, a ruined tower on a rock above it, a pro-
montory, and a mountain-ash waving its red berries.
He went home, and wove the whole together into a
poetical description." After a pause Wordsworth resumed with a flashing eye and impassioned voice:
"But Nature does not permit an inventory to be made
of her charms! He should have left his pencil and
notebook at home; fixed his eye, as he walked, with
a reverent attention on all that surrounded him, and
taken all into a heart that could understand and enjoy.
Then, after several days had passed by, he should have
interrogated his memory as to the scene. He would
have discovered that while much of what he had admired was preserved to him, much was also most wisely
obliterated. That which remained—the picture surviving in his mind—would have presented the ideal
and essential truth of the scene, and done so, in a
large part, by discarding much which, though in itself
striking, was not characteristic. In every scene many
of the most brilliant details are but accidental. A true
eye for Nature does not note them, or at least does not
dwell on them." On the same occasion he remarked:
"Scott misquoted in one of his novels my lines on
Yarrow. He makes me write—

> "The swans on sweet St. Mary's lake
> Float double, swans and shadow.

but I wrote—

> "The *swan* on *still* St. Mary's lake.

Never could I have written 'swans' in the plural. The scene when I saw it, with its still and dim lake, under the dusky hills, was one of utter loneliness; there was *one* swan, and one only, stemming the water, and the pathetic loneliness of the region gave importance to the one companion of that swan—its own white image in the water. It was for that reason that I recorded the swan and the shadow. Had there been many swans and many shadows, they would have implied nothing as regards the character of the place, and I should have said nothing about them." He proceeded to remark that many who could descant with eloquence on Nature cared little for her, and that many more who truly loved her had yet no eye to discern her—which he regarded as a sort of "spiritual discernment." He continued: "Indeed, I have hardly ever known any one but myself who had a true eye for Nature—one that thoroughly understood her meanings and her teachings—except" (here he interrupted himself) "one person. There was a young clergyman called Frederick Faber,[1] who resided at Ambleside. He had not only as good an eye for Nature as I have, but even a better one ; and he sometimes pointed out to me on the mountains effects which, with all my great experience, I had never detected."

Truth, he used to say—that is, truth in its largest sense, as a thing at once real and ideal, a truth including exact and accurate detail, and yet everywhere

---

[1] Afterwards Father Faber of the Oratory. His "Sir Launcelot" abounds in admirable descriptions of Nature.

subordinating mere detail to the spirit of the whole,—this, he affirmed, was the soul and essence not only of descriptive poetry, but of all poetry. He had often, he told me, intended to write an essay on poetry, setting forth this principle, and illustrating it by references to the chief representatives of poetry in its various departments. It was this twofold truth which made Shakespeare the greatest of all poets. "It was well for Shakespeare," he remarked, "that he gave himself to the drama. It was that which forced him to be sufficiently human. His poems would otherwise, from the extraordinarily metaphysical character of his genius, have been too recondite to be understood. His youthful poems, in spite of their unfortunate and unworthy subjects, and his sonnets also, reveal this tendency. Nothing can surpass the greatness of Shakespeare where he is at his greatest; but it is wrong to speak of him as if even he were perfect. He had serious defects, and not those only proceeding from carelessness. For instance, in his delineations of character he does not assign as large a place to religious sentiment as enters into the constitution of human nature under normal circumstances. If his dramas had more religion in them, they would be truer representations of man, as well as more elevated and of a more searching interest." Wordsworth used to warn young poets against writing poetry remote from human interest. Dante he admitted to be an exception; but he considered that Shelley, and almost all others who had endeavoured to outsoar the humanities, had suffered deplorably from the attempt. I once heard him say: "I have often been asked for advice by young poets. All the advice I can give may be expressed in two counsels. First, let Nature be your habitual and pleasurable study—human nature and material nature; secondly, study carefully those first-class poets whose fame is universal, not local, and learn from them:—learn from them especially how to observe and how to interpret Nature."

Those who knew Wordsworth only from his poetry might have supposed that he dwelt ever in a region too serene to admit of human agitations. This was not the fact. He was a man of strong affections—strong enough on one sorrowful occasion to withdraw him for a time from poetry.[1] Referring once to two young children who had died about forty years previously, he described minute details of their illnesses with an exactness and an impetuosity of troubled excitement such as might have been expected if the bereavement had taken place but a few weeks before. The lapse of time appeared to have left the sorrow submerged indeed, but still in all its first freshness. Yet I afterwards heard that at the time of the illness, at least in the case of one of the two children, it was impossible to rouse his attention to the danger. He chanced to be then under the immediate spell of one of those fits of poetic inspiration which descended on him like a cloud. Till the cloud had drifted he could

---

[1] "For us the stream of fiction ceased to flow" (dedicatory stanzas to "The White Doe of Rylstone").

see nothing beyond. Under the level of the calm there was, however, the precinct of the storm. It expressed itself rarely but vehemently, partaking sometimes of the character both of indignation and sorrow. All at once the trouble would pass away and his countenance bask in its habitual calm, like a cloudless summer sky. His indignation flamed out vehemently when he heard of a base action. "I could kick such a man across England with my naked foot," I heard him exclaim on such an occasion. The more impassioned part of his nature connected itself especially with his political feelings. He regarded his own intellect as one which united some of the faculties which belong to the statesman with those which belong to the poet; and public affairs interested him not less deeply than poetry. It was as patriot, not poet, that he ventured to claim fellowship with Dante.[1] He did not accept the term "reformer," because it implied an organic change in our institutions, and this he deemed both needless and dangerous; but he used to say that, while he was a decided conservative, he remembered that to preserve our institutions we must be ever improving them. He was, indeed, from first to last, pre-eminently a patriot—an impassioned as well as a thoughtful one. Yet his political sympathies were not with his own country only, but with the progress of humanity. Till disenchanted by the excesses and follies of the first French Revolution, his hopes and

---

[1] See his sonnet on the seat of Dante, close to the Duomo at Florence (*Poems of Early and Late Years*).

sympathies associated themselves ardently with the new order of things created by it ; and I have heard him say that he did not know how any generous-minded *young* man, entering on life at the time of that great uprising, could have escaped the illusion. To the end his sympathies were ever with the cottage hearth far more than with the palace. If he became a strong supporter of what has been called "the hierarchy of society," it was chiefly because he believed the principle of "equality" to be fatal to the wellbeing and the true dignity of the poor. Moreover, in siding politically with the crown and the coronets, he considered himself to be siding with the weaker party in our democratic days.

It has been observed that the religion of Wordsworth's poetry, at least of his earlier poetry, is not as distinctly "revealed religion" as might have been expected from this poet's well-known adherence to what he has called emphatically "The Lord and mighty Paramount of Truths." He once remarked to me himself on this circumstance, and explained it by stating that when in youth his imagination was shaping for itself the channel in which it was to flow, his religious convictions were less definite and less strong than they had become on more mature thought ; and that, when his poetic mind and manner had once been formed, he feared lest he might, in attempting to modify them, become constrained. He added that on religious matters he ever wrote with great diffidence, remembering that if there were many subjects too low for song, there were some too high. Wordsworth's general confidence in his own powers, which was strong, though far from exaggerated, rendered more striking and more touching his humility in all that concerned religion. It used to remind me of what I once heard Mr. Rogers say—viz. "There is a special character of *greatness* about humility; for it implies that a man can, in an unusual degree, estimate the *greatness* of what is above us." Fortunately, his diffidence did not keep Wordsworth silent on sacred themes. His later poems include many distinct as well as beautiful confessions of Christian faith; and one of them, "The Primrose of the Rock," is as distinctly Wordsworthian in its inspiration as it is Christian in its doctrine. Wordsworth was a "High Churchman," and also, in his prose mind, strongly anti-Roman Catholic, largely on political grounds; but that it was otherwise as regards his mind poetic is obvious from many passages in his Christian poetry, especially those which refer to the monastic system and the Schoolmen, and his sonnet on the Blessed Virgin, whom he addresses as

Our tainted nature's solitary boast.

He used to say that the idea of one who was both Virgin and Mother had sunk so deep into the heart of humanity that there it must ever remain fixed.

Wordsworth's estimate of his contemporaries was not generally high. I remember his once saying to me: "I have known many that might be called very *clever* men, and a good many of real and vigorous *abilities*, but few of genius; and only one whom I should call 'wonderful.' That one was Coleridge. At any hour of the day or night he would talk by the hour, if there chanced to be *any* sympathetic listener, and talk better than the best page of his writings; for a pen half paralysed his genius. A child would sit quietly at his feet and wonder, till the torrent had passed by. The only other wonderful man whom I have known is Sir William Hamilton, of Dublin : and he is very like Coleridge." I remember that when I recited by his fireside Alfred Tennyson's two political poems, "You ask me why, though ill at ease," and "Of old sat Freedom on the heights," the old bard listened with a deepening attention, and when I had ended, said after a pause, "I must acknowledge that those two poems are very solid and noble in thought. Their diction also seems singularly stately." He was a great admirer of Philip van Artevelde. Of my father he said to me, "I consider his sonnets to be certainly the best English sonnets of modern times;" adding, "Of course I am not including my own in any comparison with those of others." He was not sanguine as to the future of English poetry. He thought that there was much to be supplied in other departments of our literature, and especially he desired a really great history of England; but he was disposed to regard the roll of English poetry as made up, and as leaving place for little more except what was likely to be eccentric or imitational.

In his younger days Wordsworth had had to fight a great battle in poetry; for both his subjects and his mode of treating them were antagonistic to the maxims then current.   It was fortunate for posterity, no doubt, that his long "militant estate" was animated by some mingling of personal ambition with his love of poetry. Speaking in an early sonnet of

> The poets, who on earth have made us heirs
> Of truth, and pure delight, by heavenly lays,

he concludes—

> Oh ! might my name be numbered among theirs,
> Then gladly would I end my mortal days.

He died at eighty, and general fame did not come to him till about fifteen years before his death.   This might perhaps have been fifteen years too soon, if he had set any inordinate value on it.   But it was not so. Shelley tells us that " Fame is love disguised "; and it was intellectual sympathy that Wordsworth had always valued far more than reputation.   "Give me thy love ; I claim no other fee," had been his demand on his reader.   When Fame had laid her tardy garland at his feet, he found on it no fresher green than his "Rydalian laurels" had always worn.   Once he said to me : " It is indeed a deep satisfaction to hope and believe that my poetry will be, while it lasts, a help to the cause of virtue and truth, especially among the young.   As for myself, it seems now of little moment how long I may be remembered.   When a man pushes off in his little boat into the great seas of Infinity and

Eternity, it signifies little how long he is kept in sight by watchers from the shore."

Such are my chief recollections of the great poet, whom I knew but in his old age, but whose heart retained its youth till his daughter Dora's death.   He seemed to me one who from boyhood had been faithful to a high vocation ; one who had esteemed it his office to minister, in an age of conventional civilisation, at Nature's altar, and who had in his later life explained and vindicated such lifelong ministration, even while he seemed to apologise for it, in the memorable confession—

> But who is innocent?   By grace divine,
> Not otherwise, *O Nature !* are we thine.[1]

It was to Nature as first created, not to Nature as corrupted by " disnatured " passions, that his song had attributed such high and healing powers.   In singing her praise he had chosen a theme loftier than most of his readers knew—loftier, as he perhaps eventually discovered, than he had at first supposed it to be. Utterly without Shakespeare's dramatic faculty, he was richer and wider in the humanities than any poet since Shakespeare.   Wholly unlike Milton in character and in opinions, he abounds in passages to be paralleled only by Milton in sublimity, and not even by Milton in pathos, and spirituality.   It was plain to those who knew Wordsworth well that he had kept his great gift pure, and used it honestly and thoroughly for that purpose for which it had been bestowed.   He had

1   " Evening Voluntary."

ever written with a conscientious reverence for that gift; but he had also written spontaneously. He had composed with care—not the exaggerated solicitude which is prompted by vanity, and which frets itself to unite incompatible excellences, but the diligence which shrinks from no toil while eradicating blemishes that confuse a poem's meaning and frustrate its purpose. He regarded poetry as an art; but he also regarded art, not as the compeer of Nature, much less her superior, but as her servant and interpreter. He wrote poetry likewise, no doubt, in a large measure, because self-utterance was an essential law of his nature. If he had a companion, he discoursed like one whose thoughts must needs run on in audible current; if he walked alone among his mountains, he murmured old songs. He was like a pine-grove—vocal ever as well as visible. But to poetry he had devoted himself as to the utterance of the highest truths brought within the range of his life's experience; and if his verse has been accused of egotism, the charge has come from those who did not perceive that it was with a human, not a mere personal, interest that he habitually watched the processes of his own mind. He drew from the fountain that was nearest at hand what he hoped might be a refreshment to those far off. He once said, speaking of a departed man of genius, who had lived an unhappy life and deplorably abused his powers, to the lasting calamity of his country; "A great poet must be a great man; and a great man must be a good man; and a good man ought to be a happy man."   To know Wordsworth was to feel sure that if he had been a great poet, it was not merely because he had been endowed with a great imagination, but because he had been a good man, a great man, and a man whose poetry had, in an especial sense, been the expression of a healthily happy moral being.

P.S.—Wordsworth was by no means without humour. When the Queen on one occasion gave a masked ball, some one said that a certain youthful poet, who has since reached a deservedly high place both in the literary and political world, but who was then known chiefly as an accomplished and amusing young man of society, was to attend it dressed in the character of the father of English poetry—grave old Chaucer. "What!" said Wordsworth, "M—— go as Chaucer! Then it only remains for me to go as M——!"

SONNET—RYDAL WITH WORDSWORTH.

BY THE LATE SIR AUBREY DE VERE.

What we beheld scarce can I now recall
In one connected picture ; images
Hurrying so swiftly their fresh witcheries
O'er the mind's mirror, that the several
Seems lost, or blended in the mighty all.
Lone lakes ; rills gushing through rock-rooted trees ;
Peaked mountains shadowing vales of peacefulness ;
Glens echoing to the flashing waterfall.
Then that sweet twilight isle ! with friends delayed
Beside a ferny bank 'neath oaks and yews ;
The moon between two mountain peaks embayed ;
Heaven and the waters dyed with sunset hues :
And he, the poet of the age and land,
Discoursing as we wandered hand in hand.

The above-written sonnet is the record of a delightful day spent by my father in 1833 with Wordsworth at Rydal, to which he went from the still more beautiful shores of Ulswater, where he had been sojourning at Halsteads. He had been one of Wordsworth's warmest admirers when their number was small, and in 1842 he dedicated a volume of poems to him.[1] He taught me when a boy of eighteen years old to admire the great bard. I had been very enthusiastically praising Lord Byron's poetry. My father replied, " Wordsworth is the great poet of modern times." Much surprised, I asked, "And what may his special merits be?" The answer was, "They are very various; as, for instance, depth, largeness, elevation, and, what is rare in modern poetry, an *entire* purity. In his noble 'Laodamia' they are chiefly majesty and pathos." A few weeks afterwards I chanced to take from the library shelves a volume of Wordsworth, and it opened on " Laodamia." Some strong, calm hand seemed to have been laid on my head, and bound me to the spot till I had come to the end. As I read, a new world, hitherto unimagined, opened itself out, stretching far away into serene infinitudes. The region was one to me unknown, but the harmony of the picture attested its reality. Above and around were indeed

> An ampler ether, a diviner air,
> And fields invested with purpureal gleams ;

---

[1] *A Song of Faith, Devout Exercises, and Sonnets* (Pickering). The dedication closed thus : "I may at least hope to be named hereafter among the friends of Wordsworth."

and when I reached the line—

>   Calm pleasures there abide—majestic pains,

I felt that no tenants less stately were fit to walk in so
lordly a precinct.   I had been translated into another
planet of song—one with larger movements and a
longer year.   A wider conception of poetry had
become mine, and the Byronian enthusiasm fell from
me like a bond broken by being outgrown.   The
incident illustrates poetry in one of its many characters—that of the "Deliverer."   The ready sympathies and inexperienced imagination of youth make
it surrender itself easily despite its better aspirations,
or in consequence of them, to a false greatness; and
the true greatness, once revealed, sets it free.   As
early as 1824 Walter Savage Landor, in his "Imaginary
Conversation" between Southey and Porson, had
pronounced Wordsworth's "Laodamia" to be "a
composition such as Sophocles might have exulted to
own, and a part of which might have been heard with
shouts of rapture in the regions he describes"—the
Elysian Fields.

Wordsworth frequently spoke of death as if it were
the taking of a new degree in the University of Life.
"I should like," he remarked to a young lady, "to
visit Italy again before I move to another planet."
He sometimes made a mistake in assuming that others
were equally philosophical.   We were once breakfast-
ing at the house of Mr. Rogers, when Wordsworth,
after gazing attentively round the room with a benig-

nant and complacent expression, turned to our host, and, wishing to compliment him, said : "Mr. Rogers, I never see this house, so perfect in its taste, so exquisite in all its arrangements, and decorated with such well-chosen pictures, without fancying it the very house imaged to himself by the Roman poet when, in illustration of man's mortality, he says : *Linquenda est domus.*"—"What is that you're saying?" replied Mr. Rogers, whose years, between eighty and ninety, had not improved his hearing. "I was remarking that your house," replied Wordsworth, "always reminds me of the ode (more properly called an elegy, though doubtless the lyrical measure not unnaturally causes it to be included among Horace's odes) in which the Roman poet writes : *Linquenda est domus ;* that is, since, ladies being present, a translation may be deemed desirable, *The house is*, or *has to be, left ;* and again, *et placens uxor*—and the pleasing wife ; though, as we must all regret, that part of the quotation is not applicable on the present occasion." The Town Bard, on whom "no angle smiled" more than the end of St. James's Place, did not enter into the views of the Bard of the Mountains. His answer was what children call "making a great face," and the ejaculation, "Don't talk Latin in the society of ladies." When I was going away, he remarked, "What a stimulus the mountain air has on the appetite! I made a sign to Edmund to hand him the cutlets a second time. I was afraid he would stick his fork into that beautiful woman who sat next him."

Wordsworth never resented a jest at his own
expense. Once when we had knocked three times
in vain at the door of a London house, I ex-
claimed, quoting his sonnet written on Westminster
Bridge—

> Dear God, the very houses seem asleep.

He laughed heartily, then smiled gravely, and lastly
recounted the occasion and described the early morning on which that sonnet was written. He did not
recite more than a part of it, to the accompaniment
of distant cab and carriage; and I thought that the
door was opened too soon.

Wordsworth, despite his dislike to great cities, was
attracted occasionally in his later years

> To the proud margin of the Thames
> And Lambeth's venerable towers,

where his society was courted by persons of the most
different character. But he complained bitterly of the
great city. It was next to impossible, he remarked,
to tell the truth in it. "Yesterday I was at S——
House; the Duchess of S——, showing me the
pictures, observed: 'Here is the portrait of my brother'
(naming him), 'and it is considered very like.' To
this I assented, partly perhaps in absence of mind, but
chiefly, I think, with an impression that her Grace's
brother was probably a person whose face every one
knew or was expected to know; so that, as I had
never met him, my answer was in fact a lie ! It is too

bad that, when more than seventy years old, I should be drawn from the mountains to London in order to tell a lie!"   He made his complaint wherever he went, laying the blame, however, not so much on himself or on the Duchess as on the corrupt city; and some of those who learned how the most truthful man in England had thus suddenly been subverted by metropolitan snares came to the conclusion that within a few years more no virtue would be left extant in the land.   He was likewise maltreated in lesser ways. "This morning I was compelled by my engagements to eat three breakfasts—one with an aged and excellent gentleman, who may justly be esteemed an accomplished man of letters, although I cannot honestly concede to him the title of a poet; one at a fashionable party; and one with an old friend whom no pressure would induce me to neglect, although for this, my first breakfast to-day, I was obliged to name the early hour of seven o'clock, as he lives in a remote part of London."

But it was only among his own mountains that Wordsworth could be understood.   He walked among them not so much to admire them as to converse with them.   They exchanged thoughts with him, in sunshine or flying shadow, giving him their own and accepting his.   Day and night, at all hours, and in all weathers, he would face them.   If it rained, he might fling his plaid over him, but would take no admonition.   He must have his way.   On such occasions, dutiful as he was in higher matters, he remained incurably wayward.

In vain one reminded him that a letter needed an answer or that the storm would soon be over. It was very necessary for him to do what he pleased; and one of his dearest friends said to me, with a smile of the most affectionate humour: "He wrote his 'Ode to Duty,' and then he had done with that matter." This very innocent form of lawlessness, corresponding with the classic expression, *Indulge genio*, belonged to his genius, not less than the sympathetic reverence with which he looked up to the higher and universal laws of Duty. Sometimes there was a battle between his reverence for Nature and his reverence for other things. The friend already alluded to was once remarking on his varying expressions of countenance: "That rough old face is capable of high and real beauty; I have seen in it an expression quite of heavenly peace and contemplative delight, as the May breeze came over him from the woods while he was slowly walking out of church on a Sunday morning, and when he had half emerged from the shadow." A flippant person present inquired: "Did you ever chance, Miss F——, to observe that heavenly expression on his countenance as he was walking *into* church on a fine May morning?" A laugh was the reply. The ways of Nature harmonised with his feelings in age as well as in youth. He could understand no estrangement. Gathering a wreath of heather on one occasion—then an old man—he murmured, as he slipped it into the ribbon which bound the golden tresses of his youthful companion—

And what if I enwreathed my own?
'Twere no offence to reason ;
The sober hills thus deck their brows
To meet the wintry season.[1]

[1] I need hardly say that when recalling Wordsworth's conversation after an interval of years, it is the substance of what he said that I record, not always his exact words.

THE END

Printed by R. & R. Clark, *Edinburgh*